The Man Who Stayed Below

The Man Who Stayed Below

ALAN GOULD

St. Martin's Press
New York

I would like to thank Les Murray, Kevin Hart, Philip and Jenna Mead for reading the manuscript of this novel and making many helpful suggestions. I would also like to thank The Geelong College for an eight week Writer-in-Residence Fellowship during 1982 during which I managed to complete the final draft, and Richard Refshauge for his legal advice concerning Chapter Four.

Acknowledgement is due to *Quadrant* in which a part of Chapter Three has been published.

NOTE

All characters in this book are entirely fictitious, and no reference is intended to any living person.

Library of Congress Cataloging in Publication Data

Gould, Alan, 1949–
    The man who stayed below.

    I. Title.
PR9619.3.G643M3   1987   823   86-24792
ISBN 0-312-00135-5

First published in Great Britain by Angus & Robertson (UK) Ltd.

First U.S. Edition

10 9 8 7 6 5 4 3 2 1

Contents

The Mood in London

His size had awed all of us. It was grotesque now. His feet, clad in thick white socks, stuck out from beneath the blankets and hung over the end of the stretcher. They looked like two oversized vegetables protruding from a wrapping. Despite the weight he'd lost it still took four men to carry him.

I remember those men. I remember how solicitous they were in their task. They murmured quiet instructions to each other and manoeuvred their burden as though it were some priceless sculpture being taken from a pharaoh's tomb. They were all bareheaded, while a fifth, who held open the iron door that led to the poop accommodation, removed his cap as the stretcher was taken through. I noticed that he kept his eyes lowered or watched those of his colleagues. They too avoided looking directly at the face of Captain Trygg. There must have been a fine drizzle at the time, for I remember someone casting an oilskin coat over the blankets as the stretcher came out of that door into the light of day.

We had detested him. When I say 'we' I speak on behalf of all but one of us; five apprentices, the fo'c'sle hands and the two mates. The one exception was Alex, our senior apprentice, and I cannot pretend, even now, to understand the dogged submissiveness he extended to this captain.

But it is hard to find a man despicable when he passes before your eyes covered by blankets and an oilskin coat, with his head sunk into pillows. We stopped the work we had in hand. Those with caps on removed them spontaneously. It was still early in the morning. The sky above the masts was the colour of an unwashed fleece. The first dockers were arriving for work. The donkey engines along the wharf had not yet erupted into life. Here and there rail wagons stood motionless on lines that were a silver scribble over the wide expanse of the wharf. It might have been a Sunday. The hum of the city behind the docklands was muted. The water in the West India Dock was as smooth as an ebony table and the masts of the ships made a winter forest.

As Captain Trygg was taken across the main deck toward our gangplank, I cast a quick glance over the faces of my companions. Some looked at the captain briefly, some kept their eyes on the ground. Either way, the reaction to his passing was not one of indifference. Though we could not say we had known him well, his involvement with us, at least, had been intimate. We had been confined with him for better than one hundred days.

For my part I had a morbid curiosity. I was nearly seventeen and had just completed my first passage at sea. I had not seen the captain since he had disappeared below on the Equator. That was five weeks before. During that time he had remained in his cabin attended only by the steward. The first mate, Mister Hallet, would not deign to go near the door of his senior's cabin. Though we had not expected the latter's condition to improve we were uncertain about the exact nature of his complaint. Not that we had much time to speculate, for from the Equator Mister Hallet worked us like slaves.

So I looked at Captain Trygg's face as the stretcher passed me. I got a fright. Not only had it been large, but it had been a well-fleshed face, solid rather than fat. The face that I saw on the pillow as it went past was skull-like and yellowish. The powerful cheeks had withdrawn under the cheekbones, and the eyes, which stared unflinchingly upwards, were rimmed with purple lids. But the beard and moustache — both freshly combed — shone lustrously. Where all else was shrinking into itself, the beard and moustache flourished. What remained in that visage was its curious stamp of scorn, the suggestion that all created things its eyes came to rest upon were utterly contemptible.

Those eyes ignored us and ignored the ship. They continued to do so as the shipmaster was lifted up over the main rail. Mister Gillard, the second mate, standing by the gangplank said 'Speedy recovery, Captain,' then looked away in embarrassment as his remark went unacknowledged. Mister

Hallet watched from the background.

There was a horse-drawn ambulance waiting on the wharf, insignificant among the cranes and rolling stock. Its roof shone like a wet, black umbrella, and the last any of us saw of Captain Trygg was his head disappearing beneath its canopy. There was a middle-aged woman standing beside it, slightly apart from the two attendants. She was a relative of the captain, a sister, I believe, who had travelled down from the north. Mister Hallet had signalled the captain's condition off Dungeness; news must have travelled quickly. She received the portmanteau and the small box of books from the seaman who had been following the stretcher, placed them in the carriage, climbed in and pulled down its canvas flap. The driver shook his reins and the ambulance moved off toward the harbour gates, disappearing from view behind a warehouse. We returned to work.

We were at our midday meal when the sergeant and the constable of police came aboard. Someone called from the midshiphouse door.

'They're here to take Alex away.'

We left our meals half-eaten and went out to watch. The two uniformed men were talking to Mister Gillard, and both became noticeably ill-at-ease as we formed a crowd around the deckhouse door. The presence of constabulary on board a ship is resented by seamen. We have the feeling we can look after our own, that the rigours of our work, good officers, and our long periods of isolation from other communities are sufficient inducements to make us sociable. These two officers of the law were an intrusion on that feeling and, alas, a sign that our code did not have the absolute reliability we imagined.

Mister Hallet approached the group and ushered them toward the same door through which Captain Trygg had been carried earlier that morning. The door clanged behind the four men. We waited.

Perhaps a minute later Mister Gillard came through and held it open. Next we saw the bewhiskered face of the police sergeant. He appeared to be struggling, for he stumbled on the iron lip at the doorway, then pulled an arm through the opening. There was Alex. He had set his feet against that lip and was resisting fiercely. With a tug he was toppled over it and dragged, with a policeman on each arm, toward the gangplank. It was absurdly theatrical. He dug in his heels, he dragged his feet. The two policemen laboured and puffed. Mister Hallet followed, while we watched in a state of dull astonishment. Alex made no sound in his resistance, though his face had crumpled up like a newspaper. It was a grimace I shan't forget, because it was a grimace so surprising on *that* face. It was an expression of extremity, of desperate intensity, somehow emptied of personality and intelligence. There had been a time when I thought Alex's was a countenance on which such an expression was impossible. It was a boyish countenance, a little humourless, but open, expressing a plain eagerness, frequently troubled, however never until this moment creased into an extreme of either anguish or mirth. It had been a suntanned face, but now it was pale after five weeks of confinement below.

Not once did he call out to us for help. We may well have gone to his aid. I don't know. At one point in this procession Mister Hallet took hold of Alex's collar and said, 'Now, now, mister. Put a brave face on it.'

But I suspect Alex did not hear this. As he was hauled bodily onto the gangplank he broke his silence. He began to howl, a terrible, endless cry of self-pity. Some of the dockers stopped what they were doing and looked at the commotion. I remember feeling embarrassed. The police sergeant, who had a doleful, sympathetic expression on his face, was making soothing sounds, but they had no more effect on Alex's behaviour than Mister Hallet's advice. At the bottom of the gangplank Alex simply sagged and whimpered quietly. He was lifted into a cart somewhat similar in appearance to that which had taken away Captain Trygg earlier. Mister Gillard went hurrying down the gangway with Alex's bag of belongings, and climbed in. He was to go to the dock watch-house to give a description of the charges. The constable climbed on top and the vehicle swayed off. The last anyone saw of Alex before the enquiry was the blotch of white that was his face, between the figures of Mister Gillard and the police sergeant.

We filed back into the midshiphouse where our meals had gone cold. No one said very much. For myself, I felt a strange mixture of feelings. He aroused, of course, an ache of sympathy in me but it was as though his distress had been fathomless, somehow unhuman. I knew the reasons for it; the obvious reasons anyway. I may have had a glimmering, even then, of other reasons, that stood like shadows behind the actual events of the previous hundred or so days, and gave such a terrible depth to Alex's distress. I understand them better now, but then, as I say, I was not yet seventeen. Most of the workaday experiences I had undergone since leaving Melbourne shortly after New Year's Day in 1913 I can say I vaguely anticipated in my boyhood daydreams about life at sea. There had been less glamour and more brutality in the actual work, certainly, but there had been unexpected kindnesses. What I had not anticipated was the other dimension, our . . . what shall I call it — our nakedness in the face of sheer human nastiness. Things had gone wrong during that voyage, badly wrong. I had been involved. I had not been prepared for how easy, how frighteningly easy, it was for me to be implicated in something nasty. I felt uneasy and subdued by the morning's events. I was perplexed. I was not the same person that had joined the ship in Melbourne some four months previously.

CHAPTER 1

The Initiation

I

I was determined to begin my working life unescorted by anyone. So, at the door of my parents' home I kissed my mother, shook hands with my father, and, with a few pounds in my pocket, took the train to Melbourne. There I bought myself the peajacket and cap that were the apprentice's uniform and, wearing these garments, I went in search of my ship. It was one of those December days when the wind blows into Melbourne from the inland. The heat was intolerable, and the gusts of hot air that blew down Bourke and Spencer streets drove the dust into my eyes and mouth. I suppose I was ridiculously overdressed, but I was headstrong and full of romantic anticipation.

The ship was berthed at Railway Pier. As I tugged my bag up the gangplank I was aware of being watched by a tall, severe-looking man at the rail. Why I thought him tall, I don't know; the ship's bulwark hid two-thirds of his length. Yet he had the face that belonged to a tall man, a face that was lean with a long bony nose and eyes that were set far back in the skull and overlaid by eyebrows that were like dark clouds. Contemplating that face now, it reminds me of a seabird, a black-browed albatross perhaps. I dropped my bag with a plomp on the deck and approached him.

'Are you the captain?' I asked. He bore no outward signs of being a ship's officer, dressed as he was in a white shirt with no collar and rolled-up sleeves, criss-crossed by a pair of braces that held up undistinguished tweed trousers. He seemed not to hear me, for he continued to gaze at the ship moored on the other side of the wharf.

'I'm looking for the captain,' I announced in a louder voice. This too had no effect. Perhaps he was deaf.

'Excuse me, but are you the captain?' I raised my voice in

the manner I used for a great-aunt of mine who was hard of hearing.

It seemed to work. He turned his head slowly and looked down on me with an expression of distaste, as though he had just observed a man wipe his nose on the back of his hand or spit a string of phlegm onto the pavement. Then he straightened himself, fixing me with his gaze all the while, and with a movement so quick I could not avoid it, he pinched the hard cartilage of my ear between his thumb and forefinger and yanked it upward some six inches. The pain was awful. I felt as though I were being plucked from my feet by a pair of massive forceps. In this undignified posture I was propelled at a smart trot to where I had dropped my luggage. Then, with his free hand, he pointed at a door in one of the two deckhouses.

'SIR,' he growled. And then, 'Report to me in half an hour.'

I tried to appear self-possessed as I walked toward the door he had indicated, but my right ear felt as though it had been torn from my head. I was indignant. How was I to know he had to be addressed as 'sir'? I had only just come on board. Was there no allowance made? I confess that despite my sixteen years and my reputation for being a brazen fellow at the school I had so recently left, my eyes were stinging with tears. Indeed I was tempted to drop my bag, bolt for the gangplank, and disappear among the clutter on Railway Pier. I hadn't pleaded with my father to sign my indentures just to have this sort of treatment meted out to me.

I didn't make a bolt for it. I was too acutely aware of a pair of eyes drilling into my back as I walked toward that deckhouse, to risk it. Here was a species of human altogether more fierce than any I had encountered hitherto. I reached the door and stood facing it for a few moments, trying to regain my composure. My eyes came to a focus on a section of wood panelling the colour of black tea. Here and there yellow flakes of varnish were peeling away, while there were dark stains around the brass rim of the porthole where the metal had discoloured the wood. I turned the doorknob and went inside.

After the oppressive Melbourne sunlight the interior of the deckhouse was very dim. At first I heard only the clink of spoons on plates, but this sound ceased when my presence at the door was noted. As my eyes became accustomed to the meagre light that fell through the odd porthole and a glazed skylight, I saw four oval shapes turned in my direction, shapes which resolved themselves into an assortment of faces, all of them young; two with very downy beards, two clean shaven. Solemnly they contemplated me.

'The tall man told me to come in here.' I wondered whether I should add a collective 'sir' just to be on the safe side, though I was addressing no one in particular. There was no response. I looked around me. Against each wall there were a number of bunks.

'Is one of these mine?' I asked. Again no one spoke. Indeed, they had resumed eating. Clearly there was nothing for it. I looked for a bunk that seemed unoccupied and plonked my bag upon it.

'That's taken, fellah,' said one of the eaters without so much as looking up from his plate. I picked my bag up and put it on a different bunk. This one also appeared to me to be unoccupied.

'So is that one,' said the same voice. A couple of the faces were smiling. I tried a third, seemingly unoccupied, bunk.

'Sorry, fellah, that's mine,' said a second voice.

'Could you tell me which bunk is free?' My question was greeted with complete silence. I looked around forlornly and tried a fourth bunk.

'No good again, fellah,' said the second voice. 'That's where Jimbo's granny sleeps.' There was uproarious laughter at this, though whether at my expense or at this Jimbo's, I could not determine. I sensed I was being made fun of.

'Where *will* I sleep?'

'Where *will* he sleep?' parroted the owner of the first voice in mock desperation, addressing his question to the owner of the second. This person leaned back on the bench and appeared to give the problem careful consideration. Then he rolled his eyeballs, stuck his head below the table, and peered in both directions among the legs.

'We could put him under the table at a squeeze,' he said, re-emerging and addressing voice number one.

'Not much chance of that, Jack,' said voice one. 'Where will the flamin' Scandinavian sleep?'

Jack took another squint below the table.

'There'd be room for the both of them down there I reckon, Jimbo.'

This Jimbo shook his head and assumed a severe expression. 'Hoff is a frightful biter and scratcher when he's asleep. I've watched him.' There was another general laugh.

'I punch your head, maybe. Then you sleep all right, I think,' said a youth with fair hair and his first beard, who was clearly the frightful biter, Hoff. His comment provoked another gust of laughter. Jimbo returned to the original subject.

'What about rigging a hammock between the davits?'

'Old Fetherston wouldn't mind, but Hallet would say it was unsightly. No, fellah,' continued Jack, turning to me, 'it's a problem to know what to do with you.' The banter ceased. I stood uncertainly while the spoons clinked on the plates.

'You vant som grob, maybe?' said the one I had assumed to be Hoff the Scandinavian. He made room for me on the bench.

I was inclined to say they could keep their food. I did not think their welcome of a new crew member had been particularly warm. They were a scruffy group, and very cocksure, I thought. In their grimy shirts and dungarees they might have been navvies. One of the four was an exception to this. He sat at the end of the table and, though dressed in what were clearly work clothes, had a smartness, a fastidiousness to his appearance. The parting in his short hair was as straight as a ruler, his shirt was unbesmirched by the tar stains, paint stains, grease stains that marked the apparel of the others, and there was a scrubbed sheen to his shaven face. I had looked at him once or twice during the banter that had greeted my arrival and noticed that he occasionally smiled but never laughed outright. I assumed from his appearance some kind of seniority. The notion of a school prefect came into my mind.

'Yes, I will, thank you.' I decided that I would, after all, accept the invitation to eat.

'Heff you sompthing to eat vith?' Hoff had put a couple of slices of bread in front of me and was reaching for a saucepan.

'No. I didn't think I'd need to bring anything.' Hoff raised his eyeballs to heaven.

'Iss alvays first thing you bring on ship. Von plate, von spoon.'

An enamel plate was found for me and, to my surprise, Jimbo the teaser took his spoon from his empty plate, wiped it on his dungarees and pushed it across to me. Hoff ladled some meat in an oily gravy onto the plate and I dug in, bravely, because the food was wretched. The other young men around the table had forgotten the recent mirth and were engaged in wiping pellets of bread around their plates to sop up the last of their meal, or draining the tea in their cups and burping. I thought how horrified my mother would be at their table manners, and became acutely conscious of the daintiness of my own.

'What do they call you, fellah?' It was Jack who asked the question.

'John Reginald Boult.' I suppose my answer was pompous. There were some guffaws and I flushed.

'John Reginald Boult, eh? That's a mouthful.' Jack thought for a moment, leaning back against the chimney of a small stove. Without having said or done anything remarkable he seemed, to my mind at least, to be the focus of the cramped deckhouse. 'Well, you'd better be Johnny to us, I reckon.' He then formally affixed a name to each of those at the table. The young man with the straight parting was called Alex Holt, and I had been right in assuming some seniority for him. He was the head apprentice. The terrifying man I had met earlier at the rail was the ship's first mate, Mister Hallet.

'He seems very savage.' I wanted an opportunity to protest about my encounter with Mister Hallet and attract some sympathy to myself. Jack would not be drawn.

'Keep on the good side of him, and he's all right. You get what you deserve from old Hallet,' he said. So it was an affectionate and respectful 'old Hallet', was it?

The apprentices were getting up from the table and strolling out into the sunlight. I remembered I had been told to report to the savage first mate in half an hour, so I rushed off in search of him.

'Late,' he grunted, when I approached him. He was still leaning on the rail where I had left him. I was sure I was not late, and remembered my father's advice to stick up for myself.

'I don't think I am, sir.' He simply turned and glared at me for a moment, then resumed his surveillance of the wharf. I stood there waiting. Perhaps a minute or two went by. He was completely ignoring my presence. No one had done this to me before. I began to feel absurd, standing there waiting for something to happen. At length he turned and stared down at me.

'We have a choice, laddie. Either what I say goes, or what you say goes. Which is it?'

'I'm sorry, sir, but I don't think I was late.' His response was to turn back and regard the pier again. Another minute or two went by. After removing it for the meal, I had put my peajacket back on, thinking I would be required to present myself in formal attire. The sun poured down upon it, roasting me inside it like the stuff of a potato inside its blackened jacket, and this only served to exacerbate the humiliation I felt as he continued to ignore me. After an interval he turned to me again and regarded me with that piercing gaze.

'Which is it?'

'What you say, sir.'

'Ah.' He went back to watching the pier. Men were emerging from margins of shade and walking out along the heatstruck arm of the pier, to resume work. Mister Hallet and I stood close to where the shrouds of the mainmast — its network of supporting ropes — came down to their rigging screws. He gave me a glance over his shoulder and pointed upwards.

'Up you go.'

I looked skyward. The height of that mast, rising in its three stages, was awesome. Actually I quite enjoyed heights, being an inveterate scrambler up trees and over roofs during my schooldays. But I had never encountered anything as lofty as this before. Besides, as I squinted upward into the criss-cross of chain and wire and cordage, I felt strong qualms growing in me. The shrouds led up the mainmast and disappeared under a crescent-shaped platform some sixty feet above my head. Another smaller set radiated upwards and outwards from the mast just below this platform to its edges. I foresaw that anyone trying to clamber onto the platform would be hanging upside down for part of his climb. I couldn't do this. I was not a fly or a spider that could crawl across a ceiling. Gravity would pluck me off and I'd fall to my death on the deck. Yet how could I confront Mister Hallet once more?

'I don't think I can go up there, sir. You see...'

'UP!' Mister Hallet's countenance literally exploded around that syllable as he lunged at me. He could move like a cat. I scrambled to do his bidding.

The first part was easy, but then I reached those outward angling shrouds and funk took hold of me. I looked down to the deck, hoping the tall mate might have gone about his business. No such luck. There he stood, smaller now, his eyes, though shaded by his hand against the sun, still fixed on me, and the finger of one hand pointing heavenward. He was enjoying this. I was hurt and frightened and angry. Did he not realise that I might be killed? Could he not see it was impossible?

'I CAN'T,' I wailed. To my horror his response was to leap up onto the ship's rail and make as if to climb the rigging behind me. This was nightmarish. Clearly my life was not of the least importance to him. Either I was to become an insect or I was to be pulled from my present perch by this demonic man behind me. I decided the first course was preferable, so I reached up and began to climb out, hand over hand, upside down.

I believe I have never been so absolutely terrified as during those few seconds in which I first negotiated futtock shrouds, though I have certainly been in situations of greater peril. As it happens, my terror was needless. It is true that I felt the tug of gravity as I pushed my body outwards, but I had mistrusted the strength in my arms. They bore my weight well, and I had soon clambered up onto the platform that was the maintop.

I peeped over the edge. There was Mister Hallet, now back on the deck and with his finger pointing skyward again. I climbed the topmast shrouds, and by the time I reached the trestle-trees at the junction of the topmast and topgallant mast I was higher than the roofs of the warehouses. I had never been so high before. My state of funk had dissolved into nervous exhilaration. Again I peeped down, and there was the mate with his finger pointing upwards. I climbed the topgallant shrouds to where these came to an end in a bight around the royal mast. I looked down. This time Mister Hallet's finger was making sideways motions, as though he wanted me to step off into thin air. It took me a moment or so to realise that what he wanted was for me to go out along the royal yard, which was just above my head.

It was about the thickness of a man's thigh. Heaving myself up to it, I pressed my belly against its wooden arm and side-stepped very cautiously out along the footrope. It wobbled. It felt distinctly unsafe. By the time I reached the end of it I found I was panting, through nervousness rather than fatigue.

So there I was, virtually no more than a schoolboy, fresh from the protection of a good middle-class home, now perched at a giddy height above the city of Melbourne and looking down on a pier and ship where humans moved about, very tiny, very busy, with their one hundred important tasks appearing rather absurd from this height. The fierce Mister Hallet was apparently satisfied that I had attained his objective, for he had vanished. I had a few minutes of peace to contemplate the ship I had joined.

II

She was one of that large number of four-masted barques built in the Scottish shipyards during the eighties and nineties. I believe she originally carried the name of some British legendary hero, but she had changed hands a few times, and she now bore the sunnier, if more ordinary name, of *Emilia Denholm*. The original Mister Denholm must have had a large family for at one time there were reckoned to have been a dozen ships surnamed Denholm sailing out of London to different parts of the world. Generally the *Emilia D.*, as we called her, took a mixed cargo out to an Australian or New Zealand port, and carried a wool or wheat cargo home. On this occasion, after discharging her general cargo in Melbourne, she was due to sail in ballast to Port Chalmers, New Zealand, where a consignment of wool destined for London was waiting in the warehouses. My father, who had investigated the ship thoroughly before agreeing to sign my indentures, told me it was under the command of a Captain

Fetherston, a fine seaman though now advanced in years.

From my perch I had a grand view of the *Emilia D.* She was a powerful old lady. In front of me rose her foremast, crossed by six very square yards. The lowest of these was at that moment cockbilled, that is, tilted at an angle and being used as a crane to haul aboard a large bucket containing gravel. This was part of the ballast, and was being taken from a barge-like vessel alongside us. The bucket swung over the rail and disappeared down the forehatch, the cable paying out as though it were a rapier vanishing down the throat of a sword swallower.

If I twisted I could see the mizzenmast behind me, also crossed by six yards, but slightly shorter than the fore and mainmasts. Behind that was the jiggermast, with no yards, but a driver-boom and gaff. At the foot of the mizzen there was a pile of tackle, wire cable, cordage, various kinds of block, and laid out in rows were several rolled sails. One of these was in the process of being hauled to its yard, while on a yard above this some men were lashing another sail to the jackstay and tucking it in a neat furl along the top of the yard.

I cast my eye along the decks. Three of the four hatches already had their tarpaulins over them and their battens wedged. Of the two deckhouses on the main deck the after-most one was the accommodation for us apprentices, while in the fore deckhouse there was a galley and berths for the ship's carpenter, sailmaker, cook and bosun. The captain and two mates lived in more spacious surroundings below the poop deck, while the seamen lived in quarters under the anchor deck in the foremost part of the ship. There was a walkway that led from the poop deck, out across the roofs of both deckhouses to the anchor deck, hinged in various places so that it could be raised when the hatches were off and the ship was loading. I'm convinced that walkway was the corner-stone of power on that ship, for it gave whatever authority was in the character of the captain and his two mates an architectural advantage. They were able to pace along it, observe any part of the deck from it, and look down upon us from a height, like hawks eyeing the industry of fieldmice.

I cannot say that I always wanted to go to sea. I fancied myself as an Antarctic explorer at one stage, and a captain in the horse artillery at another. But I can say that ships impinged on my imagination from a very early age, and that images of ships, for some reason, form my earliest memories. I can remember, for instance, watching a large sailing ship come to her anchorage in Corio Bay. I was four, I think. The wind across the bay was tugging my mother's skirt on one side of me, and compelling my father to keep his hand up to his hat on the other. I was enthralled. The ship seemed to move as if by magic, propelled as it was by the invisible strength of the wind. There seemed to be a darkness all around it, my mother's dark skirts and my father's dark suit, a darkness in the sky as a rain squall moved across the bay, a darkness on the water. But as it exists in my imagination, that ship seems caught in a pool of brilliance with its green hull and duck-white sails. Then I saw the yards swinging and the foresails taken aback and blown against the mast, while other sails seemed to shrink upward into themselves. I could not, of course, discern the labour or hear the shouts that were going on aboard that ship while she completed her manoeuvre. To my four-year-old mind it was as if the ship behaved of her own accord, magically and with the instinctive grace of a Pacific gull coming in to land. Now, as I write this memoir, out of work and in my mid-thirties, the image of that ship still haunts me as something utterly still in time; beautiful, and a little ominous.

By the age of seven I was clambering among the timber piles of Geelong wharf with a scared playmate, grazing myself on the incrustations and slipping on the silky, treacherous weed that clung to the timber. I crept into lighters and pilot boats moored there, and was chased off by burly men with loud voices. Later, in a schoolroom, while my classmates confronted barbarous problems of algebra, or were lulled to drowsiness by the recital of a poem, I was drawing ships; ships of all sizes, ships from all ages. More than once one of Nelson's great battle fleet, majestic in the final stages of its composition, was ripped from beneath my fingers and torn to shreds, while I, the unhappy admiral, was hauled by my ear to a corner and ordered to face the wall.

About the age of fourteen my preoccupation with the sea changed subtly. I still studied ships with an unabated passion, but that passion now involved an image of myself. I had met on the Geelong promenade a man who had been to sea in ships, both sail and steam. He was a stocky fellow in his late forties whose ginger beard was turning grey in places, and whose eyes were underlined by dark, delicate purses of skin, the result, I suspect now, of ruinous drinking. He spoke with a cockney accent, and its effect, when he reeled off the names of the places he had been to — Iquique, Antofagasta, Puget Sound, Algoa Bay, Port Jackson — was a curious mixture of the homely and the exotic. His quiet tones always suggested he was talking as much to himself as he was to me, yet how that London voice, with its surprising suggestion of cosiness, infected me. There was such a richness, such an abundance of experience that it conveyed. Geelong is a small town, at least it was then; yet there, in that kindly ex-seaman's head, was a coil of life that wound throughout the world. I don't suppose my existence was of much importance to him, but I worshipped what he was and wanted to embark upon the same way of life in order to attain the same kind of character. To lean on a rail at some future date, to cast a casual eye on my audience, to talk quietly from a generous store of anecdotes, to be the vessel of a rich and vivid existence, that seemed to me at fourteen to be the highest ambition in the world.

I remember one afternoon quizzing him about the ship-masters he had served under. He drew a picture of a formidable breed of man.

'You see, there's no law at sea, son, no courts, no constabulary. There's only the captain's word. If he says pile the ship up on them there rocks, you do it. If he says crack on sail so that the masts come down around your ears, you do it. Not that I ever met one who did that. It's a hard certificate to get, a Master Mariner's ticket, and most of the ones I worked for were pretty sound on top. They're tough, mind, but stable. Some may hit the bottle hard — it's a lonely job — but they can usually walk without swaying. It doesn't do their tempers or their livers much good. Some take to the Bible rather than the grog, with the same effect on their tempers, if not their livers.'

He talked about the fighting skippers of the old American clippers, and the furious British tea-clipper captains racing their ships home from Foochow, Whampoa, or Canton.

One day he was no longer there. I was disappointed. I had come to rely on his daily habit of leaning on that promenade rail and gazing out over the bay. Perhaps he had grown tired of all my questions. Perhaps he had gone back to sea. It was some weeks later that I learnt actual news of him. I was standing quite close to where I used to encounter him. One of the regular fishermen came past and stopped.

'You heard what happened to him?'

I hadn't heard.

'He died. Oh, three weeks ago now. Very sudden.'

Died? How could he? I think my reaction was more one of shock than grief. It was the first time someone had actually died on me. Of course I lived in a city where there were cemeteries, funerals, death notices in the newspapers. But that a man I had met, had listened to at such-and-such a place only a few weeks before, that he should be abruptly dead, gone irrecoverably from my world, that *was* a shock. How could a man with such a vivid experience coiled within him just cease to exist? As I say, it was the first time someone had died on me, and it produced an alarm that I have never since completely freed my mind of, and which I think is lodged in the minds of most of us, the feeling that our existences are, somehow, foreclosed from the outset.

I am still not certain exactly what my father's job was. He worked for a firm, though I know he neither made things nor sold them. I believe he had something to do with inspecting them. Whatever it was, he was in contact with import companies and shipping companies. By sixteen I was determined he should sign my indentures and get me a place on a sailing ship. He grumbled that he had paid for my education to suit me to better things than mucking about in ships. He called my preoccupation with the sea 'obsessive', but he signed them, and secured me a place on the *Emilia D.* where he had been told there were other apprentices of Australian extraction.

So there I was, ready to begin adult life. For the first time since coming aboard I felt exhilarated. This was the ship, with its white masts and black spars, the discreet colours of a seabird, with its deck accommodations of varnished mahogany, its capstans, winches, pumps, its chain and cordage, its halyard-blocks, gin-blocks, lift-blocks, buntline-blocks, its

crescent-shaped tops and its long spreaders, all part of a
sublime and practical unity. And I was now a part of it, now,
at the outset of my working life. Yes, the earth spread out in
all directions beneath my perch on that royal yard, and they
were *my* directions. I was intoxicated with glamorous possibilities. I descended that mast.

III

There was not much glamour, not in the first couple of days
certainly. When I reached the deck Alex was waiting for me.
'I've been told to give you a job. But you can't do it in that
clobber. You'd better come with me. Did you bring any
working clothes?'
I told him I had and we went to the midshiphouse. I was
grateful for being taken in hand. As I changed, Alex said,
'You don't want to take much notice of Jimbo and Jack. They
were teasing you. They do it to every newcomer.' He waited
for me to assure him that I had guessed as much before
continuing. 'Did you decide on a bunk? Well, you can have
this one. And here, a spoon, a cup and a plate. You should
have your own knife.' Clearly, during my absence up the
mainmast Alex had been arranging things. There was a
fastidiousness in his manner that I found reassuring, for in
truth I had been worried by little things such as where I
should sleep and what I should eat from. Alex dissolved these
worries one by one. There was something rather maternal
about his consideration. He was a soothing, organising
presence, bustling about the deckhouse on my behalf.
I had hoped that I would be set to work with the other
members of the crew hauling the sails to the mizzen yards,
but the job that was given to me was to grease the royal,
topgallant and topmasts, so that the parrels — the collars
which fastened the yards to the masts — would slide easily on
them. Alex showed me how to rig a bosun's chair with a line
and plank in such a way that I could raise and lower myself;
then he left me to the task.
It was a filthy job. The black grease smothered my hands
and forearms; gobbets of it got into my hair and eyes and
mouth. The bosun's chair was awkward to manage. No one
was there to help me. The hours of the afternoon and early

evening dragged. I slopped the awful black jelly onto the upper masts in a gulf of misery. This was not what I had decided to go to sea for. I thought of my home in Geelong and how comfortable it was. I thought of the school holidays my classmates were enjoying, and how free they were. I was not happy.

The sun went down, the twilight darkened. I worked on. Finally Jimbo called up to me.

'Knock-off time, fellah.' I clambered down. 'Eugh, you're a sight.' He provided me with a bucket. 'You'll need plenty of water to get that lot off you,' he advised, then left me. I went to where there was a water pump and began to scrub. But instead of removing the sliminess, I succeeded only in spreading it as a film over my entire body. I must have splashed about a bit for I did not hear the approach of someone behind me. It was as I was pumping a fresh quantity of water into the bucket that a hand seized my hair and wrenched me backwards, while I heard the half-full bucket being kicked away angrily.

'What special rights do you think you have, laddie?' Mister Hallet glared down at me.

'I'm washing the grease off me, sir.'

There then followed a furious lesson on the use of fresh water on a sailing ship. Did I not know that fresh water was more precious than my paltry life on a ship? Did I not know that the bucket I was fouling was used to fetch the drinking water for twelve men?

'What must I do?'

It was demonstrated what I must damned well do. My ear was once more pinched in those powerful forceps and I was taken to where a tin can with a length of cord was stowed. With this in my hand I was next led by my ear to the rail. The tin can was dropped into the waters of Port Phillip Bay and hauled up. *That* was my damned bath water, and I was told to perform my damned ablutions in the waterways because if I fouled up Mister Hallet's deck in the same manner as I had done by that pump, he, Mister Hallet, would see I cleaned it up with my tongue. Now, I could get a swab and get the damned grease off that deck. With this parting instruction the first mate strode off.

I suppose I listened to that tirade, but if so it was from some deep recess of despair. While it was going on I was dimly aware of members of the crew passing back and forth and exchanging grins. I found a mop and swabbed down his precious deck, and as I did so I wept tears of hopelessness, tears of bitter humiliation. This was adult life? I was resolved I would leave the hideous ship, its inhuman first mate and its cocksure apprentices that night.

I went into the deckhouse where the apprentices were having their evening meal. I noted that the place I had occupied at midday was untaken, and that the plate, spoon and cup that Alex had provided for me were laid there.

'Supper time, Johnny,' said Alex.

'I'm not hungry,' I muttered, hardly able to conceal the desolation I felt. To my relief I was not bothered by any further attentions; apparently no one felt my despondency was a cause for either teasing or sympathy. With my clothes on and the sliminess of the grease all about my skin, I lay down on my bunk and gave myself entirely to self-commiseration.

The working hours of a sailing ship in port in those days were from sunrise to sunset, and that long working day was a convenience to me that night. Quite soon after the meal was finished three of my four fellow apprentices retired to their bunks. Alex pored over a rather battered tome, and occasionally wrote things into an exercise book, but he too retired eventually, and the deckhouse fell silent save for some light snoring and the occasional somnolent mutter.

I pulled my bag from its corner and stole out. There seemed to be nobody about. Two lamps shone above the doors to the poop accommodation, and there was one shining for'ard. The harbour water slopped rhythmically against the hull like the tongue of a ruminant creature, while in the distance was the hum of Melbourne's night traffic. I reached the gangplank in a moment. Once I stubbed my toe on a runner and nearly toppled into the thin wedge of oily water between the wharf piles and the ship's slab side. I shuddered at the thought of being crushed in there. Ahead was terra firma. The pier with its derricks and engines was lit by a three-quarter moon. I made for a patch of shadow beneath one of the derricks.

'Breaking ship, young man?'

I believe I gave some involuntary exclamation, and froze. There was a shortish man confronting me. I could discern a pointed white beard. I had practically walked into his arms. How in the world had he got there? He continued in his quiet, measured voice.

'The harbour gate is that way.' He pointed with his arm in a direction slightly different to the one I had intended to take. 'And the next tram will be at...' he took out a fob watch from his pocket, '...six a.m. That is to say, in a bit over six hours' time. You'll have a long wait.' I looked at him dumbly. It crossed my mind that he might be a policeman, for there were brass buttons on his dark coat, but policemen in my experience were taller and bulkier than the kempt figure before me. Nevertheless his presence exerted some powerful constraint on me, for I simply stood there, my will to act paralysed.

'Follow me,' he said, after watching me for a moment, and marched briskly up the gangplank and across the deck to the poop doors. So this was Captain Fetherston. The realisation suddenly made me feel very guilty. It was an effect that headmasters had had on me at different times. We went through an iron door and passed along a corridor with doors on both sides, then through a panelled door with a cut-glass handle into a spacious well-furnished room. A kerosene lantern had been left burning on an oval table that occupied the centre of the chamber. Against two of the walls there were couches, built into the third was a cabinet, and through the fourth a staircase climbed to the poop deck above. This was the stateroom, and very sumptuous after the cramped conditions of the midshiphouse.

'Stand there.' Captain Fetherston busied himself putting away various papers that he had been carrying, and lighting a second kerosene lamp. Then he sat down and contemplated me.

'Do you have a name, young man?'

'John Boult, sir.'

'Ah yes. Well, John Boult. It seems you have been caught in the act of deserting a merchant ship.' He allowed this time to sink in. 'Now, you are not a schoolboy any longer, so I shall tell you what I am empowered to do to you, or anyone else who tries to jump ship after he's signed on. I can lock you in a room and feed you two slices of bread and one glass of water per day until the ship is at sea.' He paused again. 'Or I can hand you over to one of the dock policemen, who will take you to court where you will be convicted, fined, and brought back here under escort. Do you understand?'

I felt foolish and miserable. I nodded dumbly.

'Speak up.'

'I understand, sir,' I mumbled.

'Speak up.'

'I understand, sir,' I said more audibly.

'Good. Now I can also pay you off tomorrow morning, though in your case you won't be collecting any actual pay. You will be free to go back to the cosy life that you came from.' There was a further pause. 'I tell you these things because I want you to realise that between now and the time that you or I leave this ship your life is entirely in my hands. Do you understand?'

'Yes, sir.'

'Aye aye, sir,' he corrected.

'Aye aye, sir.'

'Good. Well, of the three options open to me, I can tell you now that I would pay you off rather than lock you up or turn you over to the courts. It's my intention to sail in three days' time, and I don't want any delays. Also, I'd rather sail short-handed than have milksops or shirkers aboard who will prove a burden to me. Is that clear?'

'Aye aye, sir.' I was stung by the word 'milksop'. He looked at me in silence for perhaps half a minute, then the stern expression on his face relaxed.

'However, even though you seem to have turned tail at the first sign of difficulty, I'm prepared to believe you are a brave enough lad. We might even make a sailor of you. I'm not going to ask what your grievances are. I don't believe you have been long enough on board to have any grievances that would interest me. What I want you to do now is to return to your berth and go to sleep. If, in the morning, you still want to leave, then come and see me. Otherwise go to work with everyone else. There'll be no need for you to be shamefaced about this episode, for my guess is that only you and I know about it. So we can behave as if it never occurred, can't we?

'Aye aye, sir.'

'Off you go.'

It's difficult to express the sudden confidence that man instilled in me. The even tone of his voice conveyed the idea that there was an orderliness in the world. He seemed to communicate a shape to my actions, and a shape to the possibilities that lay before me. He had been uncompromising, yet somehow he had also been kindly. I closed the iron poop door softly behind me and crossed the deck. Certainly my grievances hadn't evaporated. But they'd shrunk. Had another adult been present at that midnight interview he might have observed to Captain Fetherston that he had given the boy a sense of perspective on things, for subtly I had been committed to remaining on the ship. I crept into my bunk and slept.

IV

In what seemed no time at all I was being shaken by Alex.

'Rise and shine, Johnny.'

It was scarcely light. I followed the other apprentices to where they were gathering at the galley door. We were each given a smoking mug of coffee, and within ten minutes were set to work.

The day that followed was interminable, and as demoralising in its tedium as the previous day had been in its rude shocks. While others continued to send up sails and rig the running tackle, I and a couple of fo'c'sle hands were lowered over the side on a plank, armed with a chipping hammer and a tin of red lead. Hour on hour I chipped at a patch of rust, covered it with red lead, chipped another, covered it, chipped, covered. Flakes of rust coated me, got into my hair and eyes. The other fellows chattered and left me to my own thoughts. Near the end of the first thousand years came breakfast, and some time in the succeeding centuries came the midday meal. In the afternoon we painted over patches of red lead with black, the colour of the hull. Finally (at the end of time) Mister Hallet's eyebrows appeared over the fo'c'sle rail.

'That'll do, gentlemen.'

The next day may have seemed shorter, perhaps because I was set to work with the other apprentices and my presence began to attract some friendly notice. The last of the ballast was in and the carpenter battened and wedged the forward hold. Mister Hallet required his decks to be restored to their original pristine splendour after the fouling they had received from the boots of harbour officials, dockers, representatives of the owners — the 'dockside riff-raff' as the mate termed them. So we rubbed the decks with sand and canvas, moving in a line on our knees from the windlass toward the poop. In this posture I came to know a little more about the irrepressible Jimbo.

As our line of deck-rubbers came abreast of the forward deckhouse, I happened to be the one nearest to the galley door. Jimbo was rubbing the patch of deck next to me. Suddenly I heard him say something.

'What?' I looked to see if his mumble had been directed at me, but Jimbo's eyes were intent on the deck and his hands were rubbing mechanically back and forth. I resumed my task, a little bewildered.

'When Hallet turns his back, swap places with me.' Again came the voice, yet when I looked Jimbo still rubbed the deck as though it absorbed all his attention.

'You haven't got leisure to admire the man next door to you, laddie.' Mister Hallet was standing on the walkway above my head. I rubbed furiously.

'Don't work so fast,' hissed Jimbo. 'We'll miss our chance.'

'What chance?' I hissed back, petrified the first mate would hear me and unleash himself.

'Swap now...come on...now.' And before I knew what was happening Jimbo had slipped across to the other side of me and elbowed me unceremoniously to one side. He continued to rub with perfect equanimity.

Terrified though I was that Mister Hallet would leap from that walkway into our midst, I was intrigued by what Jimbo was up to. I was too new to the ship, and to the wiles of apprentices, to have paid any importance to our proximity to the galley. I swear I scarcely took the corner of my eye off Jimbo as I rubbed, but suddenly he was thrusting something into the pocket of my dungarees.

'A present. Shhhh!'

I suspected a practical joke to embarrass me, something trivial and annoying. I went to put my hand in my pocket.

'Not here, weevil-brains. That cook'll be out in a minute.'
Jimbo moved back to his original place in the line. He was
right. The cook emerged and stood watching from the galley
door. I felt most of his attention focused on me, and went hot
with anxiety. He waited, like a man trying to decide something, then shrugged and went inside.

We knocked off for the midday meal and I put my hand in
my pocket. It was full of squashy, sticky things. I took out a
few. Raisins: my pocket was full of raisins. I put one in my
mouth.

'Here, give us a handful.' Jimbo had come up behind me
and dived his hand in my pocket.

'I thought you were playing some practical joke.' My
remark caused Jimbo to look at me with an expression of
theatrical disgust.

'Gratitude! You'll be kissing my feet for the small comforts
my talents procure for you by the time we've been at sea a
week or two, my most unthankful son.'

Jimbo was an accomplished galley-thief. He was in the third
year of our four-year apprenticeships, and with Jack had
joined the *Emilia Denholm* in London. Previously both had
sailed from Newcastle, New South Wales, to San Francisco,
thence to Taltal, back to 'Frisco, where they had joined an
oregon carrier for London.

'We didn't last long on that one,' said Jack ruefully as we
ate our meal. 'She was a good ship, but the cook told the
captain he would resign rather than go to sea in the same
vessel as Jimbo again. Damned thieving rascal he called him.
Alas, that bloke was a good ship's cook, one of the very rare
ones, so it was Jimbo that went.'

'But why did you go too, Jack?' I asked.

'Aw, look at him, will you. How could he ever look after
himself?'

I did observe him. He was grinning at Jack's sardonic dis-
paragement with an expression of genuine pride. He had
broad, tanned features that were more boyish than Jack's,
with a spigot of blonde hair at the top and a lopsided grin at
the bottom. It was the sort of face that charms shop assistants
and old ladies but arouses instant suspicion in policemen. For
the rest, Jimbo had huge hands — not a thief's hands at all;
he was stocky, with long arms and short legs, a little ape-like

indeed, and this resemblance he exploited. For he was incurably comic and mischievous and at odd times in the voyage he made us laugh to the point of tears with his grotesque parodies of our behaviour.

Jack and Jimbo were inseparables. They had begun their apprenticeships together and had always contrived to secure a berth on the same ship. I had the impression at the time, wrong as it turned out to be, that neither of them could take anyone or anything very seriously. They certainly took very little of what they themselves did seriously.

We were knocking off at the end of the day. Jack and Jimbo were walking behind me.

'What makes you think Johnny has difficulty getting a job where he works with his hands, Jack?' said Jimbo, clearly pitching his question for my ears.

'You tell me, mate,' said Jack.

'Look at him, will you. He treads on them as he walks.'

The two guffawed, and I was uncertain as to whether I should be amused or offended. Hoff passed the pair of them at that moment.

'Of course with Hoff it's more of a co-ordination problem. Clap your hands together, you Scandinavian monkey; like this, see.' And Jimbo turned his face into a mask of idiocy, flailing his hands in the air.

'I vill coorbinate your nose vith my fist, maybe,' rejoined Hoff, glancing back over his shoulder.

'Coorbinate, coorbinate,' crowed Jimbo, leaping onto Hoff's back and compelling the apprentice to carry him piggyback. They lurched about the deck like tipsy revellers until their frolic concluded in a mock sparring. The banter continued over the evening meal.

I noticed that Alex was never the subject of this chiacking. He was in the fourth year of his apprenticeship and was due to sit for his second mate's certificate when the ship reached London. It would have been foolhardy to speculate what kind of a ship's officer the scurrilous Jimbo would have made, but there were no doubts at that time that Alex was the ideal candidate for those rigorous Board of Trade examinations.

V

It was clear, even as we stood waiting for our coffee before sunrise on the third day, that a new air of expectancy was abroad. Captain Fetherston, Mister Hallet, and Mister Gillard, who had joined the ship late the previous night, were holding conference in a group on the flying bridge. The ballast lighter had gone.

We were set to work rigging the last of the running tackle and lashing the headsails and staysails to the iron hanks by which they ran up the stays. As we worked, Alex named and described every part to me with a thoroughness that was a little pedantic. Not that I minded. I was breathing in the heady smells of canvas, hemp and manilla.

In the middle of the afternoon a tugboat arrived and we took on board its cable. Mister Gillard leaned negligently against the fo'c'sle rail as the seamen worked without apparent supervision, flinging a line to the tug, hauling back a stout cable and securing it around a towing bitt. Our mooring hawsers were cast off by men along the wharf who communicated with us by a variety of signals with cap and hand which to my mind resembled more a mysterious ritual than the exchange of information. The wharf moved away behind us as though it were the world that withdrew from us and we who were stationary. I was entranced. It was, I recall, a Saturday afternoon, and Port Phillip Bay was alive with small sails blown this way and that, as though the wind had taken a ream of paper and scattered it.

As the city slipped further behind us the grey of ware-houses, the ochreous colour of towers and steeples, the red-brick office buildings merged to a misty blue colour. We passed an encrusted channel marker on which a cormorant was drying its wings, statuesque and sooty black in the late afternoon sunshine. I looked out to starboard and tried to discern Corio Bay and Geelong. Was that the spire of the Catholic Cathedral? I could not be sure. All that I had known — my parents' home, my school, the waterfront with its yachts and fishermen's boats — all were dropping away from me like clothes I had grown out of. Yes, I was entranced. . .and rather smug.

I looked up to where the yards moved against the sky with their sails waiting to be broken out. I looked ahead to where the little tug ploughed gamely on towards the bay's entrance like a squat farmer leading an immense piebald horse. A plume of dirty smoke flew from its funnel and dissolved eastward. Flocks of scavenging gulls careered in its wake and ours. I was sailing away. I was a part of a ship's inexorable motion. It was an outset, an exotic outset. Did I think it would change me? Dimly perhaps. But I was too alive to immediate sensation that brilliant afternoon to pay much attention to the future. For a few hours I was inexpressibly buoyant.

The crew were called to the break of the poop where we were divided into watches. There were twenty-eight of us, three ship's officers, the 'day men' as the carpenter, sailmaker, cook and steward were called, sixteen seamen, and we five apprentices. Mister Gillard's watch was made up entirely from the fo'c'sle, while the five of us and seven seamen made up Mister Hallet's watch. We were, if anything, a little shorthanded, for the bosun who had been with the ship from London had been taken ill in Melbourne, and Captain Fetherston had not appointed another.

I glanced around the assembled faces. At one time I may have been able to recall the names of the able seamen, but with the exception of Big MacPherson they have now gone from my memory. As apprentices, and future ship's officers we were not encouraged to fraternise with the fo'c'sle crowd, though of course we did, for it was the repository of too much lore and too many yarns for us, cubs as we were, to stand on dignity. Besides, for all practical purposes, our work was identical with theirs.

'Break out upper and lower topsails, if you please, Mister Hallet,' instructed Captain Fetherston. Mister Hallet bellowed and we leapt to life. Buntlines, clew and spilling lines were thrown off their pins and set free for running. We went aloft and loosed the gaskets holding the sails, while others below sheeted the lower topsails home. Then down we came, and with a few turns around the handiest capstan, we hauled each of the three great upper topsail yards to the sheaves on their respective masts.

'Fore and maincourses,' bellowed Mister Hallet. These two sails, the largest on the ship, fell away from their gaskets. We were passing through the Rip, with the lights of Queenscliff off to starboard and those of Sorrento further off to port. As we entered the waters of Bass Strait the motion of the vessel changed from a smooth gliding to a long and regular up-and-down.

'Brace and trim the yards. Inner and outer jibs.'

We were given no moment for reflection. In a long line we hauled the braces, and as each yard was brought around, the sail relinquished its languorous flapping and assumed the shape of a vast ovular belly. For'ard, the headsails climbed their respective stays and were sheeted home. The little tug ploughed on ahead of us, but now we were beginning to move under our own power and the heavy tow-rope sagged and disappeared in the water every now and then.

Here was man's work. I was sixteen, and it was my first taste of it. Each of the tasks we performed was straightforward enough; our instructions were crisp. I can't say that my pleasure on that late afternoon derived from the thrill of knowing very much of what I was doing. I spent most of my time following what others did, grabbing at the end of ropes that others had picked out. I suppose it was the joy of having entered into a mystery, one of the very old mysteries, that intelligent involvement with things, that self-forgetfulness we call work. Maybe. And maybe there wasn't very much at all inside my head as I scrambled up and down those masts or hauled on this and that with a boyish heartiness I now remember with slight embarrassment. But I do have an image of that first afternoon's real work (I didn't count the drudgery of the previous two days) that is delicious and poignant to savour now.

'Break out the upper and lower topgallants.' As we climbed, the masts were writing small circles against the evening sky. The ship was easily overhauling the tug by this time and the order was given to cast off. The hawser dropped from us. The vessel had heeled slightly to port and rode the powerful waters of the strait in a slow-motion gallop. There was a long *carrrush* as the bow wave parted from our stem and folded itself backwards and sideways in a tuck of white lace. The sky behind us had a cherry tinge near its horizon, while ahead, toward New Zealand, it was dark. The weather, Alex told me, was unusually benign for Bass Strait. With the ship now making her own way, Mister Hallet's watch was stood down. We were to be called at midnight.

By that hour the wind had freshened slightly, but Captain Fetherston had cracked on royals and topgallant staysails. I was detailed as lookout with instructions to stare ahead and call the mate if I saw any ships or obstructions.

'There are skerries and islands all over this part of the strait, to say nothing of the shipping. If I see any ship or other object you've not told me about first, you'll be shark's dinner, laddie.' Mister Hallet's special gift was that of making life terrifying. I strained to look into the darkness ahead. With the first mate's impressive threat in mind, my imagination naturally conjured all manner of lights and obstacles on the shifting surface of the sea, while the apprehension of arousing his ire, should what I had seen prove illusory, inhibited me from summoning him. Was that an outcrop of rocks just then — there, above the mobile contours of the sea? Was that a light, or the reflection of a star, or a trick my eyes were playing? The fact that there was a good moon shining did not help my unaccustomed gaze. If only I could have shared the vigil with someone else, someone more at home with the task. On one occasion I did tentatively sound the bell that I knew would bring Mister Hallet, and when he came I pointed to what I thought were rocks ahead and to starboard. He took one glance and grunted negatively. I tried to forestall an outburst of ill temper.

'I'm sorry I brought you up here on a false errand, sir.' He looked at me from the darkness and I could just discern his eyebrows sinking over his eyes.

'Laddie,' he said, 'if you bring me up here too often on false errands, I'll box your ears. But if we bump into anything you've not told me about, I'll feed you to the sharks.' So saying, he marched away and left me to reflect on the alternatives. Yet I was learning. Mister Hallet's manner was disconcerting, but there was an impersonality about it that suggested it was not vindictive. I called him again when I saw a pinprick of green light in the distance, which he immediately identified as one of the Hobart fruit schooners, though how, on the evidence of one navigation light he could be so confident of this, I don't know. After what seemed a cold eternity, Jack relieved me, and I went to stand with the rest of the watch in the lee of the deckhouse, to await whatever instructions might issue from the poop. I looked back toward the helm and could make out against the darkness the blacker figures of Mister Hallet, Captain Fetherston and the man at the wheel.

'Does Captain Fetherston stay up all night?' I asked Alex.

'Until we've cleared Flinders Island. He'll probably want to see us through the various skerries in this part of the strait; the Hogans, the Curtis Group, and others. Captain Fetherston has never lost a ship. He's one of the very best,' said Alex.

'But how will he know when we've cleared Flinders Island?'

'We'll be sighting the Deal Island light, shortly, I expect. It won't be long after that we're in open water.'

I was impressed. I felt entirely safe. There was the clockwork of our rostering, the scrupulous tidiness of our ship, the crisp flow of instructions issuing from the poop. So he had never lost a ship. There was something reassuringly parental about the man. All around us the sea moved in its black gulfs, gathered itself up and fell away again as if always on the point of forming some crude sculpture, then changing its mind. And through that shapelessness we moved, parting the water with the same deliberate slowness that a tailor has as he cuts through a length of cloth. *Carrrush*, sang the sea, as it divided at our stem, and then again *carrrush*. We were solid, the substantial moving upon the insubstantial. I remember that contrast pleased me at the time. And at the centre of our existence was this shortish man with his quiet voice, scarcely the demonic driver my Geelong sailor had described to me. Alex's confidence in him was infectious. Yes, I felt secure.

VI

We were relieved at four a.m. I slept the sleep of the dead, was roused, and emerged muzzy-headed and bewildered for the forenoon watch at eight a.m. During those brief hours below, the ship had cleared Flinders Island, and Captain Fetherston had set a course for the Foveaux Passage. With the perils of Bass Strait behind him, that serene man had gone below. He had been on deck for twenty-three hours.

For nine days we held our east-south-easterly course. The wind remained unusually moderate for those waters. The sky, by day, was a deep Australasian blue on which our four masts inscribed their slow spirals. The sun rose from behind New Zealand and fell behind Tasmania. Each morning and afternoon the oblongs of shade cast by our sails performed their gradual progress across the decks of our ship. It was a fitting background to our own routine of watch-on, watch-off. We swabbed down the decks and paintwork, we sweated down those ropes that had worked slack in the night, we trimmed the great yards where necessary and we ran out the logline to calculate our progress. This latter worked out to be an average of one hundred and fifty miles a day, which may have caused Mister Hallet to chafe, but which I, with no premiums to worry about, was delighted by. It was a leisurely, carefree pace, and all — or at least most — of the details of my existence conspired to make these first days halcyon.

Each midday Captain Fetherston took a reading of the sun, plotted our position, and spent an hour or so making various observations to us apprentices about navigation and seamanship. All of us were given the sextant in order to make our own readings. They were sessions of 'What do you do if...' What do you do if your anchor drags or your cable parts? What do you do if your ship is on its beam ends? Our questions, I recall, had a bias toward situations of extreme peril, but they were answered and illustrated by the captain with the same seriousness as questions that involved less dire circumstances. We sat cross-legged at his feet around the saloon skylight as he spoke. It was the only formal part of our training.

Within a day or so of leaving Melbourne I did my first stint at the helm, and did not escape falling foul again of Mister Hallet. I approached the wheel with some trepidation. The barque was suddenly very long and very lofty, and I was very small. Anything might happen.

'The wind is southerly at the present, laddie, just forward of our beam,' said Mister Hallet. He pointed at the mizzen royal. 'Watch the compass card, and keep a weather eye on the luff of that sail. If you see it tremble, adjust the helm, like so. Stay awake.'

I took the spokes gingerly and tried to do as I had been told. I concentrated very hard — at first. If the compass needle wandered a degree, I corrected. If the royal showed any signs of trembling, I corrected. The ship responded to my touch. Here was control. My initial hesitation changed to elation. The barque obeyed me, as though it were a huge animal, sensitive and willing. My confidence grew. I became rather blithe and began to daydream a bit. I began to rather fancy myself as an experienced mariner, and took sidelong glances at the sea. How fast we were moving.

Ouch! My head felt as though it had been cracked with a gin-block. I twisted my neck to see what had struck me, and faced the glowering Hallet. He grasped me by the hair and jerked my head in the direction it should have been.

'You've twenty-eight lives in your care, boy. Take your eye off the job again and I'll thrash the liver out of you.'

I stared miserably ahead. I remember seeing Captain Fetherston turning to discover what the commotion was about, and smiling, presumably at the pained expression on my features. I felt momentarily betrayed. Mister Hallet was Mister Hallet, but I had assumed the captain to be a protective ally. Not necessarily so, I learned.

But the incident made no lasting dent in the feeling of content I experienced during the crossing of the Tasman. I was temporarily injured, but not aggrieved, and I suppose this was because I no longer felt alone as I did on my first day aboard. I had my fellows. Furthermore my body had adapted surprisingly quickly to the change in sleeping pattern entailed by the four hours on, four hours off. The drowsiness that beset my first couple of days vanished.

Besides, the days were crowded with new sensations. One morning Alex called me to the cat-head.

'Look there,' he said. I followed where he pointed into the white fold of our bow wave. 'Dolphins. There's four of them, I think.' Out of the white disturbed water I caught a momentary glimpse of a head with what appeared to be a deep hole in the middle of its forehead.

I had seen dolphins before, but only at a distance on some of the ocean beaches south of Geelong. There they would gambol up and down some two hundred yards out, moving with the slow, regular motion of the painted animals of a merry-go-round. But this was different. The creature emerged briefly again, shooting forward, then veering outward into unbroken water. It was like a submerged rocket, trailing a silvery plume of air and water behind it. The distended blow-hole on its forehead made it seem very vulnerable. And there was another, and there!

'Some of the fellows like to try and spear them. I prefer to let them be. There's something wrong in harming them, I think. It's different with other fish; with sharks, say.' Alex furrowed his brow. He knew a lot about dolphins and spoke of the creatures with great affection.

'You sound as if you wish you were one, Alex.' I meant the remark light-heartedly.

'I sometimes think they could teach us a few things. But wishing won't stop the fellows spearing them, will it?' he said, with a quick smile. It was curious how he took the burden of other creatures' sorrows upon himself.

Alex set out to teach me how to do the various splices, whippings and knots. He was a patient, remorseless teacher. We sat on the sunny side of the deckhouse surrounded by pieces of old rope. It was all a matter of procedure, he told me.

'Step one: unstrand about four inches. Step two: fold the middle strand back. Step three: take the right hand strand...' and so on. The finished product, in this case a back-splice, was inevitably as well groomed as its maker. Then it was my turn. Following a procedure has never been one of my talents; for some reason imagination always obstructed my good intentions. Thus my efforts to copy Alex's splice were ugly at best, and botched more generally. Alex would watch my fumbling intently and give a curious, pained laugh when I had finished.

'No, you didn't do it as I showed you.'

'I did all the things I could remember.'

'Here, I'll splice it again.'

'Let's give it a rest, Alex.'

'We might as well finish it, Johnny. Then it's done with.'

'I'll do it tomorrow.' I got up to go, but the momentary expression of injury that registered on Alex's face made me change my mind. He looked down at the rope in his hand, as if to hide his face.

'All right. Let's do it now. Show me again.' Alex once more produced a perfectly finished back-splice, then gave me the other end of the rope to do. Mister Hallet came by as I finished.

'What's that, laddie?'

'A back-splice, sir.'

He took it and twirled it in his fingers, then gave it back with a grim smile, and said to Alex, 'You'd better keep him at

it, mister.' He strode off. Despite his lack of enthusiasm for
my handiwork, the impression I gained from this exchange
was one of friendliness, albeit remote.

'Alex, is Mister Hallet fierce all the time?'

'That's not real fierceness, not fierce fierceness. He can be a
bit gruff, but you expect that in a mate.' We were silent for a
while.

'Why isn't he captain of his own ship?'

Alex looked at the odds and ends of twine and rope that
lay around us. He paused for a moment or two before
answering my question.

'You've got to be over a certain age before you can sit for
your Master's Certificate.'

'But Mister Hallet must be over forty. Is that too young?'

'Yes.' He looked at me quickly and it was quite transparent
that he had lied. He had a strange face. It changed so rapidly
from an expression of intent eagerness to one of troubled perplexity. At nineteen he was the eldest, as well as the senior,
apprentice, yet there was something uncomfortably boyish in
his face.

I let the matter drop, but later I spoke to Jack. We had
completed a session on the pumps, and were stowing the
crank-handles.

'Jack, how old do you have to be before you can become a
captain?'

'Depends, fellah. Some get their tickets before they're
twenty-five. Old Fetherston's been a Master for thirty-five
years or more, so he must have got his at about that age. He
used to be on the China tea run before it was taken over by
steam.'

'But Mister Hallet's over twenty-five. Why hasn't he got a
ship?'

'He did have one once.' This was a revelation.

'Why doesn't he have one any more?'

'Aw, one reason and another. He may well take over here
before we get to London, though he'll probably turn it down;
he's done so in the past.'

'Take over here? How do you mean?'

'Didn't you know? Old Fetherston's retiring from the sea
when we get to Port Chalmers. He's got family up near
Christchurch somewhere. I believe he's thinking of farming.

He's a spry old fellah for sixty-plus, don't you think?'

I didn't like the news of this one bit. I was getting used to the idea of the *Emilia D.* being run by Captain Fetherston. He couldn't just walk out on me. We sailed before a benevolent wind on a benign sea, but I knew we were bound for the scarifying waters of Cape Horn. Without really being conscious of it, I had assumed that Cape was going to be somehow climacteric for me. I remembered the tales of my retired sailor on the Geelong Promenade. And Captain Fetherston had never lost a ship. I felt vaguely alarmed. He had inspired me to trust him. I had done so completely for the seven days that had elapsed between clearing Port Phillip Heads and being told the news of the captain's retirement by Jack. Seven days! It seemed much longer to me at the time. I felt as though I had sailed with old Fetherston for an age. Not that I was sharply conscious of his sedate presence. I was too taken up with objects, a capstan bar in the hand or a jackstay pressed into my belly. But he was the background and the nexus of those days, and the news that we were to lose him made me realise with a shock how much I had taken for granted the influence of his personality on my sense of well-being, and the well-being of others.

I was puzzled by something too. Why had Alex misled me about Mister Hallet's having once been a captain? In the light of what Jack had told me, Alex's seemed such a pointless and naked lie to claim the first mate was not a captain because he was not yet old enough to obtain a Master Mariner's Certificate. And if Mister Hallet was once a skipper, why was he not one any more? There was a mystery here that neither Jack nor Alex seemed willing to answer. I broached the subject with Jimbo one morning. We were up on a yard splicing some new gaskets onto their jackstay eyes.

'Will Hallet become skipper when Captain Fetherston leaves the ship at Port Chalmers?'

'Nah, mate.'

'Why not?'

'Why not? Because they're considering you for the post, weevil-brains.' Jimbo gave a wild cackle and yanked hard on the strands of the splice he had just completed. I was being fobbed off. Clearly there was some information that was privileged and I was not to be admitted to the cabal that was privy to it. I let the matter drop.

So we sailed on. The southerlies turned to westerlies which blew with equal mildness over our quarter, while the sea's blue intensity seemed to impinge on my consciousness more deeply with each passing day until it was no longer an object, but a condition of existence at whose exact centre we constantly moved. Once a solitary small cloud tailed us for a morning, then vanished. We worked in shirtsleeves. Captain Fetherston sat on the skylight bench in his sunhat and smoked his pipe. Mister Hallet swore that this was the fairest he'd ever known the Tasman, while the apprentices and crew enjoyed an idleness that would not be our lot again for the rest of the voyage. The daily duties involved in maintaining the ship took little more than a morning, and Captain Fetherston's navigation classes — they were more like chats than classes — rarely lasted more than an hour. During our afternoons, when not on watch, we sat in the sun, engaged on fancy rope-work, or reading. Some, Alex among them, were ardent ship modellers, and from off-cuts scrounged from the carpenter, whittled hulls and erected miniature rigging. Yes, they were carefree days.

One afternoon we held a chain-wrestling match. This involved a dozen or so of us sitting in a circle on an old sail. In the middle two combatants wrestled with each other. When one had had enough he would do his best to crawl to the edge of the circle and tag someone to take on his opponent. The rules were simple. The wrestling had to be conducted from a kneeling or a sitting position. There was no punching, no kicking, and if tagged, you were obliged to fight. It was an entertainment that gave rise to much hilarity and good-natured mischief, especially when Jimbo found himself pitted against the burly Scot, MacPherson. The former was very quick, crawling around the edge of the ring like a squirrel circling a grizzly bear. Now and then the seaman lunged, and missed catching Jimbo's ankle by a hair's breadth, causing us to roar with approval and merriment. However, Jimbo's ankle was finally snared, and he was dragged on his belly into the centre of the ring, where the grizzly proceeded to tie him in knots. Jimbo howled, the seaman grinned, we cheered and laughed. At last MacPherson tossed Jimbo toward the side of the ring as though he were a child's discarded plaything, whereupon Jimbo crawled to the edge, tagged Jack, and the entertainment continued.

Jack was good. Though much younger and slighter than MacPherson, he knew the holds and the counter holds. MacPherson could gain no advantage, and so retired, unbeaten. He tagged Alex with the jibe 'Theer, let the bairnies tickle one anither.' Alex and Jack wrestled for a long time, neither gaining very much advantage. Jack retired, more bored than exhausted, and tagged Hoff. Alex and Hoff fought for a long time, and the interest of the spectators began to pale. It was the comedy of unequal adversaries that made the contest amusing. Hoff retired, panting, and tagged me. Some of those in the circle were getting up and wandering off.

I had beginners' luck. In fending off one of Alex's moves, I scrambled to one side and yanked on his arm. He fell with a thump on his stomach, and the remaining spectators roared their approval. When he rose to his knees again Alex was smiling with apparent good humour.

'That was a lucky one, Johnny.'

He made another attack, and this time I was not quick enough. I was tossed onto my belly, whereupon Alex sat on me, and, clenching his fingers together, used them as a belt around my forehead to force my head backward. I found I couldn't breathe. My neck was arched so far back that it closed my windpipe. I tried to croak 'enough' but I could make no articulate sound. I could not move from underneath his weight. I must say I panicked. Didn't he know he was choking me?

Now, one of the conventions of our chain-wrestling was that the man who was winning had to change his grip once he had accomplished a particular manoeuvre and it was clear his opponent couldn't escape. For one thing, this gave the underdog a sporting chance to tag someone else, or even to try a move himself. Also, the game was primarily theatrical, and the goal was the cheers of the spectators rather than actual victory. It was a delicate form of entertainment, to the extent that it relied on goodwill and our sense of fellowship to moderate its inevitably competitive and aggressive character.

Alex would not release his grip on me. I tried kicking hard at his back with my heel, which was against the rules, but he only held on the more firmly. I tried bucking, but his weight was too great. I tried to release his fingers with my free hand, but they were an immovable clamp around my forehead. Why would he not let me go? People were shouting things at him. There was a red mist forming before my eyes.

I was relieved, but the rules had to be broken before this could happen. Jack reached his arm into the circle, and by stretching out my free hand I could just reach his fingers. Even so Alex tried to prevent this. But we touched, and I crawled to the edge, exhausted and shaken. While I was recovering my breath I heard the cheers of the circle, and looked up to see that Jack had manoeuvred Alex into the same hold that the latter had held on me. He must have been as strong or as quick as a panther, for Alex was no lightweight. Abruptly he released his hold on the senior apprentice, rested his hand on his shoulder briefly and said, 'Let's give it away, mate.'

Thus the game ended. As we dispersed, I approached Alex.

'You were killing me there for a moment, Alex. Didn't you realise?' I tried to make light of it, but I was piqued and I had been a little scared.

'Was I? No, I didn't realise, Johnny. I'm sorry. I don't know my own strength.' He laughed and clapped me on the back. There was something excessively jocular in his laugh. He probably was a bit sorry, but I never completely trusted him again.

That night we closed with the New Zealand coastline. The wind became more variable and our labours increased as a result. Early in the forenoon watch, the lights of Bluff were on the port beam. Eleven days out from Melbourne we picked up a pilot and a tug outside Taiaroa Heads, and we were towed to the ballast grounds off Port Chalmers. The waters of Otago Harbour were like a mirror, and a gauze-like cloud diffused the brilliance of the sun. The wharves of the port radiated out like the fingers of an open hand from the collection of buildings that were the town. There were some masts and tall funnels in dock. Behind them rose the spire of a church and surrounding all were the low hills of the Otago Peninsula.

For three days we worked like slaves in the hold of the ship, shovelling the gravel ballast into a wicker basket, which was then hauled up and swung to the rail, where it was tipped over the side. The work was backbreaking and monotonous.

From sunrise to sunset the entire crew was set to the task. Occasionally some of the shovellers below exchanged jobs with the haulers and tippers above. When there was no longer light to see by, Mister Hallet's head would appear over the coaming.

'That'll do, gentlemen.'

Then we would climb out of that hold, wash down, eat, sleep, rise, start work again. Other things were going on while we slaved in that pit. Captain Fetherston had been ashore and visited the company offices. The wool cargo was in the warehouse and could be loaded immediately. A replacement had been found for the captain, a man by the name of Trygg, who was believed to be in Dunedin at that time, but who had not, as yet, made an appearance at the offices.

Unexpectedly on the third morning the first mate's head appeared above us.

'All hands on deck. Look smart.' We climbed out. There was a steam launch alongside.

'What's going on, Hoff?' I asked.

'We say goodbye to Captain.'

We stood in a group around the accommodation ladder. Captain Fetherston emerged from below. He no longer wore any vestige of the ship's officer's uniform, but instead was clad in a worsted suit and a bowler hat. He might have been an elderly bank-teller, with his portmanteau in one hand and a wooden box containing his sextant in the other. He shook hands with each of us. When he came to Alex he handed him the box containing his sextant.

'Here you are, young man. This will be more use to you than me.'

Alex's polished features flushed and he thanked the captain profusely. The old man smiled, picked up his portmanteau, descended the accommodation ladder and climbed into the launch. This vessel coughed out a tree of smoke and set off for the shore. We watched from the rail. Captain Fetherston had seated himself in the sternsheets, and though we waved and called out I noticed he did not once look back at the ship. Finally we lost sight of the launch behind a wharf.

'Back to work, gentlemen. Smartly now.'

CHAPTER 2

Captain Trygg

I

For two weeks this Captain Trygg made no appearance. It was unaccountable. He made one brief visit to the company offices in Dunedin. He was known to be in the vicinity, yet no enquiries could track him down. Daily we expected a man to step on board and start issuing instructions, yet, while we lay moored in the ballast grounds and later during the week alongside a wharf loading the cargo of wool, no such event took place. Some of the older hands began to talk about a prolonged stay at anchorage off the port, and such talk was dispiriting. We needed a sense of our momentum, a sense that however far away our destination was in space, it was daily approaching nearer in time. It gave our efforts some meaning, it was the factor that gave our work its purpose, that gave us our willingness to work. The high morale that I had taken for granted during our crossing of the Tasman began to seep away.

Thanks to the arrangements Captain Fetherston had made before leaving, the wool was loaded in six days. During this time the ship was again invaded by Mister Hallet's 'harbour riff-raff', and the two mates spent most of their time supervising the lading by the teams of dockers. We, the crew, were set to the unending task of chipping rust and painting on red lead, and, with the mates preoccupied below for long periods, we were left alone to our labours.

It's a desultory job, chipping rust. Maritime housework is a good term for it; it is work that is never complete. The salt sea has one intention with regard to iron and steel; to rust them to a nothing. No matter how small the chink in the paint-work, it will find its way in and begin that process of corruption. So we chipped and red-leaded. Were we to ignore those brown flowers that bloomed beneath the paintwork, how long would it be before the ship disintegrated beneath our feet? A year? Ten?

The mind gravitates toward such mundane questions when you sit on a plank faced by the vast slab side of a ship and chip at it with a little hammer. What did it matter how long the ship would last? It was a result posited for a remote future, and when the work is monotonous enough, as ours was beside that wharf, there is no future; there is only the remembered tedium of a long past, the futility and limbo of the present. How long before we, the chippers, disintegrated as a company into nothing? Some tempers grew snappish. Jimbo took to skimming flakes of rust at those on neighbouring planks. His mischief provoked irritation rather than jollity.

Our evenings were spent reading and re-reading a few battered and ancient magazines that the midshiphouse had inherited from previous occupants. Sometimes we played interminable games of cards with a grubby pack. Alex pored over a manual of seamanship. Occasionally he would look up, his lips moving slightly as he committed some procedure to memory. Once or twice he took out Captain Fetherston's sextant, dismantled it and cleaned each piece meticulously.

One afternoon the rumour spread that we were to be given a few shillings advance on our pay and granted a night's shore leave. There was jubilation, and Alex buttonholed me.

'We'll get ourselves a slap-up feed in Port Chalmers, Johnny.'

Now, ever since Jimbo had plunged that handful of raisins into my dungarees pocket, I had come to realise more and more what a powerful sensual delight there was in meditating upon food. The meals that we had on board were of two kinds: the edible and the barely edible. Thus food was the stuff of our fantasies. We would tantalise each other with remembered or imagined menus, particularly at meal times. It was the cruellest of tortures. The imagined meal would issue from the tormentor's imagination and be displayed before our drooling fancies until someone cried 'enough'. And now there was an opportunity to fulfil those fantasies. I accepted Alex's suggestion with enthusiasm.

We dressed in our shore-going clothes and gathered at the break of the poop where Mister Hallet doled out our advance.

'Bring him home sober, mister.' The mate had the ghost of a smile on his face as he addressed this remark to Alex. The senior apprentice grinned with pleasure.

A few coins in pocket, the crew disappeared up the streets of Port Chalmers. Jack, Jimbo and Hoff were determined to sample the night-life of the City of Dunedin.

'Are you coming for a spree, Johnny?' called Jimbo from across a street. I noticed Alex cast his glance to the ground.

'Aw, a slap-up feed will do for me,' I yelled back. Actually, now that there was a choice between two things I would rather have gone to Dunedin, but I was committed. Jimbo shrugged, and the three of them made off.

The eating-house Alex chose was the first one we came to; we could see the masts of the ship from the window. The bare boards of the tables and the grimy lampshades around the electric lights were far from the image of gleaming white table-cloths and chandeliers that I had conjured up for this night out, but the food was welcome enough. Bacon, sausages, black pudding, real eggs. Alex talked at length about the examinations he would sit for on our arrival in London, and the advantages of sail over steam. I remember he became quite heated when I parrotted something Jimbo had said in passing, that the days of sailing ships were just about over. But I was not interested enough to pursue the topic, so for the most part I let him talk on. It was still light when we left, and we were at a loose end.

'Alex, why don't we track down the other three in Dunedin?' I suggested. I wanted adventure, horseplay, perhaps even to meet and talk to some girls. Teaming up with Jack, Jimbo, and Hoff offered this. The evening so far had turned out to be rather flat.

'They'll only be getting themselves into trouble. We're best off sticking around here. Besides, I promised the mate I'd bring you home sober.' Alex grinned quickly.

'I thought he meant that as a joke,' I said despondently.

We walked up and down an unremarkable main street, climbed to a lookout above the town, sat on a bench, came down again, looked into some shop windows. We were back on board by ten o'clock.

It must have been close to dawn when Jack, Jimbo and Hoff came back, for the portholes were circles of grey light. Their clatter and giggles woke me.

'Hey, Johnny. You awake?'

'Yes.'

'Light one of those lamps.'

I fumbled for matches and lit one of the hurricane lamps. In its glimmer I saw the grinning faces of the three apprentices. Jimbo's left eye was heavily bruised, and the rest of his face was badly marked and scratched. As for Hoff, there were dark streaks of blood in the blonde hairs of his moustache and beard, and a smear of it across his cheek where a hand had wiped the blood that had evidently quite recently poured from his nose. They stank of beer and their shirts were wet.

'How did you get that?'

'It's a beauty, isn't it?' said Jack, turning Jimbo's face to the light. It looked more like a voodoo mask than a human countenance. 'Mind you, the fellah that gave it to him will still be picking bits of bottle out of his hair, I reckon.'

They all chuckled. It had been a wild adventure, and each told me his part in it in an excited whisper. There had been a group of larrikins in a bar, a disparaging remark, a glass of beer flicked in the face, a brawl.

'Then this big fellow, he com for Jimbo. I heff this in my pocket,' and Hoff showed me a handkerchief with a round stone tied in it. 'So I giff him one. Poom! He gets ferry angry. "You bahstard," he says. "Ooh, you bahstard." So I giff him another, quick. Poom! So he go and sit down and rub his head and say, "Ooh, you bahstard, you bahstard." Wah wah wah, he begin to cry like a bebbi. He not want to fight any more I think.' They all giggled again.

'How come you don't look as bad as the other two, Jack?' I asked.

'Jack, he look after himself good,' said Hoff, slapping Jack on the back. Jack grinned deferentially. I felt very envious of them.

'I wish I'd been there.'

'You were offered, fellah.'

I was a little disquieted too. Fisticuffs in the schoolyard was one thing, but the image of a man picking bits of glass out of his skull was quite another. There was something barbarous about that. Hearing their account of the fray made me feel I had been sheltered all my life. Here was a glimpse of something savage, something with no restraints upon it. Yes, I was envious of their adventure, and a little scared by it. Someone might have been killed; or done a murder.

We were given no further shore leave. On the following day the *Emilia D.* was towed out into the stream to wait at anchorage until the new captain arrived. The damaged condition of Jimbo and Hoff on the early morning muster did little for the temper of Mister Hallet, nor did the delay of three days in the stream waiting for the captain.

Late one afternoon Alex and I were chipping rust under the main rail. Almost everyone else was down below performing the same task, so we were the only two to see the launch approach the barque.

It was a perfectly still afternoon. The wind had dropped completely, Otago Harbour was like a tray of glass in which the hills, the town, and ourselves were embedded. A pale yellow light suffused the cloud that hung about the hills of the peninsula. It was hard to believe that all around us lay a world where events actually happened, where people were actually swept up into them and changed for better or for worse. We were in limbo. And then, suddenly, there, like a blemish on the glassiness, was the small steam launch, its stem pointing resolutely toward us, pushing a bow wave that had the appearance of a short black moustache.

'We've got company, Alex.' We stood up from our task and watched the launch draw nearer. In it were three figures, a man at the tiller, a bow-man, and a third person dressed in an oilskin coat and with a peaked cap pulled down over his forehead. He looked overdressed, in fact, for the afternoon was dull rather than cold. He had pulled the collar of his coat up and sat on the thwart with a hunched, contemplative appearance, more like a man departing from something than arriving somewhere.

The launch bumped alongside and the bow-man made fast to the companion. It was only when the man wearing the coat stood up that his bulk became apparent. He towered above the other two in the boat, and, as if this made the task of keeping balance more delicate, he stepped onto the companion and remained a moment holding the rope rail and steadying himself. Alex turned to me.

'Come on, Johnny. We'd better do the honours.' He stationed himself at the top of the companion and waited for the man to reach the top. As he did so, Alex held out his hand.

'Alex Holt, sir. I'm senior apprentice. Welcome aboard. Allow me to give you a hand with your dunnage.' The new arrival paused at the top of the companion, ignoring the proffered hand. He seemed to regard Alex for a moment, though his gaze, I noticed then, and later, was ambiguous. He *seemed* to regard Alex, yet his expression suggested that he saw some object of inner reflection. There was a suggestion of amusement in that expression. Alex withdrew his hand in some confusion and began to descend the stairway to pick up the items of the captain's luggage. The captain waved his hand.

'Go on, clear off.'

I saw the surprise that passed across Alex's face. He even went a step or two further down, as though he believed himself to have misheard. Then he stopped and looked back at the captain. The latter had walked some way toward the poop hatch, but he halted and turned. Meanwhile the bow-man had picked up the bits and pieces of the captain's belongings and was coming up the steps of the companion. Alex was in the way.

'Go on, clear off.' It was said this time perhaps with a bit more impatience, but without any anger in the voice, only an unfathomable scorn. The bow-man gave Alex a sheepish look as he passed him and followed the captain aft. Both men disappeared below.

'That was a bit rough, Alex. You were only trying to be helpful.' It was true, he had tried to be helpful, but the captain's manner toward him had made his welcoming offer appear obsequious.

'I suppose I had better try to find Mister Hallet.' He looked troubled. No, he looked positively shocked. Alex may have learned his knots and splices in the four years he had spent at sea, but clearly he had never experienced anything like this before. He went off in search of the first mate, and I waited by the rail. The man who had been at the tiller was struggling up the companion with a tea-chest on his shoulder. As he passed me he tilted his head back, curled his hand and stuck up his thumb to imitate the shape of a bottle, and pretended to pour liquid down his throat. Then, catching my eye, he indicated the tea-chest with a nod. So there was grog in it; a fair quantity of it too, if the case was full. The tiller-man staggered off towards the saloon, reappeared a few moments later with his confederate, and together the two of them got back into their launch, cast off, and set out for the shore. Mister Hallet hurried past me, bound for the saloon, and behind him came Alex. I told him about the tiller-man's gestures. He furrowed his brow, then tried to make light of the incident.

'That's not unusual. Skippers often bring a fair quantity of liquor on board with them. It supplements the steward's stores.'

'But what if he turns out to be an old drunk, Alex?' It was a half-hearted attempt to tease him. I was a little weary of his sensibleness, and disappointed too — disappointed that he seemed to have swallowed the captain's rudeness to him so blithely. He could at least have passed some comment to me such as 'this is a swine we've got landed with' or 'he'll get a hard time if he keeps up that sort of attitude'. I was thinking what sort of a response the captain might have drawn from Jack or Jimbo had his dismissive first utterance been directed at either of them. I began to fear I would come to find Alex irksome. Certainly my attempt to tease him was wasted.

'Look, Johnny. This is an inter-colonial merchant vessel. There are regulations and procedures governing all that we do. It's not just anyone who can walk on board and...' I was spared what promised to be a sermon by the appearance of Mister Hallet, who sprang out of the poop hatch. He bellowed at us. I was to muster the hands, while Alex was to run up a signal requesting a pilot and tugboat to take us out on the first convenient ebb tide.

The hands were brought together under the break of the poop and waited for the captain to address the few customary words to them. He made no appearance, and after a quarter of an hour a slightly flustered Mister Gillard appeared from below and whispered something in Mister Hallet's ear, whereupon the first mate dismissed us without giving any reason for the captain's absence.

That first convenient tide was at six a.m. the following

morning. By the middle of the forenoon watch we had slid past Taiaroa Heads, bedded and unshackled the anchors, and made all sail for our passage of the South Pacific.

II

I have had twenty years to think about the man who, on that dull afternoon, stepped from that launch and into our lives. I should say that for most of those years my own life has been lucky. Apart from a short swim in the South Atlantic one fine evening after my ship was torpedoed, I came unscathed through The Great War. At a time during the previous decade when the deepwater sailers were being laid up and turned into coal hulks, I managed to find work and promotion among the shrinking number that still plied a trade. I suppose I was insouciant about my luck, but I think I always trusted it. More to the point, I always trusted my sense of an outset, the inexplicable conviction that sweeps over one quite suddenly when, say, a hawser goes splash and one catches oneself smiling inadvertently and thinking 'yes, this will turn out well'.

It's an elusive spirit. And there is, of course, its opposite, that equally inexplicable black foreboding that can attend an outset. Both seem to play deep down in the consciousness, twin powers that are prophetic in character, almost as though they were a residual glimmer of those sad powers we used to ascribe to gods and call 'all-seeing' or 'all-knowing'. It was the darker twin that awoke and began its disquieting play in my mind on that afternoon. As our new captain steadied himself against the handrail, then ascended the companion of the *Emilia Denholm*, I believe the spirit of mischief itself came to reside with us.

He went below and remained in his cabin for the first two days out of Port Chalmers. As I've indicated, it is customary, even for the least zealous skipper, to walk around a new command soon after he comes aboard and to take stock of what he now controls. Apart from the psychological advantage of being seen by the likes of us to have assumed authority, there is the practical necessity of ascertaining what state of repair the vessel is in. After all, his life depends on it as much as ours.

But Captain Trygg made no such tour of inspection. Perhaps he was confined to his cabin through seasickness, we thought. It is true that even some of the hardiest mariners suffer from this malady on the first few days of a voyage. We came to this charitable conclusion, and made sly jokes about it. Mister Hallet made all the preparations for our tow out to sea, set our course for Drake Passage, and gave the instructions necessary for the daily running of the ship. And where our daily life was normal, our reaction to the new captain's reticence was tolerant, if mildly disrespectful. We assumed he would take over his role on the ship as soon as he found his sea-legs.

The moderate weather that had attended our crossing of the Tasman remained with us for a further week. A vast canopy of cloud roofed us in between horizons each day, but the winds were rarely stronger than force four, blowing either from west-south-west or west-north-west. However, we were kept busy. The gales that gave their names to the roaring forties and the shrieking fifties may have been uncharacteristically shy with us, but no one doubted that they would fall with a vengeance sooner or later. Thus we were set to work rigging lifelines and safety nets. We assisted the carpenter in fitting heavy reinforcing timbers across each of the hatches and rigged stout wire cables across these. We overhauled pendants and fitted extra robands to the sails. It was daylight work and Mister Gillard supervised both watches in these tasks.

Mister Gillard was popular with everyone. 'Old Gil', as the members of his watch called him, was scarcely twenty-two, and this was but his second voyage as the junior mate of the *Emilia D.* Previously he had been the senior apprentice on the ship. His flair for navigation and the fine tuning of the rigging had been, I gather, precocious. Captain Fetherston had adopted the young man and, with his coaching, Mister Gillard had distinguished himself in the Board of Trade examinations. He was a bright young man, as they say. In appearance he was not unlike Alex, slimmer and more delicately featured, perhaps, but with the same boyish earnestness in his expression, the high forehead, the alert carriage and the high tone of his turnout. Yet there was a confidence in Mister Gillard's manner, and a composure that was absent in Alex. There was a difference in the way the two men smiled too. Behind Alex's smile I always felt there was a nervousness, like the unease you sometimes detect on the face of a child who is apprehensive that a brusque voice will ask him what the hell he is smiling for. Behind Mister Gillard's amused smile I sensed always an icy self-possession. 'Old Gil' was a name for Mister Gillard designed as much to assure us that he really was a decent stick, as it was a tribute to his easygoing style of authority. Alex was not Mister Gillard's direct successor as the senior apprentice on the *Emilia D*; there had been another, who left the ship before it departed from London for a second mate's berth elsewhere. But I have not resisted the temptation to compare the two — Alex and Mister Gillard — not only because of some physical resemblance in my mind, but because the events in this story led them in such utterly different directions.

This style of Mister Gillard's was quite distinct from Mister Hallet's. I can put it best by saying that, though I have heard Mister Gillard's voice above the din of a storm, I never heard him bellow. Mister Hallet's style of direction was one of snap and shock and clips on the ear. It worked and, I now admit ruefully, it didn't make anyone inconsolably unhappy. Old Gil's was a style at an opposite pole. You might say it was modern. 'How would you fellows like to put a lick of paint on the lifeboat davits,' he'd say, or 'We'd better get that outer jib off her, gentlemen.' We obeyed smartly enough. As I say, Mister Gillard was well liked.

It was at five o'clock on the morning of the third day that we first became aware of our captain venturing beyond his cabin. We had been mustered an hour earlier for the morning watch, and by five we were gathered around the galley door for the mug of coffee with which the working day began. Hoff brought his coffee over to where a group of us stood.

'You hear him last night?'

'Hear who, you Scandinavian monkey?' growled Jimbo.

'This new kept'n vee heff. I vake up. It is ferry dark. Then I see him. He sway as if he is sick. I think: Don' puke your dinner ofer me, Kept'n. It is not so fonny, I tell you. He looks arount like this and this, as though he try to find som person. "Who iss there?" I say. Then he iss ferry still and I think, he iss looking at me very hard somvare there. Then he says,

"This place, it stinks," and he goes out. I think perheps he iss
not right up here.' He tapped his forehead.

One of the seamen confirmed this nocturnal behaviour of
the captain.

'I seen 'im knockin' about the fo'c'sle first night out. Like
'avin' a flamin' elephant in your bedroom.'

'Aw, he's a crazy,' said Jimbo. 'Nothing to worry about.'
And with that he began one of his chimpanzee acts that took
him capering out of sight behind the galley. Of course we
knew virtually nothing about Captain Trygg at this time, but
Jimbo's gloss that the man was a bit touched was the most
acceptable simplification available. We elaborated the private
jokes we made about him.

It became quite common to see him about the ship at night.
Despite his threatening bulk he had a knack of being at your
elbow before you realised he was there. This happened to me
one night when I was at the helm. My mind had been wholly
occupied on concentrating on the compass card for about
twenty minutes. Vaguely outside this focus I was aware of the
sound of the sea as it shushed below our quarters, and that
Mister Hallet was somewhere for'ard near the poop rail.
Then unaccountably there was a vertical line of glints at the
very edge of my field of vision. I got quite a fright and for an
instant I suffered the hallucination that they were a shore
installation of some sort. We would go aground! Then I
recognised them to be the brass buttons of a very large-sized
jacket, illuminated by the glow that came from the binnacle
light. I glanced quickly to the side. Captain Trygg was
standing perhaps a yard from my elbow. He'd managed to
come up very close without my being aware of it. It was my
first encounter with him since Port Chalmers.

'You made me jump, sir,' I said, trying to make light of my
unease. I received no reply, not even a grunt. But I did have
the uncanny idea that there was a smile on his face — a self-
absorbed kind of smile. I refocused my attention on the
compass card, gazing at it, then taking quick squints ahead.
But I did so now with the self-consciousness of one being
minutely scrutinised. Because I neither heard nor saw him go
off, I assumed him to be still there. For some five minutes I
did not dare cast a glance to the side. When at length I did,
he had gone. Yet how could he move so unobtrusively?

Needless to say there was no mention made of continuing those midday navigation and seamanship sessions that we had enjoyed under Captain Fetherston while crossing the Tasman. Had the winds during that first week been livelier, our work would have been cut out and we would not have missed them. But the weather was moderate, and we *did* have time on our hands during the daylight watches.

Now, there may have been a grain of mischief in Jimbo's suggestion that Alex open the subject with Captain Trygg. The captain's only exchange with Alex so far had been decidedly cool, and Jimbo knew this. We were helping the sailmaker repair some of the fairweather canvas on the main deck. Jimbo brought the topic up.

'I reckon you ought to approach him about it, mate,' he said, speaking to Alex. 'You are the senior apprentice, after all.'

The sailmaker, a leathery old Norwegian who wore thick-rimmed spectacles and had sailed in British and inter-colonial ships for most of his working life, pulled his needle through the cloth on his knees and shook his head.

'I think best you leave this new kept'n alone.'

'I don't see why, Sails. We're obliged to receive some education. That's why we're apprentices.' Then, turning to Alex: 'Well, are you the senior apprentice or not?'

'I'll mention it to him,' said Alex, continuing to ply his needle.

'Now's as good a time as any, I reckon,' persisted Jimbo. Subtly the suggestion had transformed into a dare, and we were looking at Alex to see if he was game to tackle the captain. The sailmaker shook his head and said nothing.

'All right. I'll do it now.' Alex got to his feet and walked aft. We watched him exchange a few words with Mister Hallet at the poop rail and then disappear below. A minute or so later he reappeared and rejoined us. He said nothing, but sat down and recommenced his sewing.

'Well?' said Jimbo.

'He's not interested.'

'What did he say?'

'Just that he's not interested.'

'But did you suggest that Old Gil might do it instead of him?'

'Yes.'

'And?'

'He's not interested.'

Jimbo shrugged and the subject was dropped. But apparently this was not all the captain had said to Alex. Later, when I was on lookout duty during the second dogwatch, the senior apprentice joined me at the rail.

'He told me to stop pestering him.'

'Who did?'

'The skipper, when I went to see him this morning. I had to speak through the closed door. Pestering! I've hardly been near him since he came on board. How can he say I pester him? I have to act for the fellows when they ask me to. That's not pestering.'

Clearly Captain Trygg's use of the word 'pestering' had been an unfortunate one to use with Alex. I pictured him waiting at that closed door with his ear close up so that he could hear the captain's grunted replies to his various questions. I knew Alex would persist until he got an answer.

'He doesn't seem to like you very much.'

'I can't see what I've done.' This was a forlorn way of looking at the incident. Why did he have to bring it back to himself?

'It's not your fault at all, Alex. He looks like he's just hard to get on with.'

No, it may not have been his fault at all, but there was something about him, nonetheless, that attracted impatience. He could irk me at times and, in truth, I had been seeking out the company of Jack, Jimbo and Hoff since the night ashore in Port Chalmers. I was aware that this was a kind of gradual betrayal of Alex — at least I knew he would regard it as such — but I had outgrown the protective, elder brother company that he afforded when I was still new to the ship. The spontaneous banter and horseplay that the company of Jimbo offered was more attractive to me. And Jack struck me as a much stronger individual than Alex.

III

Thus it was that for the first three days out of Port Chalmers our new captain remained invisible by day and virtually so by night. We smirked at this uncommon shyness but there was a curiosity in our jokes about him, or rather an anticipation. Daily we expected him to emerge clearly before our eyes and to impose his particular personality on our lives and the running of the ship. He was the captain. What was it that kept him cooped up in his quarters? Grog? He didn't rave. No one actually discerned the smell of liquor on his breath on those occasions he was spied about the decks during the night hours. Yet we knew he had a good supply aboard. Why would he not show himself? The only evidence we had of his existence was a couple of coldly dismissive utterances, and a succession of unsettling apparitions after nightfall in various parts of the ship. The man stayed unseen, like a god. Certainly his huge frame in the darkness suggested something superhuman to us, but then we rather enjoyed ascribing a Gothic exaggeration to our captain.

At noon on the fourth day out Captain Trygg's face emerged unannounced from the poop hatch and frowned, as one unaccustomed to the light. After a momentary pause, the head was followed by the entire body. Jack saw him first. The two of us were running out the logline, Jack with an hourglass in his hand, and I with a line streaming out from a drum held above my head. Nearby Mister Gillard was plotting our midday position on a chart, using the skylight as an improvised table.

'Hello, here he comes at last,' said Jack in a low voice. I glanced over my shoulder as the drum spun in my hands, and was in time to catch the captain's frown. He took no notice of our activities, but passed up the poop deck and stood leaning against the rail near the jiggermast shrouds.

When the sand ran out, Jack read off the length of line that had streamed out behind the barque, replaced the hourglass in its locker and informed Mister Gillard of our speed through the water. The second mate completed his chartwork, rolled up the chart and strolled over to where the captain leant on the rail. I was still engaged in winding in the logline.

'I have our noon position and the distance covered in twenty-four hours, Captain. It's dead reckoning, I'm afraid. The sun has not obliged us.'

Captain Trygg stared down at the water that rushed past

our counter. Mister Gillard gave our position and the distance covered.

'We should cross the hundred and eightieth meridian some time tonight.' The second mate leaned against the rail and put his hands in his pockets — the preparations of a man wishing to slip into conversation with another. 'We'll get two Mondays,' he said, chattily. There was no response from the large man beside him.

'Mind you, we could use a bit more wind. One hundred and thirty-seven miles since noon yesterday...it's not going to be a record passage by any means.' Mister Gillard failed to penetrate the captain's absorption. 'Not like our 1909 passage. Did you know the old girl did the trip in eighty-nine days? Geelong to Belfast. She flew.'

As if mention of the trip had finally deflected the captain's private contemplation, the large head turned and looked down at the second mate.

'You have done very creditably, Mister Gillard.' The remark had an utter finality about it. I was overhearing all this, and I remember being surprised that Captain Trygg even knew the name of his second mate, given the amount of interest he had shown in the ship hitherto. And it also struck me, as I glanced covertly at his face, how derisive the effect of the moustache was. Mister Gillard was at a loss for words.

'I didn't mean...it wasn't my aim to draw attention to my own performance, Captain.' But the captain was no longer listening.

He took to visiting the decks during daylight quite often, though he seldom remained very long among us. His behaviour, on those occasions, was puzzling. We could not, for instance, fathom the detachment with which he seemed to regard our work. It was as if he considered he had no part in it. He behaved more like a paying passenger than the source of authority on the vessel. No, it was more than mere detachment. He seemed to have a hearty contempt for purpose and the demonstration of purpose. He would stroll the deck, head and shoulders higher than us, utterly self-absorbed. We would look at him covertly. Then abruptly he would stop and regard what we were up to.

There was an occasion, for instance, when Mister Hallet's watch was at a capstan. The wind had shifted a few points, and we were bracing the yards round and taking in the sheets of the lower sails. Captain Trygg stopped in the middle of one of his perambulations and leaned against the flywheel of the pumps. My shipmates trod in their slow dance around the capstan. I was to one side taking in the fall of the sheet, and so able to observe the captain's face.

The expressions of the men around the capstan were distorted with that fixity that the human countenance assumes when the muscles are under strain. I saw that the captain was smiling broadly at the spectacle of my shipmates performing their slow-motion rigmarole. And it was a subversive smile, because suddenly I saw their performance as ludicrous too. I looked at it as if I had no part in it.

'What are you flamin' smiling at?' said Jimbo, as his intent face swung past me in the circle he trod.

'Nothing. Sorry.'

'You will be sorry in a moment.'

Yet despite his detachment, his scorn, there *was* an authority about the man. Who could not be impressed by the statuesque torso, the huge hands, the broad forehead with its crown of lank grey hair, the regal beard and moustache. It may have been his very scorn that conveyed that ineffable air of authority, as though it were founded on some realisation, incomprehensible to the likes of us, of our intrinsic inferiority.

At the end of the first week I had my own direct brush with him. I had arrived at the helm to relieve Hoff. The wind had been picking up steadily during the second watch and by three a.m. was blowing at force seven. The barometer had been falling gradually all night, and instead of the steady snoring of water along the keel there was a concussion and tremor, as though the ship were some dull cymbal that was being struck every ten seconds or so. Before I could take the spokes Mister Hallet turned to me.

'Slip below, laddie, and tell Captain Trygg it's coming on to blow. I'm taking the royals off her. Wake him if necessary.'

'Aye aye, sir.'

I went down into the saloon. There was a needle of light shining from beneath the captain's cabin door. The saloon and the adjacent rooms were in darkness. Mister Gillard was presumably asleep in one of them, and Gus, the steward, was snoring in the tiny cubicle allotted to him next to the pantry. I knocked on the captain's door. There was no answer. I knocked louder, thinking he might be asleep. Again no answer. I decided to open the door and look in. It was unlocked. I put my head through.

'Captain Trygg, sir? Are you awake?'

There was no reply. The bed was behind the open door so I went right into the cabin to ascertain whether the captain was sleeping. He was not there.

Now it was my intention to go straight into that cabin, deliver my message, and return to the helm. But, as I've mentioned, we were all curious about our new skipper, and I was not a little conscious of how the odd titbits of information I might pick up about the man might increase my popularity in the deckhouse. So I had resolved to keep my eyes wide open while delivering my message, particularly to see what had happened to the consignment of liquor that had come aboard with him. The opportunity was too good to miss.

I cast quickly about me. The bed was creased, but still made up, indicating it had been lain on but not slept in. There was an untidiness about the cabin that was odd, because it suggested that the steward had not been carrying out his duties here. Some books lay in piles on a table. One, a large volume, was open at a page that illustrated one of the brilliantly coloured Australian parrots — one of the rosellas, I recall. Clearly the captain was given to having his evening meal in his cabin rather than in the saloon with his two officers, for the plate with a good proportion of the food uneaten, had been left on top of a locker. Again this was odd. It was three o'clock in the morning. The evening meal was hours ago. Why hadn't Gus collected the plate?

In my brief glance around the room I could not see alcohol much in evidence. A teacup with perhaps a quarter of an inch of brown liquid stood on the table beside the book, but this could easily have been the dregs of coffee, or something medicinal. The trunk of liquors that had come aboard with Captain Trygg was not immediately visible. I remembered my commission and made to leave the cabin. Clearly the captain was elsewhere at that moment.

He was facing me as I re-entered the corridor. He looked as

if he had stood waiting for the occupant of his cabin to show himself for some moments. I was flustered.

'Mister Hallet told me to come down here, sir.' I waited for a 'what does Mister Hallet want', but none was forthcoming. 'He said it's going to blow and he intends to take in the royals. He said to rouse you if necessary, sir.' The man who was our captain merely regarded me without taking any notice of what I had said.

'That's the reason I was in your cabin, sir,' I added lamely. Being suddenly confronted by his huge bulk in the dark corridor had made me feel at first alarmed, then uneasy about being seen coming out of his cabin, as if I had been caught in the act of spying on him. I suppose this had some truth in it. I was now anxious to get away from him, yet I wanted some dismissive remark that assured me I was not talking to a ghost. His continued silence was unnerving me.

At length he said, 'Show me your hands.' I was mystified by this, but did so. He pushed me into a position where the light from the doorway illuminated my outstretched palms. He glanced at them briefly, then strode past me and into his cabin muttering 'I can see I must lock this.'

The door closed behind him. It was some moments before I realised an accusation had been made. Did he think I had gone into his cabin to pilfer something? I felt outraged. I had come with a message from the officer of the watch. I had delivered it. I had expected some answer that recognised our professional relationship, something like 'Very good, young man. Tell Mister Hallet I will be on deck presently,' or 'Tell Mister Hallet to carry on.' Instead I had been dismissed with an insinuation about my honesty.

And there was more to it too. Like the man's smile as he watched my shipmates at the capstan the day before, there was something subversive and mischievous about his remark. I hadn't gone into the room to purloin anything. It hadn't entered my head. But his remark made me sharply conscious that I might have entered his cabin with just such an intention, and this possibility somehow transposed itself in my mind into an actual intention. I felt guilty. I knew I was as innocent as a new born babe, yet I flushed hotly and angrily as I climbed back on deck. He had made me feel like a thief.

Mister Hallet's face was lit up in the glow of the binnacle light like the mask of a medicine man.

'Where the devil have you been?' he growled, as I took the wheel from Hoff. I told him what had happened.

'Shouldn't I have entered the cabin, sir?' I asked. The first mate pretended not to hear, but walked forward and disappeared down the poop companion.

CHAPTER 3

Ordeal by Weather

I

'All hands.'

I started awake. A man from Mister Gillard's watch was moving from bunk to bunk shaking the sleepers. It was light outside. The motion of the ship was somehow different. I could hear a deep-sounding *pommmfff* as the barque's stem pushed into a wall of sea, rising slowly to let it pass beneath. Then it would dip on its fulcrum only to rise again toward the next concussion of sea and hull.

I tumbled from my bunk. There was water slopping about the deckhouse floor. I found my sea-boots afloat in a far corner, then joined the rush to muster below the poop rail, still tucking my trousers into the tops of my boots. The appearance of the deck gave me a surprise. It was not just damp, as after the dawn mop-down, but sopping, with streams running down the waterways, and the main rail dripping. The reason for this became suddenly apparent as the *Emilia D.* began one of her long dips and tilted her bulwarks to port. A huge sea welled up high above the rail and poured aboard. I was abruptly shoulder-high in white water and clutching about for something to hold on to as the surge carried me to the waterways. I must have felt fairly safe for some reason as my first big sea sucked me toward a washport, because I remember grinning and thinking 'this is a lark'. As it happens I was not in immediate danger; the tons of water poured from the ports, draining the deck and leaving me in a heap under the main pinrail.

I looked up at the masts. Not only had the royals been taken in, but also the upper topgallants and some of the staysails. The calligraphy of the masts against the sky was wilder than the sedate loops of the previous weeks. There was a voice yelling something from aft. It was Mister Hallet from the break of the poop, and his yell was apparently directed at me. Then I felt the port waterways dipping beneath me again and I was at once engulfed in a rushing world of whiteness that plucked and swirled me across the deck toward the mainmast, banging my head, my shins, my elbows on various obstacles before sucking me back to the bulwarks. There I clasped the first solid object my hands could fall upon.

Bruised and shaken, I pulled myself to my feet and looked about. My sweater hung sodden on my shoulders, heavy as a suit of chainmail. My boots squelched. Ahead of me the bowsprit was alternately pointing at a ragged sky, or nosing toward a dark sea that was flecked with white horses for as far ahead as I could make out. Absurdly I noticed it was raining. When I looked aft toward the poop I saw Jimbo gesturing at me in his extravagant way. I took his motions to be a summons and began going hand over hand along the safety rope toward the poop companion. Another big sea came aboard as she rolled her side under for the third time, and for a moment there was no intercession between myself, attached horizontally to the safety line, and the heaving body of the Southern Ocean outside the ship. This was scary.

'Thought we'd lost you for a moment there, Fisheyes,' said Jimbo as I reached the top of the poop companion and joined the rest of the watch. I noticed that there were two men on the helm now, and no sign of the captain. Mister Hallet stood waiting among us as the members of Mister Gillard's watch struggled aft to join us. They had been taking in the outer jib. The first mate had a rather pleased expression on his face, like that of a boxer who has just come face to face with an opponent he knows he can beat.

'Get the cro'jack off her,' he roared, pointing at the huge sail immediately above our heads on the mizzen yard.

The cro'jack was one of the largest sails on the ship and it needed the entire crew to furl it. We descended to the frothing main deck again, some making for the weather pinrail and some for the lee pinrail, hand over hand along the safety rope. I remember we shouted and laughed a bit. Mister Hallet's good mood was infective. At last, here were the big winds. Now we would fly! A glassy hillock of sea teetered toward the lee bulwark and crashed aboard. All at once, where there had been twelve men, there were but twelve heads bobbing in a snowy, surging field. The water drained around us and we were at the mizzen pinrail before another sea could crash on board.

'Ease off your weather sheet.'

Though I now knew my way from rope to rope on the *Emilia D.* this was my first experience of working in heavy conditions. I felt exhilarated. I was working shoulder to shoulder with men in an ancient craft, a craft that each knew and performed unhesitantly. There were the instinctive divisions of labour as some went for this line, some for that. There was the grace, the vigour, the timing of their exertions as they threw off the pins and hauled. There were the curt instructions given by the mate. It was a lovely, ineffable sensation to be working in the midst of this.

As two men slacked off the weather sheet, others hauled on the clew and buntlines. The great sail bellied outwards then collapsed upward and into itself. We waited by the lee rail for our moment.

'Ease off your lee sheet.' This was done, and as we put our weight onto the lee clew-garnet and buntlines our half of the sail puckered into itself.

'Aloft and furl.' As I waited behind Jimbo to scramble up onto the ratlines, I saw Captain Trygg standing on the catwalk contemplating us. What an eerie knack he had of just materialising. I nudged Jimbo.

'Surprise surprise,' yelled Jimbo in my ear. 'I always thought snakes hibernated when it got cold.' Jimbo's attitude toward the captain had changed from a tolerant to an aggressive disrespect in recent days.

Once aloft we lay out along the yard and gasketed the bunched canvas in a neat furl behind the jackstay. The effect was to take some of the roll off the ship. Down we came and mustered at the poop rail again for orders. Unless Mister Hallet wanted one of the courses taken off, which was unlikely, we anticipated that we would be sent below for the remainder of our off-duty watch. Not much more than half an hour of it was left, too short to go back to sleep, but time enough to have a smoke and get into dry clothes and oilskins.

Captain Trygg was in conversation with his first mate near the jiggermast shrouds. Abruptly the latter broke off the conversation and strode toward us. The captain followed for some paces and watched. The good humour on Mister Hallet's face had vanished.

'Clap the cro'jack back on.'

The faces of the crew showed disbelief. We had just taken the sail in. The wind had not abated at all. What was Mister Hallet playing at? No one *made* work for a crew in heavy conditions. There was quite enough to do as it was.

'We've no but ta'en the damned thing off,' protested Big MacPherson.

'Well now you put the damned thing back on again. And when you've done that, you'll come back here and I'll tell you to get it off again, except this time you'll do it smartly. Now MOVE!'

There was no option but to obey. Sullenly we returned to our stations at the mizzen pinrail. Mister Gillard made encouraging noises.

'Come on, fellows. Let's do it with a will.' Up we went, cast off the gaskets, down again and hauled the sheets home, then mustered for the order to take it in. We were angry with the futility of the rigmarole. The sail was taken in for a second time, and by the time the operation was finished we were into the forenoon watch. So much for a smoke and a change of clothes. Mister Gillard's watch were sent to their breakfasts and we sheltered beneath the flying bridge to await orders.

'What's old Hallet up to? We took that cro'jack in smart enough the first time round,' I complained.

'It's not his style to make the men do a job over. Not when the wind's up — it's dangerous,' said a seaman.

'Of course it's not his flamin' style,' growled Jimbo. 'It's the snake we picked up in Port Chalmers who was behind the idea.'

'You don't *know* that,' said Alex. Jimbo looked at him in surprise.

'Of course I flamin' know that. Weren't you watching him having a word in Hallet's ear when we came back from furling the sail first time? He's a snake.' Jimbo dug his hands in his pockets and hunched his shoulders. We were all cold. I had suddenly remembered Jimbo's remarks at the shrouds. Surely the captain could not have overheard him, and decided to punish the crew collectively for Jimbo's disrespect.

'He's the skipper and knows how to run the ship better

than the likes of us. Talk like yours ends up making everyone unhappy.' Alex was wearing one of his earnest expressions.

'He's a snake, and you know it.'

'He's the skipper and we are his crew. It makes things worse to complain.'

'Argh, get the grease out of your mouth. So he's the skipper. He's also a flamin' snake, and he'll give us a hard time unless we stand up for ourselves.'

'That sort of talk is mutinous.' Alex was becoming heated.

'And you're a flamin' apology for a senior apprentice. I bet you didn't even see him about restarting those navigation lessons we used to have under old Fetherston.'

I knew this was unfair. I thought for a moment that Alex was going to strike Jimbo, but he controlled himself, and said deliberately, 'If you make statements like that I will consider reporting you to the mate.'

'Knock it off, you fellahs.' Jack had been leaning against a stanchion rolling a cigarette during this exchange. He strolled forward and handed the finished product to Jimbo, and lit it.

Jimbo scowled, drew on the cigarette, and wandered off. His mood was still black when we were relieved in order to get our breakfasts. We had already started when he came in and sat down. He began to eat surlily. Jack leaned across the table toward Hoff.

'You know, mate, I could get money for Jimbo's face if I put it in a circus.'

'Iss true, Jeck. Jimbo does not look ferry heppy.'

'Mind you, I'd have to teach him to behave proper when he's in company.' Jack turned to Jimbo. 'You...want... work...in...the...circus...little man?'

'Get lost.' At this response Jack turned to Hoff with a look of feigned outrage.

'Well. He's a rude little man, this one. I think we must smack his knuckles with a spoon.' And he made as if to do so. Jimbo seized the spoon, then flung it to a corner of the deck-house. He left the table and went out, slamming the door.

'Iss not so much in the mood for jokes, perheps,' said Hoff with a grin. Jack shrugged and resumed eating.

Later, as we were putting on our oilskins, Jimbo came back into the deckhouse and approached Jack sheepishly.

'Look mate, I'm sorry I flew at you. It's just that that swine has got under my craw.'

'Which swine is that, mate?' Jack asked.

'The new skipper.'

Jack grinned. 'Well, you're a silly beggar to let him do that, aren't you?'

'Yeah, yeah,' said Jimbo, and smiled wanly.

Jack leaned toward Jimbo's ear.

'I reckon you should play it carefully with old Alex, mate. He's a humourless beggar, but he's all right.'

'Yeah, mate. Yeah, sure.'

II

Mister Denholm's *Emilia* was to take a further twenty-seven days to pass the meridian of Cape Horn. I know that because fifteen years after the voyage, and at a time when I had determined to write this account of it, I visited the offices of the Denholm Steamship Co. as it was then known, and consulted the ship's logbook. By the end of that period, when we were in the waters off Cape Horn, my exhaustion had quite deadened my sense of the passage of time. We may as well have taken twenty-seven years.

As we pushed on for South America that first gale established a rough pattern for our existence that was to persist until we had passed the Falkland Islands on the other side. The grey ocean breathed and bulged around us angrily. Our forefoot ploughed gamely into each long sea, dividing it and creating an instantaneous crochet on each side of the ship. Occasionally there were periods of icy blue sky when the chilly sunlight would illumine the spindrift as though it were a bride's veil. Mostly it was overcast, the daylight sky having the same off-whiteness as our sails, a whiteness of soiled bandages.

The winds veered anywhere from south-west to north-west; we were constantly at the braces trimming the yards a point or two. On one occasion in those first two days it reached force ten and we sailed under lower topgallants with all three courses furled. (We were to experience a force eleven gale before we cleared the Horn.) Hoff passed me shortly after noon on the second day, water streaming down his face, and announced exultantly that we had done two hundred and seventy miles in the twenty-four hours. This was more like it!

The gale blew itself out that afternoon and we gained the first of what were usually twenty-four-hour respites. We reset the courses, upper topgallants and royals. By the evening meal everyone was ravenous and buoyant, and the earlier disgruntlement with our skipper had been forgotten.

He was standing in the midshiphouse waiting for us. As each of the five of us filed through the midshiphouse door and became aware of the captain's presence, we fell silent. Captain Trygg's head was sunk on his chest and his arms were folded. He seemed absorbed in meditation, like a man going over the words of a speech in his mind. The apprentices stood in a knot around the door. It was strange how we all instinctively kept as far away from the man as possible. He watched for the last man to come in, then surveyed us for a few moments.

'This place won't do,' he said.

I suppose it was a mess. There had been water slopping about the floors for nearly two days, and it had washed all manner of rubbish from the inaccessible corners of our accommodation; crusts of bread, a screwed-up ball of paper, the sodden remains of a magazine, a sock or two. I should say that its messiness at that point was exceptional. As a rule we lived tidily and had regulated ourselves in these matters, taking our independence for granted. The midshiphouse was our precinct, our refuge.

'It stinks.' He cast his eye from one face to another. No one felt inclined to disagree. The sheer physical size of the man gave his utterances a finality, and clearly he was intent on driving home a lesson now. 'It's a disgrace.'

'It's been blowing for two days, Captain. The place has been inundated. We generally keep it shipshape,' said Jack. The captain regarded him for a few seconds, then, ignoring his remarks, continued.

'Where's the senior apprentice?'

'I'm here, Captain.' Alex stepped out from our midst. He had been nearest to the door. There was another interval as Captain Trygg contemplated him.

'Hiding?' The question was put almost politely. Alex looked as if he had not understood it.

'I. . .I was the last to come in, sir.'

'Ah.' He indulged in another of his long pauses. There was something intelligent and calculated about his provocation. He had contrived that restrained tone of the schoolmaster interviewing delinquent boys. The resentment in each of our five breasts was almost tangible. We could be shouted at, cursed, driven, but not taken for less than we were, namely men in an employment. The shipmaster's word was law; we all knew that; it was the central article of faith in our calling. If called upon, we would work like slaves, but apprentices or not, we would be treated like men, and our deckhouse would be sovereign to our own arrangements. It was a matter of tact. And there was something in the way he spoke that made us sense that he knew what the balance of tact was and that he flouted it deliberately, that he acted from perversity rather than ignorance. He stared coolly at Alex and Alex stared back — to his credit — unflinchingly at him.

'Is this how you carry out your responsibilities, young man?' He prodded with his shoe a bedraggled sock that lay on the floor. Alex flushed, realising now that he was to be shown up in front of his fellows.

'We thought we'd leave the clean-up till after supper, Captain. You see, we've got some messy eaters among this lot.' Jack grinned as he said this, and a few of us attempted a smile too. The captain ignored him again, not taking his eyes off Alex.

'When do you sit for your ticket, mister?' he asked, quietly.

'After we get to London, sir.'

'And you expect to do well?'

'I certainly hope so, sir.'

'He do ferry good, Kept'n. Hes big brains,' added Hoff, with an attempt at cheeriness. The captain ignored the interjection.

'And you'll expect me to write a reference for you?' Alex was silent. His gaze never budged from the captain's, but there was a bafflement and an appeal in his eyes now.

'Well?'

'I hope you will, sir.' The words were no less distinct than Alex's previous answers, but they came out as though they had been forced.

'But how can you expect a reference when this is how you

discharge your duties?' The captain again prodded the sodden sock as if to underline the reasonableness of his question. Another pause.

'I can't, sir.'

'Ah.' Captain Trygg seemed to savour this point in the exchange. 'Then what must you do about it?'

'I'll see it's cleaned up immediately, sir.'

'You'll do a damned sight more than that, young man.' He left his intentions unspoken, as if waiting to see whether Alex would divine them. The senior apprentice searched the captain's countenance for any clue as to his meaning.

'What else, sir?'

The captain straightened himself for the first time. 'While these gentlemen wait outside for their supper, you'll clear out this sewer outlet yourself. When you think you've done the job, you come and tell me, and I'll tell you whether it meets a standard of decency.' He waited. We looked at each other uncertainly, then filed out of the door. Alex went off in search of mop and pail. The captain strode away aft.

'Swine,' said Jimbo, and spat on the deck. We stood desultorily for some moments, then Jimbo acted. 'Come on, let's all get stuck into this.' He went in and was followed by the rest of us. We were all, it seemed, prepared to defy the captain's order to stay out. By the time Alex returned most of the garbage had been thrown over the side, and the items of sodden clothing had found homes.

'He'll wonder why it took such a short time,' said Alex.

'Just mop her down, mate. That should satisfy the bastard. Come on, Johnny, let's go and see what's happened to our feed.' I went with Jack to the galley to collect the evening meal. When we came back Jimbo and Hoff were standing outside waiting for the captain. Alex reappeared without him.

'I couldn't get a grunt out of him. I think he's in his cabin.'

'To hell with him. This'll get cold.' We went in to our supper.

It was an uneasy meal. We expected him to turn up at the door and make life unpleasant once more. But he didn't come and indeed he never did inspect our quarters after that tidying up. It made me wonder whether the object of his intrusion was to achieve a tidy deckhouse or to humiliate one of our number. I did not then suspect that Alex was the particular object of his dislike. I assumed he might just as easily have picked on any of us.

But then that ten minutes he spent in our quarters was typical of his vagaries. He might be observed taking the occasional noon sighting, or spending a short spell on the poop issuing routine directions to brace up, take in, or clap on sail; directions that Mister Hallet would relay to us with his customary bellow. In fairness, not all his bouts of interest in shipboard life were of the same acrimonious character as his exchange with Alex that evening, and there was enough evidence in them to suggest that he was not bogus, that he was not in reality a passenger masquerading as a shipmaster.

Still, within a fortnight of Port Chalmers we despised him heartily. His very proximity was enough to still our talk or inhibit the chanteyman as we hauled at this and that. Although he was to become the central preoccupation of our lives as we sailed northward in the South Atlantic, he was never the inspiration of our activity. Rather he was an aloof and discomfiting presence on the edge of it.

Meanwhile our course was east-south-east, and as the *Emilia D.* pushed toward Drake Passage, so we crossed the latitudes of the early fifties and the temperatures dropped. As if fulfilling Jimbo's irreverent prediction, the cold seemed to drive our captain more and more to his cabin. This of course meant that Mister Hallet and Mister Gillard were spending as long as twenty hours a day on deck, sharing the responsibilities of shipmaster as well as carrying out their own duties as first and second mates. Initially, however, the hibernation of our skipper was welcomed as a lesser evil to his unsettling influence above deck.

I had my own private anxiety at this time. The thought of Cape Horn filled me with disquiet. It dwelt in my imagination like the prospect of a difficult examination for which I knew I was ill-prepared. Certainly I had a sounder confidence in myself than when I stepped aboard in Melbourne, but I had not been confronted with anything dangerous in the six-odd weeks I had been at sea.

My disquiet was not helped by my shipmates. During my vaguely surreptitious visits to the fo'c'sle I had listened to the sailors talk about the place, that most southerly place where the Pacific and the Atlantic meet in the narrow stretch of water called Drake's Passage. Those who had already doubled the Cape spoke of gargantuan following seas rearing up around a ship as though the mountain ranges of earth had been set in crazy motion. They spoke of winds that made speech useless, winds that would flex our huge iron mainyard as though it were a longbow. They spoke of Desolation Island and Staten Island on whose beaches were the skeletons of ships, and not just of ships either. Of course they spiced their stories to terrify me. As youngest and newest I was fair game.

'Yah, you're just trying to scare me. I bet we get becalmed within sight of the Horn.'

They would look at each other in mock surprise.

'Am I not telling the boy the truth?' one would ask.

'Gospel,' would say another.

It was gospel, too. I was apprehensive enough, and for more complex and (I'll call them) Australian reasons. It was not just the ultimates of sea and wind that worried me. It was more to do with where the Cape was; where it was in my imagination. Remember, I had been born and brought up in the city of Geelong. As a boy, whenever I thought of the outside world, my thoughts had a northward orientation. Northward, a short train-ride away, was Melbourne with its shop windows, libraries, ponderous state buildings, tides of people, and clatter of traffic. Further north was the world of hearsay: Sydney, the Orient, Europe. I had grown up with a picture of Sydney's harbour on a biscuit box. It had always reminded me of an intricate sea-shell, the blue whorls of the bays rimmed by the red and white incrustations of the houses, fabulous, exotic. My associations, then, with the simple compass bearing, north, were those of a populous, vivid and substantial world.

Of course I had looked at maps, and as a youngster I had stood on the beaches south of my city and watched the Southern Ocean sparkling in the sunshine. I knew in my mind that across the water was the great Antarctic continent and that men perished there. And that was the connection in my imagination. Northward life intensified and southward it diminished; whitened; ceased. The south fulfilled a picture in my child's mind of the nethermost places. One sailed south into deadly perils, awful loneliness, annulment.

As a child I had this association very powerfully, and the

apprehension that took root in my mind as we made further east-south-east each day was more than a vestigial remnant of it. My trouble was that I was too fanciful. Perhaps I had spent too much time drawing ships in the classroom when I should have been concentrating on geometry or algebra. Well, I was no longer in the classroom. Bound east-south-east I was approaching the real thing now. It was not that I felt I was hell-bound, exactly, but I felt I was making for an edge of some sort, or perhaps a frontier. I could not envisage myself beyond Cape Horn. I knew that if I came through I would have left something of myself behind. What, exactly, I didn't know. Perhaps I thought I would be more like Jack and the others, who had all been around the Horn at least once.

So I feared the experience, and longed for it. Maybe what I mean is that I longed to be able to boast of the experience in hindsight. Needless to say I took pains to keep these feelings to myself.

III

It was dark and once more someone had shaken me awake. This must have been some time after midnight for, as my eyes jerked open, I knew only that my watch had come off duty at that hour. It seemed like three minutes ago. Outside the walls of my sleeping sack there was a terrific racket going on. I remember wondering dully how I had gotten into my oilskins and boots, then realising I had not taken them off when I had turned in, that, indeed, I had scarcely taken them off for the previous seven days. The clothing beneath them was sodden and half-warm, clinging to me like an extra skin.

I tumbled out for the muster below the poop rail. Darkness; noise; my stupefied brain would allow no further information to register. Time seemed to have no meaning any more. I could not believe that day followed night. There was only the iron-darkness of the sub-Antarctic night and the demoralising suspicion that it would never get any brighter. The muscles of my eyes ached. In a gap between the lifeboats I glimpsed the lookout's lantern for'ard. It was rearing skyward then plunging downward in long seesaw motions. The barque was dipping her leeward bulwarks and scooping great cauldrons of water from an ocean that was the colour of a photographic negative. The surge turned luminous white around my waist and I no longer cared what the seas did to me. I was content to be urged this way and that like a sea-growth. It must have been cold, but if so it did not bite through my stupor as I stood waiting for orders.

'Main course!' Though he bellowed just above our heads, Mister Hallet's order was scarcely audible above the shriek of the wind and the crashing of the sea. Mister Gillard led us forward and, seizing the weather sheet, began to unbelay it. Two of us tailed on behind him to help pay it out while others formed a clump around the clew-garnet and buntlines. I could not see how a coherent action could issue from that clumsy scrum of figures, but magically the weather half of the sail slow-crumpled upwards. We crossed to do the same with the lee half. Once I was submerged completely, my sole sensation being that of a stupid demonic pressure dashing me this way and that in its efforts to dislodge me from the line I gripped. When I emerged there were figures teetering like drunks all around me.

'Aloft and furl!' Mister Gillard hurried us up the ratlines and out along the yard. Though clewed and bunted up to the yard the sail still had enough freedom to thrash wildly. The thing was lunatic. It welled up in front of me and seemed determined to flick me from the yard. There was nothing to grip the wet canvas with. How could the wretched thing be furled? I flailed and clawed with no hope of achievement, past tears, almost past thought. Perhaps an hour, perhaps an aeon and the job was done. Whether I had any part in it I neither knew nor cared.

No sooner were we down on deck than the order came to get the forecourse in. A second gulf of misery ensued. By the end of the watch we were running under topsails and lower topgallants. Mister Gillard's watch were sent below, while my watch, like the exhausted survivors of some catastrophe, huddled under the anchor deck for shelter.

'Bring in your lower t'gallants.' Some imbecile was yelling from near the forehatch. There was a faint light now, by which objects could be partly discerned. Through all the ages of man Mister Hallet's watch had sat like statues around the windlass below the anchor deck. No one had said anything. I thought I had been awake during that entire period. I had noticed nothing. Yet here it was suddenly lighter. How I had longed to sleep. Despite their sodden condition some of the able seamen dozed immediately. I recall one bearded face opposite me that belonged to a small Glaswegian. It lay tilted to one side on his hand, which in turn was propped on his knee. He slept! And there was actually a smile on his face, as though he were listening to some calm melody.

Crash had come each concussion on our bows, sending a shudder through our iron plates. Someone had shifted his position beside me, hunching deeper into his oilskins. The wind had war-whooped through the rigging, as though we were not at sea at all, as though the night was alive with millions of savages who kept up their frenzied howling in a half-darkness that had no end.

Yet I must have slept, for here, suddenly, the light outside had a translucent quality it had not had before and someone was yelling for the lower topgallants to be taken in. Mister Gillard's watch were coming up through the fo'c'sle hatch. I followed, I hauled, I clambered, I grappled. The iron yard was brutally cold. I clawed and clawed and gathered the topgallant under my belly. Dimly I was aware of Hoff's arms doing the same thing on one side of me and a seaman doing likewise on the other.

As I waited for the seaman to start moving back along the yard I looked ahead and around and below me. There seemed to be no colour, only movement; no distinct sounds, only din. The black geometry of the cordage scribbled crazy lines back and forth across the horizons, now becoming feebly brighter. On the fore and main topgallant yards I could see five or six men still at work, perched and swaying like sparrows on telegraph wires. There was no land. There was no other ship; indeed we had not sighted one for weeks. When the *Emilia D.*'s bulwarks dipped, letting tons of water flood on board, the long barque simply became part of that turbulent ocean with nothing more than its deckhouses, masts, fo'c'sle and poop visible. As I gripped the jackstay and began to shuffle along the footrope, I had the recognition, dimly and far down in my consciousness, of belonging to a fragment that was fearfully unreal. The sea was all but swallowing the ship for long intervals. The towering vessel that had so awed me at Railway Pier had diminished amidst the tumult to a frail insect-like structure to which I, an atom, was temporarily clinging. That recognition stayed with me. It was salutary. No matter how solid the ground beneath my feet I have never quite taken my life for granted again. Had I suddenly passed into adulthood? Maybe. Why it should have been that moment above the ship, however, which was, in fact, not the most perilous I encountered on that voyage, I don't know. It was a something that came into my mind without warning and negligently broke off one of the fundamental assumptions of my childhood, the assumption that I, who am central and continuous, was invulnerable to death.

'Iss lifely,' screamed Hoff in my ear as I crossed from footrope to shrouds. He yelled again and I caught 'rom vith coffee', as he jerked his thumb downwards, pointing at the poop deck where Mister Hallet stood like a fixture near the wheel.

The aspect of the sea was even more fearsome from the deck. To glance ahead where the bowsprit made its sawing motions on the skyline, was to see sudden sierras. They seemed to tower and be impassable. If you looked away for a few moments, then looked again, they were gone and the ship had sky all around it. These following seas were momentous. They appalled and entranced me. The *Emilia D.* would slide down into the trough of a wave, and in that trough there was an illusion of calm...calm! Our lower sails would fall slack, while ahead of us, perhaps a quarter of a mile away, those tottering, bulging sierras stretched in gigantic chains. Then she would rise, and as the masts came clear of the wind-shadow the three lower topsails would crack into shape once more. Up and down, up and down in those long crests and valleys in the approach to the tip of South America: if you had asked me how long we had spent in the longitudes between 72° and 65° doubling Cape Horn, or whether it was between a Wednesday and a Sunday, I could not have told you. Presumably Captain Trygg or Mister Hallet was recording this information in the logbook. For me there was light, there was darkness, there was a perpetual shrieking, there was white water swirling around my stomach or welling up over my head as I hauled with others on this and that.

And there were others. Someone's hand was under my

armpit as I gasped for breath and tried to find my footing. There was the straining back of someone hauling in front of me and the curses of someone hauling behind. And once or twice there was someone handing me a mug with a powerful tasting liquid in it that sent a shock of heat down into my stomach and which, a few moments later, had somehow impelled me to chuckle and speak with unaccountable loudness as I lurched with other gigglers to the bunks.

We seemed to have fallen into a dimension of existence quite outside time. I came to expect no end to it. I could barely remember a thing before it. When we could clap a sail back on, we did. When we were told to take it off again, we did so, before the wind blew it to rags. I recall we lost one staysail; taut as a bladder one moment, then bang! gone as if by sorcery. Nothing left except the triangle of the bolt-rope through which the sky showed and to which some forlorn rags of canvas still adhered, flapping madly.

If we lost more sails, then I am unaware of it. How Mister Hallet decided the moment a sail should come in was one of those mysteries of craft beyond me then. For days he had scarcely left the deck, seemingly immune to fatigue. His powers of mental alertness must have been phenomenal, yet I, and everyone else, seemed to take his indefatigability for granted.

As for myself, I suppose I must have slept on odd occasions, but I have no memory of being asleep, or awake, during that period.

IV

One event stands out starkly in my memory. Even now, this long after, it gives me a shudder to think about it. It was the nearest we ever came to going down, and the nearest thing to a compliment I ever received from the stern first mate.

I was called to relieve the helm and made my way aft in company with the burly MacPherson. It must have been one of the night watches for I have the indelible impression that I glimpsed the moon as I passed along the main deck. The wind shrieked, the seas tumbled aboard, and above there was cloud scudding eastward as though part of a celestial rout. But once or twice, I'm sure of it, I saw the moon, unmoved by the convulsions all around us, sailing high, like a prospect of serenity.

'You'll need to hang on,' shouted Jack in my ear as I took the spokes from him. I soon found out what he meant. The rudder was given to bucking violently and without warning, with the result that the wheel would want to kick upwards savagely. I embraced it, trying to anchor my legs so that I could not be lifted bodily when it jumped. On the other side MacPherson stood with his feet apart, similarly bracing himself. The movement of the ship at its very stern was, of course, exaggerated. Up rose the counter, up up up, with the same heart-stopping sensation of a ferris wheel at a fairground. Then down it came with that sickening sugges- tion of a descent that would not end. It was terrifying, yet every time her stern seemed to ride those seas as buoyantly as a cork.

I stared fixedly at the compass but my mind was on other things. To lift us like that, those seas behind must be huge. They fascinated my imagination in much the same way that the rearing cobra must hypnotise the attention of the mouse. I had to look. I felt the stern sinking into a trough. When it came to what seemed the end of its descent I stole a glance behind me. Just visible against the dark sky, with the broken water of its crest faintly phosphorescent, the welling sea seemed colossal beyond all perspective. It was impossible to tell how far away from the taffrail it was. It seemed imminent, and yet terribly slow. I was moved. I looked again, but as I turned my head a hand grasped me by the scruff and rudely redirected my eyes at the compass card while I heard a voice so close it could have been talking inside me.

'If you look backwards, laddie, we're all dead.'

I fixed my eyes on the card and gripped the wheel with the strength of terror. That sea broke over our poop. The stern of the vessel rose and rose as the bulk of the wave slid beneath our keel. Then crash. I was plucked from the helm as though I was a straw doll cast from the hand of a petulant child. As I was hurled forward, I momentarily glimpsed Mister Hallet's large, flailing body swept away for'ard, black limbs sprawling in a luminous welter. My own forward rush was halted by the skylight, and I lay there with my nose an inch or two from a deck-seam. I remember thinking 'It'll be safer if I lie low here,' but I was also thinking, 'No, there is something wrong, something mentioned in our chats with Old Fetherston.' Something unfamiliar was beginning to happen. I sensed the stern sliding down the reverse side of that sea. I popped my head up and looked aft. There was another great wave just distinguishable, but the white broken water of its crest was no longer directly behind us, where it should have been. Instead it was out on the starboard quarter. The barque was broaching. The helm! It was unmanned. I struggled to my feet and lunged for the spokes. I peered at the compass card. This was not right. I tried hauling on the spokes, but I could make no impression. It seemed to be jammed. O why did I have to be alone there? No sooner had I thought this than I noticed MacPherson had clawed his way back to the other side of the wheel. He was putting all his weight on a spoke and crying 'O mother, O Jesus, O mother,' in a voice quite loud enough to hear over the sea's crescendo. I added my own desperate strength. The helm moved. Far in the distance the foremast and bowsprit gave the impression they were travelling in a slow arc. The ship was responding. It had sunk into the trough of the previous wave by this time and the stern was beginning to rise again. I hunched my back against what I anticipated was coming. I waited to be plucked and tumbled away again. But this time we were left alone. The wave passed entirely beneath us. Mister Hallet was struggling up the poop deck, limping slightly. He must have been carried to the poop rail or beyond. Now he stood beside me and I was aware of him trying to regain his breath. There was a hand on my shoulder and I heard him saying between gasps, 'Bravely...bravely done.'

It is only in retrospect that I know what a close shave we had during those moments when the helm stood unmanned. If the ship had yawed further we would have been hit broadside on by those seas. We would have been bowled over like a toy — on our beam-ends, as the expression is — helpless as the ocean pummelled aboard, sweeping our decks clear of their lifeboats and accommodations, staving in our hatches and flooding below.

Perhaps one wave in twenty — it was impossible to detect a rhythm in it — was so mountainous that its crest swept over the counter, crashing down on my hunched back. Mister

Hallet had taken the slack of the spanker sheet and lashed both myself and MacPherson to the wheelbox after that first experience. If we went, then so did the entire apparatus of the helm.

I have said that during those days my consciousness had shrunk the world to an irreducible core of elemental sensations. Darkness, light, noise, sodden discomfort. Yes. But I surprised myself at the helm that night. I became a nugget of mental concentration for the remainder of that trick with MacPherson. My ears, my eyes, whatever that other sense is that registers movement, have never since worked on such tenterhooks. Sitting here at my table, with the cat gazing at me from its perch on the window-sill and the children of a neighbourhood school shrieking in their playground, I picture a long ship depending on the strength and alertness of one burly Scot and one boy for its existence.

But then, at *that* time, I was aware of nothing and of everything. There was no ship, simply the grating I stood on, the spokes I grasped in my hand and the yellow-glowing compass card that periodically disappeared beneath an avalanche of water. There was MacPherson, who might just as well have been anonymous, for I knew nothing about him except that he was burly and was a Scot. I had exchanged perhaps thirty words with him that voyage. Yet for an hour we worked in complete accord, clawing the helm round a point or two every time we sensed those immense following seas were shifting from dead astern to our quarter.

And there was Mister Hallet, braced against the twin doors that led below, staring ahead, sometimes casting a glance behind and roaring above that maelstrom, 'Watch out for yourselves,' as a mountain prepared to break its snowy back upon our heads.

If he had not stood so squarely in front of me, would I have deserted the helm and sought the safest corner of the ship I could find? I don't know. I was terrified enough, terrified of the random power that had plucked me once already from my station. Before such a power I was helpless. My life no longer belonged to me. It was utterly in the hands of chance. One of those slow gigantic seas might easily tear me and the wheelbox and MacPherson from where we stood and bundle us overboard. I had never been in such an exposed situation before. Barely eight weeks had elapsed since I had been a schoolboy. I had always assumed that people died or got hurt because they allowed control to slip from their fingers. But here there was no possibility of control. I would be a beetle-like flailing figure who might pass briefly before the eyes of another flailing figure before being extinguished utterly.

But this is hindsight. It didn't occur to me to run away. I was too preoccupied with what was given. Mister Hallet stood there. MacPherson and I stood there. The binnacle stood there. We *were* the vessel. Captain Trygg was presumably below. Mister Gillard was somewhere for'ard with the hands. They might just as well have been on Neptune. The three of us were utterly alone in that turmoil, but we didn't scream for the loneliness of our plight. There was no opportunity. We stood, we stayed, as though we were the only sentient beings in the Universe.

So that spell on the helm passed; so we were relieved and discovered other creatures existed in the darkness and noise. We came off watch. We slept like the dead in our reefer jackets and boots on our sodden mattresses. We were called. We clapped on a topgallant. We coiled down ropes that the sea had washed away from their pins. We slept. We took off a topgallant. And all the time the mighty continents of water moved around us, throwing up their sierras, throwing down their broad valleys, dissolving them, re-forming them, as though here was the firmament and now the epoch of up-heavals, and we a unique and privileged mote on the surface of still volatile matter.

It came to an end, of course, except that in my case this occurred more abruptly than it did for my shipmates.

Crack! A flurry. Where was I being taken? What was happening to me? Horrible confusion. Rest. I was there. I was flat on my back in the middle of an afternoon. My foot seemed to be caught in something that pinned it like a bear-trap, and I was being tossed this way and that like kelp in the tide. My mouth was filling with a warm liquid which I could do nothing but swallow. Blood, I suppposed. Still, I felt comfortable enough, though I could not get my eyes to focus properly, and there was a pain beginning to develop in my shoulder. The fierce hold whatever it was had on my ankle was too remote, I thought then, to worry about. I decided to get to my feet. I couldn't. Why should I not be able to accomplish this? It was irritating.

My hands cast about for something to grasp. A man was shouting. There was white sky above my head and water about my ears. All right, I would just lie back. Blood was still coming into my mouth from somewhere. Now the same voice was shouting from closer at hand. A pair of arms was being pushed under my shoulders and there was a head that swam briefly above mine. Then all at once there was a great deal of water. I was lifted by it, but it brought a sharp pain from my ankle. Water ran over my face. I was being held by that trapped ankle, and I began to feel panicky. The sea subsided. I tried to free the ankle, but could not. The pain in my shoulder had spread to my head. Hands were groping about near my ankles. Ah, my foot was free. Again that head swam into view and arms grappled under my shoulders. It was Alex. I was being moved. Now that my foot was free I didn't want to be moved. Not at all. Why could I not be left to myself? I had worked hard. I deserved to be left alone for a bit. I remember trying to wriggle from the grip of those benevolent arms beneath my shoulders. Then there were more hands, more faces, obliterated suddenly as another deluge of water swept over me. My panic of being held under returned. The water drained. A second voice behind my head was shouting (why did he have to shout?) 'Take him to the saloon.' Mister Hallet's face crossed my patch of sky briefly. How comically severe it looked. The pain in my head was growing, though that in my ankle had gone temporarily. I was borne up and carried aft. As I was shifted, I retched. There was darkness over my head. I was being laid down on a couch. I was now very drowsy and there was a voice in my mind saying, 'Retreat. Your troubles are overwhelming. Retreat into yourself.'

From the moment I found myself lying in that waterway I can remember with an eerie clarity, but I have no recollection whatever of how I came to be there or how I was injured. One moment I was passing along the safety rope toward the fo'c'sle — I think I had a message, though I've no idea what it was — then there I was, lying happily in the scuppers as the seas washed over me.

Hoff later reconstructed what happened. A big sea had

come over the side and I had lost my footing, while hanging onto the wire rope. During the time I was submerged something had come along and walloped me on the shoulder and side of the head with considerable force. That 'something' was probably one of the iron pump handles that had become unshipped. Anyway, Mister Hallet assumed this was the cause, for he blasted the exhausted watch when he found it was missing from its place. Once wallopped, I had obviously let go of the safety line and had been carried to the waterways where my foot had become caught behind a bulwark stanchion and one of the heavy iron washports. There Alex had spotted me and raised the alarm.

As I say, all this I learnt later. For the moment I drifted into a nightmarish state about which I can remember little now except that my mind was filled with rushing, pell-mell images and whatever shapes I saw had a great deal of red splashed about them.

CHAPTER 4

Laid Up

I

By one clonk on the head I managed to transfer the tumult that was raging outside and around me to within me. My sensations were similar to those I imagine a drowning man has during his last moments. I had the dim consciousness that there was a surface above which events happened and from which I was very remote. I inhabited a frightening unreality. At one time there was what seemed to be a red forest through which I was being chased, terrified. At another I swam in a broad, fast-flowing river; there was a current taking me downstream, and the source of my anxiety in this dream was my willingness to be carried along by the current. Somewhere on that river I knew there was a waterfall that was bottomless and that was also known as 'World's End', but whether it lay before me or behind me I did not know.

Now and then I fought my way to the surface. The saloon was incongruously tranquil. Outside the thin plates of the hull I was aware that the ocean seethed, the masts slow-wagged across the sky, men scurried hither and thither. But within the saloon the table stood bolted to the deck, the chairs were lashed together, and only a hurricane lamp above the flag-locker slewed hypnotically in rhythm with the grand movements of the ship.

On one of the occasions that I surfaced I found my oilskins and wet clothes were being peeled from me by Captain Trygg and the steward. At the time it did not strike me as the slightest bit odd that our derisive skipper should have been sociable enough to succour a damaged man. Indeed I was immensely comforted by his ministrations, for he and Gus seemed to set about their task of divesting me with great gentleness. At one point in the manoeuvring of my prostrate form, the captain's large face hovered above my own, and it seemed, to my mind, to wear an expression that was exaggerated and ludicrous in its kindliness. It could have been the model for a cartoonist seeking to illustrate a benevolent giant in a folk tale. Once stripped of my sodden and fouled clothing, I was reclothed in borrowed trousers and a huge sweater that could only have belonged to Captain Trygg, then sheathed in a sleeping sack. Gratefully I curled into its dark warmth.

I was brought to the surface rudely again. The din around the ship had somehow penetrated the saloon, there was a cold blast of air coming from somewhere, and water was slopping about the floor. Men clattered down the poop stairway and I found myself being lifted by persons unknown. I was rushed along a corridor, and the rough handling I received sent a shooting pain through my shoulder. There was a wait in darkness as my bearers swayed with the motions of the ship. Then someone yelled 'Now', a door clanged open and I was being propelled through daylight at what seemed extraordinary speed. At one point I was borne upwards and milky water boiled around me while vehement curses issued from the mouths of those holding me aloft. I believe I giggled. Then I was hurtled forward again. A door banged open. Once more there was darkness above my head. I was laid on a bunk. My carriers rushed out. The door slammed shut.

For how long I lay in my dopey state I don't know. It was probably only a day or so, though I felt I was experiencing the passage of centuries. Whenever I woke, Captain Trygg seemed to be in the room, standing at a distance from me. Once I remember him saying, 'Staten Island is abeam of us.' I have the impression he may have said more, that he gave me a commentary on our progress in a low, self-absorbed voice. Again it didn't occur to me how strange it was for the captain of a vessel to be spending so much of his time with an extremely groggy first-year apprentice. My whole outlook was so utterly dislocated that this detail of it did not trouble me in the least.

I was later told the reason for my removal. A big following sea, like the one that had hurled MacPherson and me from the helm, had smashed over the counter, surging forward and staving the poop hatch. Water had flooded below, and the captain had ordered my immediate transfer to the forward deckhouse.

'I've never seen him act so smartly. You don't know your own luck, Johnny,' said Gus, when he was trying to coax me into accepting some watery soup. 'He's scarcely done anything towards the running of this ship, but he was mighty insistent you be kept dry. Oooh, mighty insistent.'

There was a spare berth in the forward deckhouse, usually occupied by the ship's bosun. Since neither Captain Fetherston nor Captain Trygg had replaced the man who left the ship in Melbourne, I now took this bunk, sharing these new quarters with the carpenter, sailmaker and cook. The forward deckhouse was reckoned to be drier than the half-deck, where we, the apprentices, had our quarters, and the fact that my three fellow occupants were 'day men' and not subject to the night watches meant that their quarters were less prone to disturbance, and therefore more appropriate to my damaged condition.

For, as Gus related, my condition had aroused considerable alarm. I had retched a great deal of blood and behaved in a particularly limp fashion. Mister Hallet had speculated that the blood might indicate some internal rupture. To this extent I was bogus. Whatever clouted me had made my nose bleed. Lying on my back as I was, the blood had flowed into my mouth. I had swallowed most of it, then vomited it back up. I suppose I must have looked pretty sick, for the first mate expressed the opinion to Gus that I might be dying. Dying! I was not ready for that. I became very anxious about those periods of consciousness when I seemed to be slipping below the surface again, and spent long hours concentrating on staying awake. But eventually I would sleep again.

I stayed in that bunk for the best part of a week.

II

It was only much later in London that I gained any inkling as to what my injuries were, and by then they were all but gone. I stayed with the family of one of my mother's cousins, and the good lady, on hearing that I had been bowled over off Cape Horn, insisted I accompany her to a doctor to check that I had not injured myself in any permanent way. This man examined my skull minutely and could find nothing, and also my shoulder, where his prodding drew a twinge at one point. His conclusion was that I had probably fractured my scapula slightly and suffered from severe concussion, and this explanation I have accepted. I must have tumbled about the deck a bit before ending up in the waterway, so it is quite likely I was walloped on at least a couple of occasions. As things turned out my injuries proved to be convenient... at first; much less so later on.

Meanwhile I lay on my bunk. By the time my grogginess had gone, Captain Trygg had disappeared. (I still wonder whether I dreamed his presence in that deckhouse.) My torso and my arm were like belligerent neighbour states for whom the slightest movement was enough to make the border area of my shoulder a battleground of outraged nerves. I lay utterly still on my back, staring at the door where the carpenter's apron swayed on its hook in rhythm with the roll and pitch of the ship. If I could stay like this, I thought, completely motionless, my torn shoulder would re-knit with the rest of my body. Shortly after breakfast on the first day after I had returned to full consciousness Mister Hallet came in and stood by the bunk. His manner was almost kindly.

'Any better, laddie?'

'A little, I think, sir.'

'Where is it sore?' I indicated shoulder and head with my good arm. He lifted the injured limb and prodded around my shoulder. I cried out involuntarily. The pain was dreadful.

'It'll mend. Rest it for a few days.' He strode out and the iron deckhouse door clanged behind him. On each of the five days I was laid up he returned at precisely the same time, asked the same two questions, reached the same conclusion, and left.

Shortly after the door clanged shut on the first of Mister Hallet's visits, it opened again, and there stood Alex, hesitating about whether he should enter.

'Good-day, Alex,' I managed to croak. I must confess I felt somewhat heroic in my stricken condition and quite welcomed the chance to be seen as such by my fellow apprentices. After all, I had doubled the Horn, and bore a glorious wound as a token of that feat.

'You were lucky,' he said, deciding to come in.

'Why?' I thought I had been particularly unlucky to sustain the clobbering I had done.

'You were nearly lost.'

'Was I? I thought I had my foot jammed in something.'

'That wouldn't have stopped you. Those seas coming aboard would have torn your foot off and taken you over the rail. You were lucky we got to you.' I thought this was a little morbid, not to say improbable. Alex's manner was curious. He appeared to be, not exactly irritated, but bothered about something, like a man in company waiting for some impropriety to be detected by his companions. I tried to change the subject.

'Where are we now, Alex?'

'It's lucky I didn't go over too. I was caught by a big one while trying to get your ankle out of the washport.'

'Yes, but where are we now?'

'I reckon you could say I saved you a long swim.' The grin on his face as he said this had the same queer contrivance as that which he flashed at me after the chain-wrestling episode, only now there was the hint of a suppressed anger behind it. It dawned on me what he wanted.

'Thanks Alex. You saved my life there.'

'There were the others too. It's lucky we got to you quickly.' He tried to brush off my gratitude, but his brow seemed to clear at my recognition of a debt to him.

'Where are we?'

'The Falklands are off to starboard. It's calmed down a bit.'

For three days Alex became my most regular caller. He spent most of his off-duty time entertaining me, and was forever coming in during slack periods when he was on watch. He was most attentive, often reading me stories; adventure tales usually, from a magazine which, I noted, was designed for boys between the ages of ten and twelve. I enjoyed them well enough. They were preferable to the hours of inertness, staring at the carpenter's swaying apron. But the enthusiasm which Alex would display in conversation about these tales was hard for me to reciprocate.

He talked about other things too. Alex, I discovered on one of his visits, was an orphan; effectively so anyway. He had been the eldest of three children, but was still very young when his father had disgraced himself in some way (Alex

could not be persuaded to elaborate on this) and walked out
on the family home. The mother decided that she could
manage two children on her own, but not three, and that it
was the two youngest that needed her attention most. She
placed Alex in an orphanage, and there he had spent his
childhood under the authority of a certain Mister Laidlaw.
This gentleman, according to Alex's account, was a strict and
God-fearing man, but even-handed in his dealings with the
boys in his charge.

'If we were caught for anything he'd take a switch of wire to
us. "Anarchists," he'd say, "fearful... little... anarchists,"'
and Alex imitated the exertions of the dour Mister Laidlaw
as he applied the rules to the upturned bottoms of his wards.
'But he was all right. You always knew where you stood with
him.'

'What happened to your mother?'

'Mum? She used to come and visit a bit in the early days,
but it was just birthdays after that. We used to go to teashops
and I could choose any kind of cake I wanted. She would've
come more if she could've.'

'Is she still alive?'

'She paid my indentures. On my fifteenth birthday Mister
Laidlaw called me to his office. There was Mum. "Now
Alex," said Mister Laidlaw, "we're going to send you to sea.
Would you like that?" "I don't know, Mister Laidlaw," I said.
To tell the truth, Johnny, I didn't like the idea at all; not
then. I didn't want to go far away, not see Mum, or my
brother and sister for years. "Do you not want to be a captain
on a ship one day, Alex?" said Mister Laidlaw. Mum was
watching me, so I said, "Yes, Mister Laidlaw, I'd like that."
"Good," he said, "because your mother is willing to pay your
indentures. Now that is a lot of money, Alex. You'll be
bound for four years, then you will sit for an exam, and
become a ship's officer. You will have to do well, and behave
yourself, to show your mother you are grateful for what she's
done for you, won't you," he said. "Yes, Mister Laidlaw," I
replied. So off to sea I went, at *that* time more because Mum
wanted it than anything else.'

'So here you are.'

'Here I am. I have to get through. All Mum's money will
have gone to nothing if I don't.'

'You will. Everyone says you will.'

During the course of this last conversation I realised some-thing: Alex had no friends on the ship. It struck me I had only ever heard him talking to the other apprentices when he was giving directions or explanations as the most senior of our number. I never knew anyone, except myself, to stop and actually chat with him. Furthermore, I had always assumed he kept himself away from our horseplay and banter out of a sense of the dignity of his position. It may equally have been out of shyness, out of a lack of assurance as to how we regarded him.

The fellow was starved of human companionship. I sud-denly saw the dimensions of his loneliness. Alex was toler-ated, but he was not, in any real sense, one of our company. With the exception of myself, all the other apprentices had made a number of voyages before joining the *Emilia D*. All of them accepted Alex's position as senior apprentice. Why not? Let him take the rap for their shortcomings and pranks. He was convenient. In the ordinary run of things we supported him. We were indignant when the captain picked on him to clean up the mess in the deckhouse. But I think it is true to say that our indignation was a reflexive outrage against tyranny in the abstract. Had we felt solidarity with Alex, sympathy for Alex? I doubt it. There was something in him that inhibited sympathy, some awkwardness. He was too confined within his own notions of success, too much the model, to attract much fellow-feeling from us, his peers.

I saw why he had been so solicitous on my account during my first weeks at sea; why he had cultivated my company. I was fair game, new to everything. He could be a mentor and, in that role, gain some of the companionship he craved. But the inevitable happened. I outgrew my mentor rapidly. What I didn't see then, but see now, is how Alex's seeking of my company subtly lowered him in the estimation of the others. I was the youngest, the ship's 'green boy'. Nothing was spoken, of course, but the hierarchy of natural authority co-existed with the formal hierarchy of the ship. By having to seek the company of the lowliest and youngest, Alex lost status. And my guess is that he knew it.

He stopped coming after the third day of my recuperation. Once, when the door had been left open to let in some air, I

saw him pass across it briefly, then come back. I called out
and he looked up, but averted his eyes quickly and did not
pass across the door again.

I was getting other visitors. One afternoon Jimbo stood
leaning against the door jamb.

'Flamin' malingerer.' He swaggered in, took something
from the pocket of his dungarees and tossed it on the bed.

'Here, stick that under the blanket.' It was a smallish flask,
half full of a brown liquid. I looked at the label on it, and saw
in the middle of an elaborate insignia the words 'Distilled
Whisky'. I was filled with alarm. Apart from the tot of rum
that was issued to us from time to time alcohol was strictly
taboo on board. Of course we knew of the existence of a few
bottles of wine, a flask or two of spirits, all jealously guarded
by Gus, and intended for the palates of the ship's officers, or
any passengers the vessel happened to be carrying.

'Jimbo! Where'd you get this?' He made no immediate
answer, but went to the door, looked out, returned to the bed
and took a swig.

'Here,' he said. 'It's good stuff.'

I followed his example. The taste of whisky (on that
occasion) I found awful, and though the sensation of heat it
radiated on my tongue and throat were not unpleasant, it
sent a spasm of pain through my still-delicate head. Jimbo
took it from me, had another quick swig and corked it.

'Hide it somewhere good. I'll get killed if it's seen.' I
indicated the underside of the palliasse I slept on.

'But where did you get it?'

'One guess.'

'From Trygg?'

'You're a genius, my boy.' He grinned.

'How?'

'Ah, that *was* a stroke of luck. Remember when we had to
shift you from the saloon?'

'Vaguely, I was feeling pretty groggy.'

'Well, a big sea came over the counter and smashed the
hatch doors. Quite a bit of water got below and rampaged
about. Everything was flooded, including Trygg's cabin. So,
while they were evacuating you for'ard, Hallet got the
carpenter to rig a tarp over the smashed doors, and got me

and Hoff to clear up below. Me! Hallet should have known better.'

'Hallet looked awful when he came in here this morning.' I had in fact been quite shocked by the signs of strain on the first mate's face. His eyes were bloodshot with puffy bags below them. He had seemed more self-absorbed than on his previous visits, though it may have been that I was too pre-occupied with my own pain to have noticed the exhaustion evident on the first mate's countenance before.

'He's done in. If Trygg did his whack, instead of skulking in his flamin' cabin. . .' Jimbo fulminated against the captain for a while. Both he and Jack were inflexibly loyal to the first mate, though his loyalty certainly earned Jimbo no favours.

'So how did you sneak this out?' I indicated the contraband below my palliasse.

'I knew he had a lot stashed away, not only from what you told me about that crate he brought aboard, but also because Gus had seen him tossing the odd bottle over the side. Well, while splashing about down there, everyone shouting, chaos going on outside, it wasn't hard to slip a little something under my oilskins. He was watching me, mind, with that flamin' imbecile expression on his face. You know, half-grin, half-sneer. . .though I reckon he's never actually looking *at* anything when he stands about like that; looking *through* something more like. He's bad, that one. I'd like to have a go at pinching the rest of the liquor he's got down there. It might ferret the snake out of his hole and up on deck where he could do more of his share of the work.'

'It's a pity Hallet isn't the captain,' I said. Jimbo got up to go. 'Jimbo, has Trygg told Alex to stop coming here?'

'Yeah, mate, I gather he has.'

'Why?'

Jimbo shrugged. 'No reason. Trygg's got it in for Alex. He's been giving him the runaround lately.'

'You don't like him much, do you?'

'Who? Trygg? He's a snake.'

'No, Alex.'

'Aw, it's hard to feel one way or another about Alex. I don't think about it much, fellah.' Jimbo was obviously loath to talk about personalities. 'Time I went. . .Here, give us another go on that flask.'

III

Another well-wisher was Jack. He ambled into the deckhouse one evening after the first dogwatch.

'How're you doing, fellah?'

'Aw, not bad. My shoulder's a bit rough.'

'You'll want to take it easy for a while.' We exchanged remarks of this nature for a time, and I basked in the glow of Jack's interest. Remember, I was sixteen. I admired Jack enormously. I had been immensely impressed by the way he had handled himself, by his return unscathed from the fray in Port Chalmers, the efficient way in which he had dealt with Alex in the chain-wrestling. I guess my attitude to him had become a kind of hero worship, though now, twenty years after he was killed, I cannot really remember what he looked like. This troubles me. Images of Jimbo, Hoff, Alex, Mister Hallet, Captain Trygg, I can conjure up in my mind with a photographic clarity. But with Jack the details are blurred, like the features of a man who moved at the instant the picture was taken. I have the impression of fair hair, a bony nose, twinkling eyes, athletic build; but these are common enough distinguishing marks. Why should his exact physical appearance elude me? Because of what happened later?

To put it simply, Jack had charisma. He seemed to be at the centre of any group. He was strong. He was just. He had a kind of modesty with it too. As far as I could see he was successful at all that he did. How do I re-create on the page these virtues? He was like a man at the centre of some electrical field. There are people like this in the world, who seem to move in an aura of grace, apparently untroubled by the frustrations and weaknesses of the rest of us. Jack stands there in my life, in that patch of shadow that divides my childhood from my adulthood, out of focus; somehow the favoured one.

'I suppose things are a bit shorthanded in Mister Hallet's watch with me out of it?'

'We can't get by without you, Johnny. We've knocked off work until you can get back.' Jack grinned.

'Hallet looks pretty done in these days.'

'He's tough as boots, fellah.'

'Why didn't he take over at Port Chalmers? Surely we would have been better off with Hallet as skipper, and a new mate?'

Jack looked at the floor for some moments. 'What do you think of Hallet?' he asked.

'He's hard. But I don't mind him...not any more. I reckon he would back us up always.' I was recalling that pat on the back and the voice saying, 'Bravely...bravely done,' back there on the approach to the Horn, which now seemed an aeon ago.

'Well, if I tell you why old Hallet won't take on a command, you'd better not change your notions of him.'

'I promise.'

Jack went to the door and looked outside. Dusk was falling on the South Atlantic, and the patch of sky I could see through my doorway had a green tinge to it near its rim. When he came back, Jack contemplated me for a few moments. At length he spoke.

'Hallet put a man in prison once...wrongfully. Kind of framed him.'

'How long ago?' It was an inane question, but Jack's disclosure had taken me by surprise. It was not so much that I was shocked. I simply had not associated Mister Hallet with any kind of past. The first mate was simply *there*, as obvious as a stanchion, or a risk to be faced daily. Alex had a past life. Jack and Jimbo had a previous ship. But Mister Hallet had no previous existence in my mind whatsoever. His life began on that hot December day I joined the ship in Melbourne, and continued until the visit he had paid me that morning.

'About five years or so. A bit less, I think.'

'What...what had the man done...the one Hallet put away?'

'Killed someone. That was the theory anyway.'

'Do you know what happened?'

'Yeah, most of it,' said Jack with no particular urge to go on. I waited to see if he would, but he remained silent.

'Did you know Hallet then?'

'Nah. I got most of it from the carpenter on my last ship. Jimbo and I had a short spell in London after we left that oregon carrier from 'Frisco. We ran into the carpenter one night, and when he heard we were going to join the *Emilia D.*

he told me all about Hallet. He'd sailed with him for years. Gus knows a bit about it too. It's not too much of a secret. The papers — the shipping papers that is — splashed it about a bit. No one talks about it much round here. Obvious reasons.'

'Tell me what happened.'

Jack contemplated me again. 'You'd better remember your flamin' promise.'

I nodded. He seemed satisfied, and began:

'Hallet was one of the brighter fellahs to come out of the old sail-trainer *Macquarie*. He got on fast. Soon he was the second, then the first mate on one of the crack wool carriers of the late eighties. He had his first mate's ticket by the time he was twenty-three, and *that* is *good*. My carpenter mate — a bloke called Cluny — began working for him at around that time.

'The owners took an interest in Hallet. He sat for his Master's ticket at the earliest time, got it, and was given a smart little three-master on the Tasmania–Europe run. Cluny then lost touch with him for about ten years. Then five or six years ago they crossed tracks in Belfast. Hallet, by then, was commanding one of Denholm's big barques. He was bound for Adelaide with railway iron and needed a carpenter. Cluny joined. Disastrous flamin' voyage that turned out to be.

'There was this character by the name of Tate in the crew; an able seaman. He was a low sort, apparently, and one of your knife artists. He quarrelled, whinged, or got others to whinge for him, started fights, shirked. Cluny reckoned one of Tate's problems was his size. He was short and skinny and always trying to make up for it. Well, the ship had a hard time down in the forties, and by the time it got to Adelaide Hallet loathed Tate with a vengeance, and made little secret of it.

'Why not get rid of Tate at Port Adelaide? Well, there was some minor gold rush being talked about. Half of Hallet's crew deserted and joined the rush. Unfortunately Tate stayed. He wasn't going to be taken in by any wild talk about gold rushes, not him. With his crew at half strength, Hallet couldn't very well throw him off. They were due to sail from Adelaide to Newcastle and load coal for Lyttelton. Hallet managed to get a few sweepings to replace the men who deserted, then sailed shorthanded for Newcastle. There were some more nasty types in the new crowd, according to Cluny, and before they'd even cleared the Backstairs Passage, Cluny had made up his mind to keep his mouth shut and his eyes open. On one thing the new crowd seemed to be agreed: they didn't like Tate either. Not one bit.

'You might have thought Tate would have cleared out in Newcastle, but he stuck like a limpet. Perhaps he liked punishment, or attracting trouble.

'They sailed from Newcastle and ran into gales in the Tasman, almost before they'd dropped the New South Wales coast. It was actually that first evening when everybody was hauling on the buntlines that the fight flared. Cluny's not sure what was said, but you know how it is, a lot of men crowded round the pinrails, all hauling, treading on everyone's toes, swearing, elbows everywhere. Suddenly, says Cluny, there was Tate, flying backwards out of the ruck, and ending up on the main hatch with a character called Ruby following after him with his fists up.

'Quick as a flash, this Tate had produced a knife from somewhere and was waving it about, threatening to open up Ruby's stomach if he came near. He'd had enough, he screamed. He wouldn't stand for their treatment any more.

'Now there are knives and there are knives. This thing of Tate's was apparently no ordinary sheath knife. It was a very fancy piece of work, with a kind of squiggly blade, a pearly handle, the kind of thing you might pick off the counter in a bazaar in Madras, or Singapore. Not designed for cutting cordage, you might say.

'Old Hallet was down from the poop like greased lightning. He found the second mate trying to talk Tate into dropping the knife, and the watch gathered round.

'"Give me that knife, Tate," says Hallet, coming through the crowd. Tate says he'd be glad to put a hole through the captain's stomach as well. Two bastards are as easy as one. Each time anyone tries to come near he brandishes this thing in their face.

'"Give me the knife, Tate, and I'll say no more about it," says Hallet. Tate tells him to go rot in hell. He looked completely pathetic, according to Cluny; this weedy little monkey crouched in the middle of all those men who loathed him. Ruby had been restrained by a couple of the others, and no one was really game to go near Tate.

'"All right. Put the knife away and we'll forget it. It'll be as if the episode never happened," said Hallet again. Tate did nothing the first time this request was made, but Hallet kept repeating that everything would be square if he put the knife down, so in the end Tate lowered the thing and made as if to put it away.

'As he did so Hallet lunged at him and, so quick that Cluny reckons he could hardly follow it, snatched the knife from Tate's hand and flung it overboard. Tate actually went after it. He was fond of that knife. He'd paid a great deal for it, and he threatened he'd blasted-well get even with Hallet for that act. Captain Hallet, as he was then, simply bawled him and the rest to the lines, then worked them for the remainder of the watch until they were ready to drop. When they knocked off, he hauled Tate and Ruby up before him, roasted them, docked three days' pay from Ruby and a couple of weeks' from Tate. That really stung.

'A couple of days later Ruby disappeared. It happened at night. The bad weather had stayed with them and there was a big sea running at the time.

'Towards the end of the first watch the helmsman, who was a young fellow like yourself, called Hallet over and said that he thought he had heard the crying of a man sweep past the stern. You don't hesitate in situations like that. Hallet ordered the ship to be hove to immediately and a boat prepared. Meanwhile the mate went to the fo'c'sle and lowered down a light. "Any empty berths?" he yelled, when he'd roused the off-duty watch. Yes, Ruby's berth was empty...and so was Tate's. The watch on deck was all accounted for.

'A search of the ship failed to find Ruby, and the boat that was lowered found nothing either. The sea was too high to have given much of a chance anyway.

'What the search did uncover was Tate. He was caught by a group of the men coming out of the sailmaker's cubby. Very convenient, that cubby, for a man who wants to get away from the rail in a hurry.'

'Why didn't the sailmaker know he was there?' I asked.

'The sailmaker's berth was in with the carpenter's and cook's in a different part of the deckhouse. The cubby was where the sailmaker kept his bolts of cloth and did most of his work. The other thing was that, since the ship had been under-manned since Adelaide, Cluny and the sailmaker had been helping out in the first mate's watch during the spell of heavy weather after Newcastle. This means that they weren't in a position to hear Tate go into the cubby on that night, or any other night.

'Tate was suspected of having got even with Ruby for the fight and the two weeks' pay he had lost. After all, men don't throw themselves overboard, particularly when they are a part of the off-duty watch and should be in their bunks. Hallet thought so anyway and locked Tate up. He then grilled the men of both watches, one at a time, to find out what had happened. He grilled Tate too.

'No one except the lookout had seen any disturbance on the deck at the time, and even he wasn't sure he'd seen anything. He thought he remembered seeing two figures beside the rail, one of them pretty small. "What time was that?" rapped Hallet. "Oh, pretty close to the time you put the helm down, sir," replied the lookout. But, says Cluny, *he wasn't sure*, not then, when the ship was still at sea. Hallet is supposed to have said to him "Well you'd damned-well better be sure by the time of the enquiry and the Admiralty Court in Lyttelton." There were one or two scraps of evidence from the off-duty watch. Someone remembered seeing Ruby get up and go out. "Was he called out?" "He could have been. There was a fair racket from the sea outside. Difficult to say."

'From Tate, Captain Hallet got a great deal, though he didn't believe any of it. Tate claimed that the crew had been giving him a hard time, and that he'd decided to go and get his kip somewhere out of their reach. The cubby was perfect as he could wrap himself up in a bit of sailcloth and sleep under the workbench.'

'What did he say the crew were doing to him?' I asked.

'Aw, they're supposed to have red-leaded the inside of his sleeping sack, among other things. They denied it when Hallet questioned them, but as I said, they were the sweepings.' Jack took out a wallet of tobacco and began to roll a cigarette.

'Then why was he coming out of the cubby when the men found him?'

'He'd heard the commotion on deck, the ship being hove to, the duty watch searching the ship, and so on. As I say, Hallet didn't believe him. He reckoned that Ruby had been the victim of foul play, and was convinced Tate was behind it.

'The ship berthed at Lyttelton, there was a preliminary enquiry and then Tate was tried for murder before an Admiralty Court. One thing the prosecutor wanted to know was how Tate managed to slip into the cubby without being missed by his own watch, and appear back with the watch when they came up on duty again. "Oh, I'll explain that," said Tate. "I'd hang about near the windlass till my watch had gone below, then slip in there when no one was looking and get my shuteye. I'd always wake at seven bells and clear out before my watch came up on deck." "You must be a very light sleeper if you always heard seven bells and never needed rousing," said the prosecutor. "Yes, I am a light sleeper, as it happens," said Mister Tate. "No matter what state of exhaustion you might be in?" "No matter what state I was in. Besides," he added, "I'd only been going in there since the fight with Ruby. They'd been threatening to fix me properly. They'd been putting filth in my sleeping sack. What would you've done, eh?"

'Well, that prosecutor established that Tate's reasons for being in the deckhouse were flimsy, to say the least. The prosecutor said, "I put it to you, Mister Tate, you went into that cubby to hide after you had somehow disabled or stabbed the man Ruby and bundled him over the side, and you went there because you had not expected Ruby's disappearance to be discovered so rapidly and you found you did not have time to get back to your own berth undetected." "That's a lie," said Tate. "They're out to get me."

'It wasn't absolutely cut and dried, for though Tate had a motive, there was no actual body. But there were the testimonies written down by Captain Hallet, among which was that of the lookout. "Lookout declares he saw Tate in company with Ruby at the rail shortly before the ship was hove to," was how the captain's written account read. Cluny admits he was a bit surprised when he heard that definite statement read out by Hallet in the court, as he can't remember the lookout being as sure as all that, but then he'd only heard what the lookout had said from hearsay and, like the rest, he assumed it *was* Tate who disposed of Ruby.

'The defence counsel asked Hallet: "Are you certain, Captain Hallet, that there was no element of doubt in the lookout's mind as to the identity of the two men at the rail?" "There was none," replied Hallet. There were lots of other questions asked, such as: Why was the lookout not directing his attention seaward to the dangers of other shipping? How could he see what was going on near the fore-shrouds if the weather was as it was? and so on. Hallet stuck to his guns, despite Tate yelling things from the box, such as: "That's a lie. He wants to nail me." The lookout himself took the stand, and of course by this time he was sure of what he'd seen at the rail. It was unmistakably Tate.

'As I say, Hallet was convinced that Tate had done away with Ruby, and no doubt he thought his small adjustment of the evidence was justified in nailing an obviously criminal type. He'd tried to use a knife on Ruby, after all. Tate had also been a thorn in Hallet's side since London, so he didn't have too much sympathy with what lay in store for him if he was found guilty. And that's what happened. He got sentenced to death. The defence lawyer lodged an appeal. Since the ship was due to sail from Lyttelton to Callao with timber, and then on to London with nitrates, it was decided to send Tate straight to England where he would be held in custody until Captain Hallet's ship docked, and the appeal could be heard. It's about the best thing that defence lawyer did, lodging that appeal; for Hallet as well as Tate.

'The appeal, see, was never heard. It turned out Tate had nothing to do with Ruby's disappearance. There'd been a plot, involving practically the entire fo'c'sle. Ruby was liked by that crowd about as much as Tate was, only he was bigger and fond of using his weight. So they *really* hated him. As well, during the time that the ship was idle in Newcastle, Ruby had won a good slice of several pay packets at cards, so five or six of the crew decided they would solve two problems in one go.

'The assumption on the night and through the trial was that it must have been someone in Ruby's watch, the off-duty watch, that had given him a shove, and since Tate was found apparently hiding, *and* had a motive, why look further? But everyone in the fo'c'sle knew Tate didn't spend his off-duty watches in the crew's quarters — that's why I say the plot involved practically the whole complement of seamen. Actually it was a couple of fellahs in the duty watch as well as two or three from below who did the deed. Ruby was called from his berth on some pretext. The pair from the duty watch approached him. I suppose it was very casual-like. They probably even passed some friendly remarks. Then hup! They bundled him overboard. The two or three from below went back to their berths, and the other two quietly rejoined the watch in the lee of the deckhouse. They were a bit surprised when Hallet suddenly ordered the ship hove to, but it hadn't taken a moment for everyone to be where he should have been.

'There were too many of them in the plot for them to get away with it. One thing that should have aroused suspicion was that a number of the crew deserted in Lyttelton, including the lookout. Not that Hallet wasn't glad to see them go. His ship sailed for Callao, and eventually he put into London with his nitrate cargo. Tate had gone back on the mail boat. Meanwhile, of those who had jumped ship in New Zealand, one had joined a ship in Wellington. This ship had to put into Rio for fresh water; one of its tanks had sprung a leak. The crew went for a spree, our man apparently said a little too much in his cups, and word got back to the ship's captain who had read something about the case in the shipping papers. The ship sailed, the captain bided his time, slipped a letter to someone in the pilot boat that met them off the Mersey, and so arranged for the constabulary to pick this character up when the ship berthed at Liverpool. To save himself, he blabbed. There was an enquiry. Tate was exonerated and released. It seems they *had* been persecuting him and his reasons for being in the cubby were the truth. I think one of the others in on it was picked up later as well.

'Hallet was lucky in one respect. He heard about the fresh evidence concerning Tate on the grapevine before he got a cable advising him to attend the Board of Enquiry. His nitrate consignment had been redirected to Nantes, and someone there had put him in the picture. He resigned his command, took the steamer to Dover, went before the enquiry and was roasted for concocting evidence he knew to be false. He made no attempt to hide or excuse his adjustments to the evidence. He had very nearly got an innocent man hanged. But still, I reckon Hallet had a lot of gumption to be as straight as Cluny says he was in the circumstances of that enquiry.

'His certificate was suspended for three years, and he went to prison for six months for perverting the course of justice. He did his time, then went back to sea, this time before the mast. But Denholm stood by him, and cajoled him into taking a first mate's berth. When the three years were up Denholm tried to get him to accept a command, but he wouldn't. Word came that the man Tate had died, not from the knife, but from natural causes, surprisingly enough, but that made no difference. Old Hallet was adamant.'

Jack had his eyes lowered to the floor during the course of this narrative; now he looked up to see the effect the story had on me.

'Won't he ever accept command of a ship, Jack?'

'I dunno, fellah. He seems to have chosen not to. Cluny, who stuck by him after his suspension, says that he never will out of a kind of grudge against himself. It may not matter. He practically runs this ship. Except that if things go wrong he doesn't have to take the blame.'

This last remark didn't convince me, and Mister Hallet's decision to refuse command seemed like a fearful price to pay for one small indiscretion. Of course I was looking at Mister Hallet's fate through the eyes of a boy with forty working years in front of him. The idea that a man's career could come to a halt through one tiny misjudgement was numbing.

'I can't see why he should be so hard on himself just for one small lie.'

'It wasn't one small lie, fellah. It was a big one. If you're a captain, you've got to be seen to be just. There's no policeman, juries or courts on a ship. The captain's word is law, and whatever comes up, he has to put right. Often he has to deal with crooks — the kind who like brandishing knives, for instance. Thieves, runaway murderers, the scrapes from fandango halls, they all find their way onto ships. It's not hard to turn good men into bad with that sort of mischief loose among them.

'The captain's got the powers of a monarch when he is at sea, only his job is lonelier. There's space enough on land to walk away from the trouble you've created. Not out here, though. You live with it. You solve it, or it gets out of control. We're going to have to watch ourselves on this ship too. There's some bad things beginning to get under way.

'You see Hallet made a bad mistake. By falsifying evidence he put a man behind bars for nearly two years for something he didn't do. He nearly got the man hanged. As a result, all but two of the culprits got away with murder. They're in the world somewhere, and while that's the case there's always the chance they'll poison the life on board some ship. Someone who bundled one man overboard will do it again easily enough. So my guess is that Hallet won't accept another command for one simple reason: he can never fully trust himself to be just. Old Hallet may be a bit fierce sometimes, but he's a sober man. He knows what he did.'

I was silent. Jack's story had taken me below another kind of surface. The first mate was no longer the straightforward phenomenon I had assumed him to be. Mister Hallet had a past — yes — and it was impossible for him ever to be free of it. That was one thing. But Jack's story had impressed on me how utterly *contained* the life on board a ship was. There was no room to duck consequences. There was no walking away.

Jack got up to go. 'Privileged information, Johnny,' he said. 'And you'd better see that shoulder heals up quick.' He went out.

CHAPTER 5

The Mischief-makers

I

On the day after Jack told his story the first mate entered my sick-quarters at his habitual time. His manner was preoccupied and his face wore an expression even more severe than usual.

'Show me.' He indicated my injured arm and I offered it. He prodded and levered it, at which I winced. It was still painful.

'Any improvement?'

'Yes, sir, I think so.'

'Get up and walk across the room.'

I had not used my legs for a week, and as I tried to manage them to traverse the narrow deckhouse they felt unfamiliar and wobbly. Mister Hallet, however, seemed satisfied.

'You'll do. Start work again tomorrow morning. Light duties. You can help the steward.' The door banged behind him.

Towards evening I dressed and tottered from the deckhouse to the rail. The winds were still westerly, though now the great yards had been braced hard against the starboard backstays to suit our north-easterly course. We had left the fiftieth parallel behind us and were sailing out into the mid-Atlantic in order to pick up the south-east trades.

The sky was pellucid and the sea rolled away from our bows in crisp collars of white on indigo. Apart from a small rectangle through the deckhouse door I had not seen the open air for a week, breathing an atmosphere saturated with the pungencies of oilcloth and sweat. To stand by the rail at that moment was a tonic. The climactic seas of the south had given way to a dark, inexpressibly haunting aspect of sea and sky. I felt I was beginning to sense things again, to come back to life. After all, I had passed into another hemisphere. The continent of South America, like a huge comma, lay between me and my home. The ship was making fine headway and carrying me further into strangeness, nearer to those continents of hearsay: Europe, North America, Africa.

But that dark sea affected my mood. For an hour or so as the evening gathered I experienced a longing for the exuberance I had felt during those days crossing the Tasman with the ship under the command of Captain Fetherston. Those days were less than eight weeks ago, yet how remote they were from the present I found myself in. Life on board had seemed halcyon during those eleven days in a way that it was now impossible to recapture. I was getting to know too much; more than I wanted to know. Mister Hallet had lied to an enquiry and been disgraced. Alex was being harassed by the captain of the ship. This captain was unaccountably perverse, reclusive, antagonising. Then there was Jack's sense of foreboding, mentioned casually perhaps, but enough to unsettle me.

In part I was simply naïve. I was sixteen. This was my first experience of being contained with adult humans. I was learning, but slowly, that men cannot be taken for granted in the same way a capstan or a fairlead can.

But there was more to my unease than that. I had an instinct that told me the unease on the ship was unusual, that something inimical was loose, and would grow before it went away. I began to look forward to reaching London with a feeling that the city might be a haven from more than just the dangers of sea and wind.

I joined my fellows for the evening meal. There was fellowship and concord enough at that table, with Hoff and Jack making sardonic comments about my return to the land of the living, and Jimbo undertaking an ape-like mimicry of my attempts to manoeuvre food onto my spoon with my uninjured arm. I noticed Alex was not at the table.

'Where's our boss-apprentice, Jack?'

'Skipper's got him on some job or other.'

'It's our dinner time. He can't do that.'

'Skipper can do anything, fellah. The ship comes first. You

know that.' There was a long pause in which nothing was said. My question seemed to dampen the banter that had greeted my return to the half-deck.

Alex came in at the end of the meal, scraped the cold remainder from the saucepan and bolted it down. As he did so, the other apprentices were getting up to muster for the second dogwatch.

'Vill be vaiting, Elex,' said Hoff, gently. Alex nodded, gulped a mouthful of tea and got up to join them. I tried to detain him. It was two or three days since I had last set eyes on him, and I was mystified as to why he had been stopped from paying me visits in my sick-quarters.

'Hey, Alex. G'day. What's the rush?' I said. He merely nodded at my greeting in an oddly formal way and went out.

'What's the hurry, Hoff?' I was bewildered. Mister Hallet expected smartness, but nothing quite as feverish as this.

Hoff had been in the act of diving into a sweater. He answered, 'Kept'n gives Elex a bad time. Must not be any seconds late on vatch or big trouble. At eight bells he vait for him, then below again kvik.'

'But why?'

'Kept'n says Elex spends too much time reading books ven you are sick. Goes in to see you during vatch. No good. Tells Hellet that Elex must be ferry smart or no reference. Iss drinking many drinks. No good.'

Hoff hurried out and Jack, who was on slop-duty, began clearing away the supper things. I felt idle and superfluous. The ship was obviously being worked hard, yet ahead of me lay a whole evening with nothing to do. I lay on my bunk and read. At eight Mister Hallet's watch came in and I heard Mister Gillard's watch tramping aft from the fo'c'sle for the eight to midnight shift. Alex came in after the rest and again I tried to engage him in conversation.

'I gather you got into trouble on my account, Alex. I'm sorry about that.' The senior apprentice shrugged. He was intent on removing his boots and had nothing to say, it appeared.

'He's a swine to pick on you just for keeping me company, don't you think?' I wanted an assurance that Alex was not offended with *me*.

'Not now, Johnny. I have to sleep.' He put his head down

on the palliasse and pulled the sleeping sack over his ears.

'How long is he going to be on your back for?'

'Not now.' There was a terrible fixity of purpose in his intention to sleep. He was applying himself to it like a candidate to an exam paper. I lay back and listened to the noises of the half-deck. In one corner Jimbo and Hoff were conducting a conversation in a subdued murmur. Jack had begun to snore lightly. I tried to hear whether there were any indications that Alex had relaxed into sleep, but no signs were forthcoming. Once he cleared his throat. But he never shifted his position and his breathing was inaudible.

I drifted off myself and was woken by six bells. From the neighbouring bunk I heard Alex putting on his boots. There was an hour to go before Mister Hallet's watch would need to muster. The apprentice went out. Why? Time below was precious. If a decent gale blew up it might be days before sleep was again possible.

Shortly before eight bells the man from Mister Gillard's watch came among the bunks rousing the sleepers. Alex followed him in and stood in the middle of the room. Anyone slow to stir was roused a second time by Alex.

'It's nearly eight bells. Come on. Now!' he hissed insistently. I remember Jimbo's grumpy response.

'All right. I heard the first time. Don't flamin' go on. *Jeeesuss*.' They tumbled out. The half-deck was silent. I slept.

II

My own work began at five a.m. when I brought the morning coffee to the officer of the watch. For the next four or five days I carried all the meals from galley to saloon. I became quite adept at balancing a loaded tray in one hand while levering open doors or hatches with foot, head, or knee. Jimbo revelled in grotesque imitations of my exertions; his object, I was sure, was that I should topple and spill the contents of my tray over Mister Hallet's precious deck. I used to dread encountering him.

On arrival I would place my tray on the saloon sideboard, and Gus would serve up. During Captain Fetherston's day there had been a stipulation that the ship's officers should take their meals together, but this civility had now gone by the board. Captain Trygg was still taking his meals in his cabin. Gus would give two knocks. The door would be opened, the meal taken within, and the door closed. More than once the meal was refused altogether. Occasionally the two mates ate in company, and these were rather stiff affairs; at such times Alex was made the duty officer. More usually they took their meals alone at the large saloon table. Mister Hallet ate rapidly, drained a glass of water and returned to the deck or to his cabin within ten minutes of commencing. He would not tolerate me standing around idly.

'Put him to something, steward. He's got one paw he can use.'

Mister Gillard took more time at his meal, and I was generally retained as a drink waiter, pouring glasses of water or bumpers of tea in the charade of gracious living we three performed when unwatched by the captain or the first mate.

'Another glass of your house special, if you please, mister.'

'House special. Aye aye, sir.'

It was my job to clear away and wash up in a bucket of sea water, though Gus usually hovered nearby, fussing, and talking half to himself, half to me.

'Captain Fetherston would never have stood for this,' said Gus, shaking his head. 'With him it was all-eat-together. You knew where you stood like that. One fuzzy rule breeds another, he used to say.' Gus was referring to Captain Trygg's used plate, which would appear on the floor outside his room an hour or so after he had received it, invariably with a good portion of the food on it untouched.

'It's the drink, Johnny. It takes away the appetite. The sooner we doss *him* in London, the better.'

Apart from meals my tasks included tidying up the saloon and cabins, issuing provisions to the cook and occasionally lending this sour gentleman a hand in the galley. When nothing else offered, Mister Hallet had me polishing the ship's brightwork with my one good paw. It was easy work. Furthermore it gave me a glimpse into a part of the ship that might otherwise have been another world.

If Mister Hallet abhorred idleness, Gus cultivated it. I suspect his approach to work would have been the same whether he was a railway porter or a government clerk. Whenever a person in authority was in the vicinity, Gus made a great bustle, and even Alex's humble authority could inspire him into activity with his duster. The steward had divined how to make up a bed or dust down a cabinet as though he were undertaking a grand and ticklish project — theatre designed for watching eyes, you understand — and on such occasions he would slip me a significant look which I could only interpret to mean that I too should behave with like gusto.

Then, as soon as the magisterial eye had returned to the deck, or otherwise passed beyond our care, Gus would pat me on the shoulder, screw his face into a grimace, and say: 'Spread the work, Johnny. Spread the work. They'll only pile on more if we finish.'

So that was our curious game. For twenty minutes at a time throughout the morning and afternoon we leant on our brooms, with one ear cocked. We stood in that saloon or in one or other of the cabins as though we were waiting for a train. Then clump clump clump came a pair of boots on the companion and presto! we were Mister Denholm's industrious and devoted employees.

As for the officers' reactions to us, Captain Trygg took no interest, which was curious given the harsh treatment he was at that time meting out to Alex for allegedly sitting down on the job. Mister Hallet would pass through wherever we were with his lips compressed and his eyes averted, as if resolved that it were best not to know whether real work was being done or not. Mister Gillard had a keener instinct for enjoyment than his two brother officers. He would approach a doorway quietly and lean against the jamb, surveying us with his icy smile. He never caught us sitting on the job — it would be impossible to catch Gus out, he had the hearing of a cat — but the second mate knew the game and would fix us with a glittering and amused gaze for anything up to half an hour. This taxed Gus's ingenuity to the limit, for it is difficult to remain productively industrious in a small space for that length of time. Sometimes Mister Gillard needed only to look as if he were going to watch us for that length of time for Gus to become agitated. Whenever he and Gus conversed, the latter would not so much as look up from his job in hand to meet the eyes of his interlocutor.

The strangest aspect of the steward's approach to his job

was that it was impelled by a sense of duty. Gus felt he owed it to himself not to work any harder than he could get away with. His reasoning was this: there were those who would work him harder than was commensurate with his wage, so there needed to be a counterbalancing restraint on his part to make what he considered to be a fair exchange of work for wage. Had Mister Hallet come into the saloon one day and announced to Gus that he had a week off on full pay, I do believe this would have distressed the steward. As it was, even during those periods when we were unwatched, Gus would rub nervously at a patch on the top of a locker with his duster. The important thing was that there was never any progress to his polishing until the eye of authority was once more upon him.

He had one overriding passion: gardening. In the long sessions of broom-leaning between one officer's intrusion and the next, I was given long explanations as to the best kind of manure for red cabbage, or the processes by which wine might be made from potatoes or dandelions.

'But, Gus, how can you keep a garden when you spend months, even years at sea?'

Ah, well, for one thing Gus had a book on the subject, much thumbed and kept on a shelf above his bed in the narrow cubicle he occupied next to the pantry. And for another, Gus had a wife and four children who lived in the English Midlands and to whom he was devoted. He wrote long letters to them from every port-of-call, letters full of gardening instructions and advice appropriate to the season of the year, which is to say the English seasons. For no matter that his ship stood in the steamy air off Singapore with the yellow pods of ripe coconuts actually visible on a plantation of palms, or that it had closed with the hot coast off Caleta Buena with its barren mountains like puckered human skin in the distance, Gus inhabited in his daydream a tiny plot of soil in the English Midlands. So, while his wife and brood may have been the de facto gardeners, he was indubitably that distant Eden's moving spirit and architect.

During a period of leave toward the end of The Great War, I went to visit Gus and his family, and I can vouch for the actuality and the goodness of that plot of ground. Gus's wife, a very jolly woman who was considerably larger in size than

her sailor husband, laid on a formidable spread of home-
grown cucumbers, tomatoes, and radishes for my benefit. It
was a hero's welcome I didn't deserve, for overall I had a very
easy war. Afterwards, in the late light of an English summer
evening, Gus showed me around his daydream, his manorial
patch, overshadowed as it was by the chimneys of textile
factories — the industrial vegetation of England. We strolled
among bamboo stakes as high as a man, which supported
burgeoning tendrils. We stooped and examined leaves and
soil. We tasted this and that. I'm no cultivator, but that
garden and the war seemed centuries apart.

Gus's eyes were small and his features resembled those of
some South American Indians, except that he was almost
bald. Any task that I found difficult with my injured
shoulder I had only to curse, and Gus would be tapping me
and making his characteristic grimace.

'Give it a rest, give it a rest,' he would say, waving his
hands in diminuendo movements. 'Any job that draws a
curse is not worth doing.' I sometimes thought that Gus
coined his own proverbs to suit the demands of the moment.
I would leave the particular job, only to find on my return an
hour or so later that it had been discreetly accomplished in
my absence.

His kindness notwithstanding, Gus was the font of gossip
and rumour on the ship. Prior to my own appointment as his
assistant, the only knowledge to be gained about what was
happening below the poop deck came through sounding out
Gus for what he knew.

Gus was overlord of the cabin stores, a responsibility that
was a constant headache to him. Everyone except the ship's
officers was a scrounger, and one, Jimbo, was an unashamed
thief. The fact that Jimbo considered himself a secure chum
of the steward is testimony to how proficient a larcenist
Jimbo was, for Gus, in fact, regarded him with intense
suspicion. My job, as Gus's offsider was, of course, a godsend
for Jimbo. A fellow apprentice with direct access to both the
galley and the officers' pantry presented opportunities too
good to miss.

As it happened, Jimbo did have an enterprise in mind, and
it did involve my privileged position. But his project was, I
think, more altruistic than I imagined.

III

'Over here, Johnny.'

Jimbo was leaning on the rail near the main shrouds, and he had turned and called out to me as I emerged from the poop accommodations. The galley had closed up for the day and the long twilight of our southerly latitude had begun.

When I joined him he offered me a few puffs on a cigarette he had been smoking. It was obvious, in retrospect, that he had been lying in wait for me.

'Looks quiet enough, don't it?' I agreed. He was silent for a time, then he said, 'What d'you think we should do about our flamin' skipper?'

'Do?' I replied. 'There's nothing we can do, is there? Except leave the ship when it reaches London.'

'That's weeks away. Something will boil over here before that.'

'How do you mean?'

'Look at the way he's hounding Alex Holt. That's one thing. And for another, have you seen how spent the mate's been looking lately? He's been both skipper and watch-keeper since Port Chalmers. Trygg's not lifted a finger. Even flamin' Hallet can't keep it up for ever.'

'Jack says Hallet is as tough as old boots. He'll last out till London, won't he?'

Jimbo looked up into the lofty web of cordage above our heads. 'A man that's dead on his feet is prone to making bad judgements. Do you want Hallet to pile the old *Emilia D.* onto a nice Cornish sandbar?' I remember thinking at the time that this was an exaggeration, but I deferred to Jimbo's wider experience of life at sea. I changed the subject.

'Why do you think Trygg hounds Alex? Hoff says it's because Alex took time off when I was in bed crook.'

'Nah, that's not the reason, not the real reason. I dunno. Perhaps Trygg fancies Alex.'

'Fancies him?'

'Yeah.' Jimbo spat over the side. He didn't elaborate on the word 'fancies'.

'Do you think we should form a delegation and tell him our grievances?' I asked pompously.

Jimbo snorted scornfully. 'Captain Trygg, sir. We the

apprentices of this here ship believe you, the captain, to be a
spiteful old boozer. Come out of your hole and do your
whack, and lay off harassing our colleague here, or we will be
most displeased. Come on, Johnny, use your brains! The
man would laugh at us. Hallet would roar and then work us
like slaves for opening our mouths. And flamin' Alex would
deny anything was going on anyway.' Jimbo spat again and
was silent for a few moments. 'No, what we need is some trick
that will drive the snake out of his cabin. What do you
reckon keeps him down there?'

'Hoff reckons he knocks back the grog all day and night.'

'Yeah. I wonder what makes him do that. Gus tells me
there's something the matter with Trygg. He hardly eats, and
he spends twenty minutes in the dunny each time he goes.
The grog must have seized up his bowels.' Jimbo chortled
maliciously.

'He won't let Gus into his cabin at all these days.'

'That'd be right. Listen, Johnny, I want us to do something.'

'What's that?'

'Steal his liquor and put it over the side.'

My mouth must have dropped, for he continued quickly.
'Look, there's nothing to it if we do the job properly. You
stay on in the saloon one night. Find an excuse — shining up
the stateroom silver or some such. Watch Trygg's cabin door.
When he goes off for a sit, or on one of his night prowls, you
come along to wherever I am, and tell me, casual-like, that
I'm wanted aft. Then we go back. I go into his cabin, find his
liquor, take it to the side and toss it over. Then back on
watch before he comes back. It's simple.'

It was horribly simple.

'You're crazy.'

'Why?'

'Well, what if he turns up while you're still in his cabin?'

'He won't. You'll be back at your silver keeping an eye
open, to warn me.'

'All right, even if he doesn't suddenly come back, as soon
as he sees his bottles are gone he'll know it would have to be
us.'

'Why?'

'Jimbo! We can't exactly go into hiding.'

'Where's the evidence? It'll all be over the side,' Jimbo grinned. 'He'll be *that* mad.'

'But it's so pointless. It won't solve anything. It's just a stupid prank.'

'Of course it will solve something. Hell, fellah, how smart are you? His liquor goes, and his reason for skulking down there goes with it. He'll have to come up and do his whack through sheer boredom. There would be no alternatives. And if he's busy, then he might lay off our boss apprentice.'

'I thought you said you didn't care one way or the other about Alex.'

'Who likes to see anyone getting pushed around?'

'But what if he's sick? Trygg, I mean. He won't come up then.'

'If he is it's probably alcoholic poisoning. We'd be doing him a favour.' Jimbo had all the answers. I felt myself being led against my instincts. The idea was idiotic.

'I can't do it. I'd be doing a dirty on Gus and Hallet. It's thieving.'

'You didn't object when I brought you that flask the other day . . . or at any of the other favours I've done you.'

This was true. But a handful of raisins in the pocket, a flask secreted from a flooded cabin, these were exploits, not thieving. Nonetheless Jimbo knew my attitude to his small larcenies was one of admiration, and he used that fact to implicate me in his scheme. He had made me feel obligated to him, and this, I'm sure he knew, was the first step in gaining my involvement.

'Why don't you try and get someone else? I've never done anything like this.'

'Like what?'

'Well, like helping to steal something.'

'Don't blow the thing out of all proportion, Johnny. We're not planning to do a murder. It's for the good of the whole boat, isn't it? Look, it's got to be you that's in on this. I've got to have a lookout, and you've got an excuse to be in the saloon.' I was beginning to feel trapped.

'I won't help. Sorry.'

'Why not?'

'What if we're caught? We're likely to have our indentures cancelled. It's a stupid idea.'

Jimbo became quite irritated. 'We're likely to have them cancelled? What do you mean? I'm the one who is taking the flamin' risks. All you've got to do is sit on your butt and flamin' watch.' I felt ashamed at my timidity.

'I'm still not prepared to be involved. I just feel it's wrong. I don't know why.' I looked down at the deck and Jimbo looked out over the side. He spat for the third time, then faced me.

'I reckon you're a cur,' he said, and walked off.

That 'cur' hurt. Had I been elsewhere I might have shrugged and dismissed Jimbo from my existence. But I was not elsewhere. My world was the ship. I had to face Jimbo over a mess-table, on deck, across the counter at the galley. So I was a cur. The sea breathed and moved all around me. I felt very lonely at that moment. I felt mean and I felt ungrateful. Jimbo had made me laugh, had clowned about, had secreted me and the rest of the apprentices one hundred and one small comforts from galley or pantry or elsewhere, invariably at some risk to himself.

I went into the half-deck where the apprentices were lying around on their bunks reading or talking. Though it is unlikely any of them were privy to Jimbo's plan, I actually imagined they were shunning me. Perhaps it *was* only funk that made me object to joining him in his escapade. That at least is what I had managed to convince myself by the time they were called for the second dogwatch. As the apprentices filed out, I went up to Jimbo.

'O.K., I'll be in it,' I said. He grinned, and there was triumph in his grin.

'I knew you'd join the side, Johnny. Tomorrow night. Some time in the first watch . . if the weather obliges us and we're not too busy . . . *and* if that bastard's bowels oblige us.' He gave me a lurid wink and went to join the muster.

IV

So I had chosen to join Jimbo's crazy plan for restoring conditions to normal aboard our barque. I saw nothing but disaster and disgrace for myself as the outcome. What if he were seen, not necessarily by Captain Trygg or either of the mates, but by any one of the crew. Hurling bottles of good liquor into the sea in the middle of the night! It would raise an eyebrow or two. This was no vast ocean liner. The entire ship's company would hear about it within minutes, the arraigning of Jimbo would follow shortly thereafter, and the incrimination of me as his accomplice would inevitably ensue. And I had chosen to do this. Why? Because I did not want to be seen to be a coward. Yet in making my choice I knew I had been weak.

Towards evening I found the courage to say to Gus: 'I think I'll give the stateroom silver a going over tonight.' As I dreaded, Gus responded by deprecating my intention.

'Never do today what you can leave until tomorrow, Johnny.'

'Best to get the job over with, Gus.' I did have some excuse as Mister Hallet had recently complained that the ship's cutlery had been looking tarnished, but Gus invariably waited for explicit instructions before acting. I could have strangled him for the good sense and solicitude he demonstrated on my behalf as he wrangled with me over my absurd intention to work after hours. In the end he let the matter drop with a shrug of his shoulders. I had been insistent. I had been strident, I was sure, and my behaviour must have appeared conspicuously criminal.

I went into the saloon at the beginning of the first watch. Mister Gillard was sitting on one of the two couches idly thumbing through an illustrated journal.

'I was going to do the silver, sir, but if you'd rather...' He waved his approval, and I commenced to lay the cutlery out, piece by piece, the one or two silver plates — trophies the ship had won for fast passages in her early days — copper kettles and tureens, condiment containers, and so on. Mister Gillard proved to be most helpful. Before going up on deck to keep the first mate company for a spell, he put several lanterns and his sextant on the table for me to clean.

'Since you're so keen...'

I worked away. I was meticulous. There was no telling when that captain might emerge from his den. He might not come out at all. In any case it was four hours until midnight, at which time Jimbo would come off watch and sleep in order to be ready for the morning watch at four a.m. There were four hours that I might have to kill. I could not afford to hurry the job. The saloon chronometer ticked. The oil in the lamps burned. Occasionally came the subdued sounds of Mister Hallet giving an instruction to the helmsman, and once there were footsteps marching the length of the poop and bellowed orders. Behind the captain's cabin door nothing stirred.

At two bells Mister Gillard descended the poop companion and retired to his cabin for three hours' rest before taking the second watch from midnight. It was a fine night outside, he deigned to tell me. There was a full moon and a bit of cloud flying about. I rubbed and polished. I dismantled the lamps and rubbed each part until it shone. When I had finished I did them again. The bits and pieces gleamed on the saloon table like a pirate's hoard. And all the while I prayed the captain's door would remain shut and that our forlorn enterprise would lapse through lack of opportunity. And if he did emerge? I toyed with the idea of not alerting Jimbo, of pretending when next I saw him that the captain had stayed locked up all the watch. It would be easy enough to tell that lie. But I remembered Jimbo's 'cur'. No. I was not going to be accused of funk. I had chosen to be in on the exploit. I would see it through. Five bells sounded. Then six. I knew someone would come down to rouse Mister Gillard shortly after seven bells. If the captain did not stir soon the opportunity would be lost. I fervently hoped it would be lost.

I was down to my last dozen spoons for the second time when the cabin door opened and Captain Trygg came out. He could not have timed it more finely. I bent my head over my task while at the same time trying to keep him in view. His face was impossible to make out in the darkness, but his head was sunk on his breast and, as he hesitated in the doorway, he gave the impression of being uncertain on his legs. He seemed unaware of, or at least uninterested in, my presence in the saloon, for he stood for some moments in deep concentration like a parody of a knight in deep sorrow. Abruptly he jerked his head up, as if remembering something, and then began to falter down the corridor. He seemed very much the worse for drink. I heard a door close and the snibbing of a lock.

So now I had to act. I gave him thirty seconds or so, then crept along the corridor, terrified that I would make some noise and he would become aware of my presence. Had anyone observed the furtive way in which I opened the heavy iron poop door there would have been no doubt whatsoever that I was guilty of something. Once outside I went in search of the watch. Mister Gillard was correct; there was a great deal of moonlight.

I found my fellows. Predictably they were sitting or standing around in the lee of the forward deckhouse. The ship was snoring along with sail set to the royals. There was little for them to do.

'Jimbo. Captain wants you in the saloon.' Jimbo looked up at me with what appeared surprise.

'You sure it was me, not Alex here, that he wanted, fellah?' he asked, getting to his feet. This quite disconcerted me, and for a moment I had the idea that I had invented the whole escapade.

'Probably wants you to join him for a nightcap, mate,' said Jack.

'Yeah, probably. The bastard.' Jimbo dug his hands in his pockets, yawned and ambled off, clearly in no hurry. I followed some way behind.

As soon as he had disappeared from view on the other side of the deckhouse Jimbo must have moved with cat-like speed, for by the time I had reached the same corner he was at the break of the poop. I just had time to glimpse the poop door close. The bulbous forms of two lifeboats on their skids obscured Mister Hallet's view of this part of the main deck from his position near the helm, otherwise I was sure the scamper of two apprentices in that flooding moonlight would not have failed to arouse his suspicions.

I slipped through the other poop door and resumed my station at the saloon table. The blood thudded violently in my head and I was wobbly with apprehension. I shot a quick glance at the door of Captain Trygg's cabin, expecting to see Jimbo slinking out of it with an armful of bottles. It was closed. Surely Jimbo would leave it open to allow for speedier transit between cabin and main rail? I listened for the sound of rummaging or the clink of bottles. I could hear nothing. And Captain Trygg? Presumably he was sitting in the darkness of the cubicle. There was no sound. The door to the captain's cabin did not open, and no Jimbo laden with contraband emerged. Again I began to doubt that the escapade existed anywhere other than in my own fancy. Had I gone to fetch Jimbo? Had he ever put the idiotic plan to me? There was silence. Seven bells had sounded a while ago. Suddenly the door of Mister Gillard's cabin opened and the second mate came out. I could have leapt from my skin. I began polishing a tablespoon. So this was it. We were in for it. If Jimbo came out of Captain Trygg's cabin now, loaded with bottles, we would both lose our indentures and be handed over to the courts when the ship reached London. It was as simple as that.

'Still here!' exclaimed Mister Gillard.

'Just about finished, sir.'

'You're a fool, son. You should be asleep.'

'Aye aye, sir.'

He went up on deck. This meant that Mister Hallet would be down shortly. It must be on the knock of eight bells. I must warn Jimbo, we must call it off, I thought.

I crept toward Captain Trygg's door, intending to tap on it gently. I strained to hear the sounds of Jimbo shuffling about within. I heard a voice. A voice! There was a voice in there. I had heard an utterance and then a silence. The voice was not Jimbo's.

I fled. I went straight to my berth and got into my sack. Where else could I go? I was in a high state of dread. Were I a landsman I could leave town hurriedly to avoid disgrace. I could go to some remote part, live under an assumed name, grow a beard and moustache to disguise myself. Here there was only my berth.

Immediately I felt myself completely to blame for Jimbo's having been caught red-handed. I had not been caught. Not yet. Yet how had the man got back into his cabin? It wasn't possible.

The deckhouse was empty. I heard the voices of Mister Gillard's hands as they made their way aft for the muster. Eight bells sounded almost simultaneously with this, and shortly afterwards Jack, Hoff and Alex came into the deckhouse. I heard the thud of bodies being flung onto bunks, then I became aware of Alex's face hovering above my own.

'Johnny, are you awake?'

'Yes.'

'Do you know where Jimbo got to?'

'Isn't he doing something for the captain?'

'Is he? All right, goodnight.'

'Goodnight.'

I lay rigid with apprehension. So the storm had not yet burst. Jimbo was still there in closed session with the ship's captain. I was not sure what procedure was followed on a ship in the case of someone caught stealing from the officers' cabins. Would Jimbo and I be locked into some cramped quarter of the ship for the remainder of the passage? Alex would know.

Why was there no commotion yet? I assumed that Jimbo's discovery would be all over the ship within minutes. But there were no shouts, no murmurs of suppressed amazement, no striding of officers this way and that with stern expressions on their faces. There was only Alex's question, the question of a senior apprentice checking up on the whereabouts of someone who, theoretically at least, was in his charge. Then what was happening back there in the saloon?

'Johnny Boult.' There was a man from Mister Gillard's watch standing near my bunk.

'Yes?'

'Hallet wants you in the saloon. Double quick.'

So all *was* discovered. I had a vision of myself returning to that decent household in Geelong and having to break the news of my disgrace to that gentle man that was my father. I got up and went aft, trying to prepare myself for the wrath of the first mate. The thought that Mister Hallet, in particular, knew me to be the accomplice of a thief was horrifying.

He was standing by the saloon table when I came in. Jimbo was not there and the door of Captain Trygg's cabin was still closed.

'What the devil is the idea of leaving all this silver about the place?' He glared at me. He was very annoyed. He'd come off watch and unaccountably here was all the ship's silver lying about. It would have annoyed a saint.

'I...er...I was shining it, sir.'

'I didn't ask you what you were doing with it. I asked you why it was left lying about.'

'I don't know, sir.'

'Clear it away!' he growled, and accompanied his instruction with one of those cuffs on my ear that left it stinging without any real pain. He watched me as I put the things into their lockers and stations. He could not know the relief that had burst upon me like sunlight. I was undiscovered, I was not implicated.

'Will that be all, sir?' I said when I had finished.

'Get out of here.' Mister Hallet disappeared into his cabin and slammed the door. For the second time I fled to my bunk, and there I lay awake.

Where was Jimbo? Why was there no upheaval?

Some time before four a.m. I must have dropped off, for I remember waking at that time and hearing Mister Hallet's watch being roused. There was the rustle of oilskins, meaning either that the seas were high or that there was rain. I had a momentary reflex to join them, but the ache in my shoulder reminded me of my light duties. They went out and I lay awake for the three-quarters of an hour before Hoff came to rouse me.

'Hup, Johnny. Hup. Hup.' I tumbled out and made my way to the galley. The cloud must have built up during the second watch, for now the sky was a dark plaster ceiling. A pale line was growing along one edge of it. Africa was in that direction, I remember thinking in that bemused state when the mind is still sleeping though the body moves in its appointed tasks. The wind had increased too, for I noticed the royals and the gaff topsail had been taken in.

Gus and the cook were pouring coffee into the enamel mugs, and the watch were assembling at the galley door for the issue. One by one they took their bumper and biscuit. Then, there before me was Jimbo.

'Slip another sugar into it, Johnny,' he said with a grin. I was astounded and relieved to see him. I was expecting to be greeted with the news that he had been locked up, yet here he was, and happy enough. Furthermore, I could detect no reproach in his tone towards me for having failed as a lookout. His face was drawn and had that peculiar wild look that comes after a person has had little or no sleep. I was mystified and could hardly contain my curiosity.

'You look pretty rough,' I said.

'Aw, do I? Why should that be?' He winked and moved off. But for that wink I could have believed there was nothing unusual to have been expected on this stormy morning. Jimbo's good humour betokened some very strange exchanges in that cabin.

V

Seeing Jimbo, a Jimbo apparently untroubled by the events of the night, was the first of two surprises that awaited me that morning. The second greeted me a few minutes later. As I prepared to take coffee to the officer of the watch, Jimbo called out:

'You'll need another, Johnny.'

He gave a self-satisfied smile and said no more. I picked up a second mug and made my way aft. Ascending the poop companion, the tray with the enamel mugs on it balanced delicately in my good hand, I saw there at the binnacle, not Mister Hallet, as I had expected, but Captain Trygg, with Alex standing nearby. I could not believe my eyes. Was Jimbo responsible for this? Had he actually cajoled our reticent skipper out of his hole for the first time in weeks? How? Here was daylight growing every minute. I half expected him to evaporate, like a phantom. Yet he was solid enough, planted there, his feet apart and his head cast back as he eyed the upper sails. What on earth could interest him up there? We knew of his scorn for mere purpose. Was he on the lookout for a tremble perhaps? An indication the ship could be borne off a point, or brought up a fraction? He looked every inch the professional, and this was as startling as finding him there at all. If I think of it now, there was even a touch of the heroic in his posture. Why, the white mash of the ship's wake streamed out behind him as if he had created it. And the peak of the gaff towered above him as he towered above me.

'Your coffee, Captain.'

He swivelled that newly discovered professional eye of his from the mizzen topgallants to my person. His face was blotchier than I remembered it, and there was a yellowness in the skin and the whites of the eyes. He was thinner around the jowls and cheeks, and, perhaps most notably, that intent, self-preoccupied smile that had seemed to be such a permanent fixture on his face had quite gone. Instead his expression had an angry aspect, though again, of a curious kind. It struck me, even at the time, that this was not an anger in any way associated with Jimbo's outrageous invasion of his cabin. It gave the impression of being more remote *and* more immediate; not involved with any irregularity to hand, but aggrieved, like the expression of a child who has been made the victim of an injustice. My recollection of his appearance that morning is indelible, the changes being so marked from the time I had last seen him, either in my concussed state in the saloon, or weeks before that when he had humiliated Alex in our accommodation.

'Will that be all, sir?'

He made no reply. I gave Alex his bumper. The helm was relieved. I stood waiting to see if the captain required anything more. Alex hovered nervously behind him, his hands clasped behind his back as though they had been scared into that position and could never again be unclasped. Carefully he avoided my enquiring glance, though every now and then he looked in the captain's direction, as if afraid to miss something that was said. Captain Trygg sipped once or twice, and winced at the black syrupy liquid. Now and then he would squint at the binnacle to check the course, then look up into the storeys of canvas that strained above us. There was every appearance here of his being in charge and, given what we had surmised of his character hitherto, this was remarkable. After some more sips he flung the rest of his coffee over the side and handed me the cup. Then without looking at Alex, he said:

'Get the watch cracking, mister.'

Alex jumped, gulped down his coffee, ran to the poop rail and shouted the orders for the morning swab-down. His alacrity was embarrassing to watch. There was such an air of obsequiousness about it.

I took the empty mugs to the galley. As I did so I passed Hoff who was in the act of dropping a bucket into the sea in order to draw water for the swab-down. I asked him where Mister Hallet was this morning.

'Goes below. Schleeps. Kept'n takes vatch. Elex is the mate for morning vatch.'

'Trygg looks foul.'

'Iss the drink. He pays for it now, I think.' Hoff seemed cheerful about this nemesis. As for myself, I was dying to find out from Jimbo what had passed between captain and apprentice in that cabin. There must have been some desperate talking on Jimbo's part; some *inspired* talking.

I got no chance to talk to him during the next thirty-six hours. To my utter frustration I was kept busy during the morning watch preparing breakfasts, while the hands were set to taking in sail. The westerly wind blew itself into a south-westerly gale. The upper and lower topgallants were taken in. At the start of the forenoon watch Mister Hallet's crowd were kept on deck and together with Mister Gillard's watch they took in the cro'jack and the foresail. Only then did the day's work begin. It seems there was a great deal of chipping below that Captain Trygg wanted done. Most of the crew disappeared one by one down a booby hatch in the mizzen hold. Alex was put in charge.

'You make them work, mister,' I heard the captain say to the apprentice.

'Aye aye, sir.' Alex seemed to have lost the habit of meeting a man's eye.

With most of the crew below, the ship might well have been abandoned. The helmsman stood at his post. Captain Trygg stood on one side of him, and Mister Gillard stationed himself near the jiggermast shrouds with one hand on a rigging screw to steady himself. The cook was in his galley, the carpenter and sailmaker in their respective cubbies, and I ran the errands along the vast main deck, seeing no one, hearing the wind *shabang* in the sails above my head, the Atlantic *shush* all around me, and twenty hammers knocking discordantly below my feet.

By midday the wind had hauled west-north-westerly and moderated considerably. The sun had appeared. I attended as Gus served the meal in the saloon. Jimbo may have induced the captain to make an appearance on deck, but he had not succeeded in persuading him to join his brother officers at the dinner table. Captain Trygg took his plate and disappeared into his cabin with it. Mister Hallet was on deck for the afternoon watch, so Mister Gillard once more ate alone. No doubt as a young officer with all his career in the Merchant Service before him, these solitary meals were galling to him. Where was the confraternity of the poop deck? Where were the professional parleys, the opportunities for a bright young man to show what he knew?

Ten minutes after he had gone into his cabin with his dinner plate Captain Trygg came out again and placed it on the table with its contents largely uneaten. Gus looked at the captain questioningly.

'Is it not to your liking, sir?'

Captain Trygg shrugged. 'I've tried worse.' He poured himself a glass of water.

'The wind is dropping, I believe, Captain.. We'll have the t'gallants and royals back on by the dogwatch,' said Mister Gillard in only the second attempt at conversation with his captain I had heard him make on the passage.

'I think not.'

'Think not, sir?' Mister Gillard raised his eyebrows in surprise.

'Pamperos, mister.'

'Pamperos?'

'This is the latitude for them, is it not?'

Mister Gillard had a look of bewilderment on his face. He took time to frame his next question delicately.

'Is there any reason to believe that one is imminent, Captain?'

'Light nor'westerly change. It'll get calm. Then it'll blow. Doesn't do to be caught napping.' The captain drank from his glass and rested his gaze on the troubled countenance of his second officer. He seemed to fill the room. He said: 'You're not in a hurry to get home, are you, mister?'

'I try to make a fast passage where it is possible, Captain.'

There was the hint of an indulgent smile on the captain's lips. 'It will spring on us tonight. Call me at the beginning of the second dogwatch.' He turned to go.

'And if the pamperos leave us alone, Captain. Do we proceed to London under topsails?' Mister Gillard's question was impertinent, there was no doubt, but it betrayed an aggravation of spirit that even I, a ten-week-old sailor, could pick. This time it was not a matter of a smile being hinted. It was broad. And our Master-under-God actually wagged his finger at his second mate, as though he were talking to a persistent child.

'You keep your men off those halyards, mister.' Then he turned, went into his cabin and shut the door. Mister Gillard stared after him for some time. Then he shrugged and gave me a direction to inform Mister Hallet to keep his men away from the halyards on account of the possibility of a pampero. There was his icy smile on his face when I left him. The first mate received the information without alteration to his countenance.

'Very good, laddie.'

When I passed on that conversation in the saloon to my fellow apprentices the captain's caution was greeted with derision. Ignominiously for an afternoon and an evening the ship dawdled along in the South Atlantic with nothing but topsails and a main course set. We thought ourselves a good crew, and the possibility that we might be sighted by another ship surging under a full press of canvas and flying a signal from the peak of her gaff that read, say, 'Do you request a tow?' aroused resentment and a feeling of dissociation from the entire enterprise. We were not responsible for this faint-heartedness. We would not be responsible.

But by seven in the evening it had gone calm and the glass was falling. Then shortly after midnight we were struck by a wind of extraordinary violence. I awoke to its shriek and the almost simultaneous bellow of someone at the half-deck door. 'All hands!' There was a stridency in the yell I had not heard before. I saw nothing of the flurry that followed, the letting go of topsail halyards, the frenzied hauling of clew-garnet, buntline, leechline. I did not see the mizzen upper topsail explode with a bang, though I saw the rags of canvas that clogged the running gear the next morning. For four hours, I'm told, the waters around the ship boiled and the wind shrieked in a kind of manic triumph at how it had made us jump and look to our lives. Extra gaskets were put on every furled sail and the ship careered through that maelstrom with nothing but a goose-winged lower topsail set. By the time I was summoned in the morning to serve the coffee issue, the pampero had departed. Captain Trygg had been right, and there were no further comments about his being a fake sailor.

Our bespectacled sailmaker even suggested darkly that our captain had conjured up the maelstrom himself, as an act of spite. I was impressed by this association of the man with supernatural powers. There was something appropriate about the idea.

'Supernatural be buggered,' said Jack. 'He's about as supernatural as breakfast.'

It would have been easier if we had been left to our derision. During the days that he spent regular periods on deck, before he disappeared permanently back into the depths near the Equator, Captain Trygg demonstrated he knew more than enough about the handling of a barque to pass muster as a shipmaster. He did not, in our youthful estimations, perform his tasks particularly well, but there was a vestigial smartness and canniness in his day-to-day seamanship that suggested he had once been very good, and that what we witnessed was the functioning of a man who possessed practical knowledge but not the zest for applying it. We could not now completely disrespect him, though we found him perverse and hateful. Nor could we give him unqualified respect. The line of deck swabbers grinned furtively at each other when the captain was seen striding above their heads early in the mornings, but at root our response to him was one of fear; fear of what he represented, and withheld.

The captain's inexplicable resumption of his duties released one other feeling among the apprentices and seamen on the *Emilia Denholm*, a feeling of relief. We did not like him, but here at least was what appeared to be a restoration of the conventional hierarchy of a merchant vessel. This was reassuring. If a captain died at sea, or was incapacitated, then it was expected the first mate would assume responsibility for the running of the ship. But for a captain to be apparently hearty while at the same time to be as superfluous a presence on the ship as a passenger, that was very odd and unsettling.

Of course no one, except me, knew that Jimbo had a role in this emergence. As I say, I was on tenterhooks to find out from him what had passed in the cabin, but opportunity did not present itself until the evening of the day our pampero left us. We were worked hard, and during any brief respites there were others present to whom Jimbo presumably did not want to divulge his secrets. One thing his negotiations with the captain had not achieved was any improvement in the latter's treatment of Alex, and before I could learn from Jimbo what occurred during the closed session with the captain, an incident took place which demonstrated this.

When the pampero departed with the same suddenness as it had arrived, it was followed by rain. Receptacles of all kinds were put out where they could catch as much rain water as possible, and this was used by us to wash ourselves and our clothes for the first time since Port Chalmers. We sloshed about, naked, in the wet summer air for a half-hour or so during the forenoon watch.

Alex was putting up a line of dripping togs between the corner of the deckhouse and the mainmast shrouds when Captain Trygg descended the poop companion and strolled up the main deck. He did not stop to regard what Alex was doing. He did not order him to take his line down. He went straight to the main shrouds and began untying the line himself. The senior apprentice stopped pegging out the garments and watched. His line sagged and the wet clothes fell with a plop on the deck.

'This is a ship, not a whore's parlour,' announced our captain. Alex looked down at the fallen line with a hangdog expression on his face. The captain waited, as if inviting protest from the apprentice, but none was forthcoming. He walked back toward the poop.

The point was made resoundingly. It was not the offence — there was no offence — it was this particular offender. Jack came up to where I was standing with Alex and the line at our feet.

'What was that all about?'

'Trygg pulled Alex's line down. He said this was a ship, not a whore's parlour,' I supplied.

Jack strode aft immediately, and we saw him in conversation with Trygg near the helm. Abruptly he turned and came back.

'What did you say to him?' I asked.

'Swine.' Jack was outraged. 'I asked him what was wrong with the damned line.'

'And what did he say?'

'Unsightly. That's all. Unsightly. He's a swine, that one.'

Alex was picking up the fallen togs.

'You let him push you around too much,' said Jack accusingly to Alex. The senior apprentice said nothing. 'I reckon you should stand up for yourself against that bastard.'

'There's no choice. He's the captain,' said Alex.

'He'll ride over you unless you kick back a bit. Do you *want* to get trodden on?' Alex was silent. 'Well, do you?' repeated Jack. 'Do you enjoy it? I can tell you I don't enjoy having to watch it. In fact I find it bloody offensive to watch. And that goes for the other fellahs too. It's painful to see the rubbish you take from that bloke.' Alex had finished picking up the garments. Jack had been standing over him with his hands on his hips as he had delivered his broadside. The senior apprentice straightened and looked quickly into Jack's face, then back to the deck.

'I want to get my reference,' he said, and walked off with his burden of clothes to the half-deck.

VI

That evening, with characteristic suddenness, Jimbo was at the galley door. The cook was present, a man unsympathetic to apprentices generally, and this pilferer particularly, so Jimbo indicated with his eyes that I should follow him as soon as practicable. I had pretty well finished.

'I'll be off, cook.' The man nodded glumly. He did seem to take very little interest in life, one reason perhaps why our meals were so indifferent. I joined Jimbo at the rail.

'You don't think I shopped you, do you?' I asked nervously.

He turned on me, grabbed my throat in one paw, set his features into an expression of exaggerated rage, and raised his other paw in a fist to my nose. Then he grinned.

'Yeah, mate.' He released me, took out his tobacco wallet and began rolling a cigarette. Then, noting my perplexity, he said, 'Relax. I know for a fact you didn't. For some reason he made a point of telling me.'

'Telling you?'

'Yeah.'

'What happened? I heard voices in there and panicked. I thought all hell would break loose. Then you turned up at morning coffee — and Trygg on deck too!'

'Weirdest night's work I've ever done, Johnny.' Jimbo looked at his large feet for a moment, then out to sea. It had continued to rain and blow moderately throughout the day, the tail-end of our pampero, no doubt. Now, as darkness came to the ocean there was still some ragged cloud flying above us, though the horizon towards Brazil was clear and tinged with pink along its rim, like litmus paper. It gave to the distant waters a strange insubstantial blue tint in comparison to the dark sea that flowed around us. Jimbo furrowed his brow.

'Mind you, I still think he's a snake,' he said, as though to mitigate some other effect the captain had made upon him.

'But what happened?'

'Well, you'll remember when I shot off in front of you I went straight to his cabin. I even had a piece of wire in case his door was locked. It wasn't, which I suppose should have put me on my guard. It was dark inside but I didn't want to strike a match for fear I'd give myself away. Besides, there was a smidgin of light from his two portholes, so I started groping around for his hideyhole. There were bottles everywhere — all flamin' empty too. He must have drunk himself paralytic on occasions. Strewth! But he'd stacked the full ones away somewhere nice and safe because I couldn't lay my hands on them.

'Then all of a sudden I thought: there's someone else in this room. I couldn't see anything, I couldn't hear anything, yet I knew someone else was in there with me.

'I could have turned into a flamin' jelly. I know he's as quiet as the grave the way he suddenly turns up on you, but this time he must have slunk in extra damned quiet. Or so I thought. I hadn't heard a thing! I assumed immediately it was him and not you. I got pretty aggravated too — at you, fellah, for not keeping a proper lookout. I waited to see what would happen. Christ, I thought, I'm done for. I was expecting him to start shouting, to work himself up, to start laying about me with a bottle or something. But all he did was stand there near the door, shuffling every now and then. I was hoping like the devil that he hadn't heard or seen me.

'Perhaps he was drunk, I thought. Yes, of course, he's so full he wouldn't know where he was. I stayed as still as a flamin' chair down there on my knees. My hand was actually in one of his drawers. Talk about a tight spot.

'But he'd heard me all right, and he wasn't lurching and, as I found out, he was far from stupid-drunk. I heard him shuffle across the cabin and I heard the creak of a chair as it took his weight. I couldn't place him accurately — how far away his chair was, whether he was facing me — as I needed to do if I was going to make a bolt for it. I began to move anyway. Can you imagine it? On my hands and knees, lifting one leg and drawing it forward, so slowly, so carefully it took me half a minute or more to shift from one leg to another.'

'You sound as if you were enjoying yourself.' He was certainly enjoying the telling of it.

'Yeah, yeah,' said Jimbo, not wanting to be interrupted. The truth was that his manner of telling his story was peculiarly complacent. It was nothing but a lark to him. I began to wonder about those moral arguments he had used to implicate me in the scheme.

'I still thought that by some wild fluke I hadn't been seen,' he continued. 'I reached the door, hoping to sweet Jesus it would be slightly ajar. It wasn't.

'I wasn't beaten. I started to rise to my feet, ver-ry slowly, ver-ry carefully. I felt as though I was playing some children's game. Then my flamin' knee-joints creaked. Would you believe it? I had my hand on the door handle and was halfway to my feet; not a sign from the man behind me whose cabin I had invaded, and my knee-joints creaked.

'I reckon he was waiting for a cue, and that was it.

'"Won't you join me?" he said. It gave me a turn to hear him actually speak. "Won't you join me?" I thought he was being sarcastic. That didn't stop me sitting down. Sarcastic or not, I took him at his word, I was that stunned. I parked my backside on something; a washstand I think. I was pretty keen to know what would happen next. I remember thinking idly to myself: Now, if I was to bolt for the door and disappear he'd never know who it was on their hands and knees in his flamin' cabin. Yet it didn't occur to me to actually do it. He just sat there somewhere, and he had me eating out of his hand to know what was coming. I had the butterflies, of course, but I was beginning to want to know what would happen; badly. I was *curious*. Me! Can you believe it? I've wriggled out of more tight corners than anyone in the service, and I simply didn't feel like making a break! "Won't you join me?" he says, and I thought he was being sarcastic.

'Sarcastic? Not on your life, because the next thing he said was "Here," and I got the idea in my head that something was being offered to me. I couldn't see a thing, and there we sat, him in his creaky chair, me on whatever it was; him holding out what was presumably a flask in the darkness, me reaching out a hand to grab it, both of us flailing about in the dark.

'"Here," he said again, and I was tempted to say "I can't flamin' see it." I could have rolled on the floor laughing at that point. It was ludicrous. Here I was, a third-year flamin' apprentice in the cabin of a ship's captain where I had been interrupted trying to snaffle his grog. And I was being offered a flask by him out of the darkness. And I couldn't see the flamin' thing. It was killing.

'"Thanks," I said, when my hand made contact with the flask. As if it were the most natural thing in the world. I took a swig and put my arm out with it. We flailed about again until he finally found it. By now I was thinking: He's lunatic, I can still squeak out of this. Keep everything low-key, keep him thinking everything is in order, that I had just popped in for a quick dram, as it were. This was pretty wild, but the whole thing struck me as being scarcely real. None of the rules seemed to be working. So I thought I could still control things.'

'Was he drunk?'

Jimbo spat into the sea. 'Difficult to say. More doped than drunk. I reckon he had put away a bit, but he was, well, not sluggish like your average sot. He seemed pretty wide awake. More so than we give him credit for. He knew something was up the moment he saw you cleaning brasses in the saloon.'

'But he didn't see me there. He didn't even look in my direction.'

'He may not have stared at you, fellah, but he knew you were there, and he made a point of telling me. "Tell your young friend to be more discreet in his spying on me," he said. It was weird listening to a voice from a face I couldn't see. Like listening to a flamin' ghost. He was silent after that, and I kept quiet also. I heard Hallet come off watch and yell for someone to fetch you. I was expecting Trygg to give some explanation of what he'd just said, but he didn't. I wanted to keep him rambling, because I felt safer like that. At last he said, "It was clear something was in the wind, so I just slipped into a corner and watched that boy go past. Then I came back in here and waited behind the door for what might turn up." He made another of his pauses during which I thought, like an idiot: Where is that flamin' flask? "And you turned up," he said finally.

'"Yeah," I said, not knowing what else to say. The cunning old snake had been in the cabin all the time! The drift of the conversation was getting a bit personal, so I tried to steer him in a different direction. Keep him chatty, I was thinking. "What was your last ship, Captain?" I asked.

'"I knew one of you pilfering gentlemen would turn up," he answered, "and it was you."

'This was a bit rough. Though I was rapidly discarding the idea that I was talking to a lunatic — he was controlling our chat too well for that — I was still fairly sure he didn't know who I was. Why should he be able to pick me out of the rest of the crew? He'd hardly been on deck since New Zealand. There wasn't enough light to see by anyway, and if I couldn't make him out, how could he know who I was? But I was unnerved. I knew that only a couple of yards across the room that fancy moustache was twitching and those starey eyes were probing the darkness.

'"You don't know who I am," I challenged.

'"James Clement Wichelo. Indentured Melbourne 1910. Previous ship the *Star of Persia*. You're the fair-haired, squat one, sonny," he said. Squat! I wasn't sure about that. But I had to admit he had a fairly definite picture of me in his mind's eye. I felt pretty glum, I can tell you. Neither of us said anything for a while. Then another "here" came out of the darkness, and that flask was being offered my way again. We groped about. He was still mellow enough to offer me a tot. I waited for him to say something for a minute or two but he didn't oblige. He was off in his own thoughts. He really didn't seem to mind having caught me in his cabin. Then at last he said:

'"There's a special kind of face you find among petty criminals. Did you know that?"

'It took me a few seconds to realise he was including me in his petty criminals. He was baffling me again. One moment I was being handed a flask, the next I was being called a petty criminal. The strangest thing was that he made me feel as though I *was* a flamin' sneak-thief. I've never felt guilty, Johnny. What I do is not thieving, it's opportunity. Yet I felt...I don't know...shamed, being down there, as if all the reasons I had previously worked out for being down there didn't amount to anything.

'"Did you know that?" he said to me again.

'"Can't say I did," I said, rather quiet-like.

'"I would have thought you, of all this crowd, would have known something about it," he said. I didn't like all this background he seemed familiar with. He was too wide awake for comfort, and I began to get a bit panicky.

'"Why don't you get out of here and do what your job is occasionally?" I flung at him. I got to thinking that if he's not drunk and not lunatic, then I'm done for. So I might as well get my say in. He didn't answer that first question. "You're a flamin' freeloader," I told him. "Why did you come onto this ship anyway? You do nothing. You might as well be a flamin' corpse for all the good you do."

'And then it hit me Johnny. In a flash. The whole picture just came together. Call it inspiration if you like. Maybe once or twice I'd said idly to myself, what if he is... but suddenly, then, it all made sense — why he didn't want people to see him, why he hit the bottle so hard all the time, why he had that preoccupied look about him. I knew it for a certainty. He had not spoken after my outburst, so I tried it.

'"That's it! You *are* as good as dead, aren't you?" I said.

'I thought he'd stopped breathing after that. But I'd hit the truth all right. Trygg's dying. He may not even make London.'

'Dying?'

'Dying.' Jimbo flicked the butt of the cigarette he'd been smoking into the sea.

'But he can't just die.'

'Too right he can. He still hadn't said anything after what I'd said. I knew I'd scored a hit. And I knew I could get out of trouble then too. "It's true, isn't it?" I said. He still said nothing. "It sticks out a mile," I said.

'"I suppose it must," he said. He was shaken up. I could tell.

'"Why try and hide it then?" I asked. He chewed on this for a long time. I thought he might have tossed me out, or called Hallet during that silence. I was pushing my luck as far as it could go, and I knew it.' Jimbo stopped and seemed to meditate upon his luck for some moments.

'What did he say?' I asked.

'He's a funny, bitter sort of a bloke. I suppose I would be too if I was in his shoes. He said, "I'm not so very keen on people's pity."

'"Why not?" I asked.

'"It's grotesque," he said, then added, "Don't you think?"

'"I've never thought about it," I replied.

'"It would be intolerable...on top of everything," he said.

'"So you want it kept dark?" I said. He didn't respond at first. Then he said:

'"I thought you said it stuck out a mile."

'"It does," I said, "but then I notice things."

'"Who else notices things?" he asked. I caught his drift.

'"Only me," I said. "I'm a bit unique." I couldn't help adding that. We sat there for a long time after that, the ship galloping along, someone's footsteps going down the poop above our heads. "Here," he said eventually. It was the flask again.

'"Do you want to know the reason I turned up here tonight?" I said to him. He was silent. "Well, I'll tell you anyway," I said. "I thought if I relieved you of your liquor supply and dumped it over the side, you might have less reason for skulking down here with nothing to do but knock it back and give my shipmates the runaround. I thought it might get you up on deck and exercising your proper function.'

'"And you got caught red-handed," he said. This was real delicate negotiating, Johnny. But I was in pretty good form.

'"True," I said, "but in a way I've caught you, haven't I?" He was silent. "I guess it would go pretty rough for you if everyone on board knew you were practically a corpse." Again he was silent. "They'd all be very sympathetic," I said. "You'd certainly notice a change, because they detest you now," I said, and let that sink in. He grunted. Then I went for the big one. "I reckon I can keep dark about one thing in return for you keeping dark about this."

'"Brave of you," he said.

'"Of course you'd have to take some of the weight off old Hallet's shoulders," I put to him next.

'"Would I?" he said. He seemed amused. "I gather you don't detest Mister Hallet."

'"He does his whack," I said.'

I interrupted Jimbo's narrative again. 'Is he going to leave Alex alone?' Jimbo squinted and looked at me quickly, then down at the ship's bow wave.

'Stop interrupting, can't you. Anyway, we talked for hours after that, or rather he did. I had heard eight bells and the change in the watch. Then one, two, three, four bells. He wasn't going to let me go. He seemed glad of the company in a funny sort of way. He's got some morbid ideas. Once he said to me:

'"Have you ever done anything you wanted to?"

'"All the time," I said.

'"That's just appetite," he said, "or whim."

'"I don't know what you mean," I replied.

'"Bringing off an effect," he said. "An effect that is all your own. Have you ever?"

'"Maybe," I said. "I've not thought about it much. What about you?"

'"Never," he said. I was tempted to add, and you won't now either, but we had become quite friendly during the course of our chat. I felt I didn't want to hurt the poor beggar any more. Still don't.'

'What's wrong with him? Why is he going to die?'

'I don't know, fellah. I just knew in an instant down there that he was done for, that he'd had that look about him ever since he came on board. Smart bit of guesswork that.'

'How did you get out of there?'

'He must have gone on for hours. I simply waited for him to stop. Then we sat in silence for a long, long time. I didn't know what was coming next. He'd been talking all kinds of rot, about how people needed a focus, one that's close to hand. "A consuming passion," he said at one point. Passion! "Too right," I said. I knew that he could still call Hallet or Gillard, though I was fairly sure I'd won by then. Occasionally his chair made the odd creak as he shifted his weight. He wasn't going to sleep, that was clear. We must have sat there at the end for ten minutes or more, utterly silent, staring at each other without seeing anything. In the end I just got up and walked out. There was only about an hour left of the watch below. I thought about rousing you, but decided not to. I lay on my bunk. There was no chance of dozing off after all that excitement, so I waited for the man to get us up for the morning watch. I was down in Trygg's cabin for four flamin' hours!'

Jimbo finished. I wanted to make some acknowledgement of the fact that the captain was dying, but something in Jimbo's casual acceptance of that fact inhibited me. I found it hard to believe. That the captain's perversity and reclusiveness might have stemmed from some sickness or some huge embitterment would not have surprised me. But to hear he was dying, that I was in the company of one who would be dead, perhaps in a matter of weeks, who was now breathing, seeing the same sights as me, registering the same impressions, that was chilling. All I could manage was a 'Poor old Trygg.' Jimbo pounced on it.

'Yeah, yeah, fellah. Don't get too carried away.'

'But you said he may not live to see London.'

'It happens, doesn't it?' said Jimbo. 'And Johnny. I let you into all this because we were in it together. You keep it utterly dark, right? Because I promised him down there that I would — kind of honour between thieves. So you promise me, fellah.'

'Of course.'

'You'd better. Wouldn't want you to go over the side.' He grinned and I grinned back, then looked at the deck. Jimbo's comment was the most terrifying moment I had on that ship. I remembered Jack's story of Ruby. And here was Jimbo, who was capable of giving me a shove as easily as blinking.

'I'll see you, fellah. I'd better get some shuteye. I'm on the first watch.' He went off with his hands deep in the pockets of his baggy dungarees. It was quite dark now, the ship rose and fell in easy movements. Behind her the wake was a long phosphorescent curve back to Melbourne. Ahead was the Equator and London.

I stayed at the rail. Here was the ship, and nothing that it contained could be avoided; nothing. That was the thought that again struck me. It seemed to me then that everything was known and inexorable. Mister Hallet's disgrace, Captain

Trygg's illness. Would the world close in on me like that? Surely not. I could see nothing of what lay ahead of me, except that Jack and the others had been talking about trouble. I could hardly visualise London, despite the pictures on the tops of biscuit tins — pictures of Big Ben, Tower Bridge, the Tower of London — that had graced the tables of my childhood. It was all rather mournful. And the captain was dying.

I stared down at the sea for a long time. It was lit only by the luminous lacework of the bow wave. At length I went to my berth. As I passed along the deck I could hear someone singing up near the fo'c'sle.

CHAPTER 6

Ordeal by Man

I

Jimbo may have wriggled out of a tight spot — he was vehement enough about his luck that evening by the main rail — but his account left me with a feeling of unease. I did not doubt that every part of it was an accurate description of what happened in Captain Trygg's cabin. Who would invent a story like that? But as I thought about it in subsequent days I could not convince myself there had ever been any *real* danger to Jimbo. What had befallen him was too removed from expectation, from the summary discipline of the Merchant Service. Was not Captain Trygg 'Shipmaster-under-God' of our ship? Yet he had entered into this curious charade with an apprentice. As the degrees and minutes of latitude passed beneath our keel I could not help thinking that the encounter had been between two confederate souls. But then, as I have said, my trouble is that I am fanciful.

I do not mean to suggest that the two of them had met by arrangement, only that their encounter in the darkness of that cabin had been, in a curious way, happy. Nothing in what Jimbo had said could give me grounds for my suspicion. But his narrative had been vivid. Unwittingly he had conveyed to me something of what *hadn't* been said. There was something they had shared, and it was more than a flask. Call it something like a common predisposition, as if two aspects of an abstract mischief, one frivolous, rebellious and daring, the other incalculable and malign, had discovered each other.

Needless to say I said nothing of this to Jimbo. For one thing I could not explain why I felt it to be true, or rather, on what level I felt it to be true. For another, I would have lost Jimbo's capricious goodwill, which was for me, as I was then, something to be valued. I did not, as I think I should have, press the question of whether Alex was discussed.

The malice at work on the *Emilia Denholm* did not, of course, date from that conclave of Trygg and Jimbo, but there it intensified, and its effect was to drive Alex further out of our company.

I was taken off light duties and returned to Mister Hallet's watch. The lean mate took my injured limb, wound it round a few times as though it were a clock-hand and, ignoring my involuntary yelp of pain, proclaimed me fit for general duties. I was willing enough. Gus was a benevolent overseer, but there had never been enough work for two, and I was eager to return to the real 'sailorising'.

The day I rejoined my watch the ship was on latitude 31° south and a few minutes west of the thirtieth meridian. The sails that had borne the ship from Melbourne were being sent down and the fairweather canvas sent up and bent to the yards in its stead. This was lighter, usually a worn suit of number one sails, and used to reduce the wear on the ship's best suit while we enjoyed the more moderate conditions we anticipated when we picked up the south-east trades.

It was daytime work, moving from yard to yard, clewing, furling, unlashing from the jackstay, sending the heavy canvas down and hauling its replacement up; then lashing, attaching sheets, buntlines, reefing gear and so on. The sun shone, the sea was blue, and the furled sails slid off their yards like pale anacondas gliding from the branches of a tree. My shoulder still twinged, but not intolerably, standing the strain of hauling and climbing well enough.

Jack told me we could expect to pick up the trades any time after crossing the thirtieth parallel. He described these south-easterlies as good winds, constant in direction and moderate in strength. With luck they would see us to the Equator within a fortnight, and our immediate prospect was warm easy days and starry nights — 'flying-fish weather'.

Whatever the trade winds did elsewhere in the March and early April of 1913, they did not blow for us with any constancy or conviction. Certainly the days were balmy, the sky blue or occasionally relieved by brush-strokes of high cirrus — 'mare's tails' as Jack termed them. I saw actual flying-fish, and there were starry nights when we slept out on deck in makeshift hammocks. But the ship dawdled in fickle winds that drove her less than forty miles in the twenty-four hours on one occasion, and becalmed her for a morning on another. She seemed to hang back, as though she were a creature reluctant about her future, prescient of some oncoming trouble hidden from us. In this way, at least, we projected our own forebodings on the ship. Mister Hallet tried this and that. We hauled on lee braces, on fore and main tacks, while the captain watched impassively. It made no difference, and this was dispiriting.

We knew that ahead lay the doldrums where our progress might well become imperceptible for days on end. The voyage had been too long already, with the slow crossing of the Tasman, the delays in Port Chalmers, and now this sluggish northing. Some blamed the length of the passage on the ship's having a foul bottom. Some blamed it on a jinxed captain. Either way the tedium was aggravated by the widespread contempt in which the shipmaster was held, the smouldering indignation at his blatant and daily humiliations of the senior apprentice, and some affront at Alex's meekness before such treatment.

I had one secret motive for wishing the voyage finished: I dreaded having to witness the actual dying of Captain Trygg. I was sixteen. I was not prepared to look at a corpse with equanimity. I didn't want the — what? — the responsibility of that horrible knowledge, the knowledge of what a dead man looks like, in the flesh, or, I suppose, what was the flesh. If he must die, I prayed, let him die after we reach London.

Daily I had to nerve myself for contact with him. It was not that I thought he bore me any ill will. On the contrary, he had been most solicitous on one occasion. But after Jimbo's story I could not regard him in the same way. He was a phenomenon now, and this I found threatening. Here was a man who knew his life had run out. How must he feel? His awareness of that one fact severed him from every living being. Severed him utterly. I suppose I must have felt this was inexpressibly sad at the time, but I recollect more that I thought the fact of his awful knowledge somehow made his behaviour, if not justifiable, excusable.

Whenever our work took me anywhere near the captain I would look at him covertly. I don't know what transformations I expected to see being enacted before my eyes — exhaustion, disintegration, the skin shrinking around the bones as though he were a dead sheep or cow?' What in fact I saw was by no means a walking corpse. I have described his blotchy face, but there was colour in it, despite the traces of jaundice. I said that my impression was that he was thinner. This was true of his face and wrists, but he was growing what seemed to be a healthy paunch at the same time. Indeed he seemed at pains to hide it by wearing his oilskin coat loose. As the days grew warmer he replaced this with a loose-fitting jacket which made him look like a banker in a Far Eastern city.

The heroic posture, with his head thrown back and his eye on the luff of the mizzen royal, as we had seen him on that first morning after Jimbo's escapade, did not last. Frequently he took the weight off his legs, sitting for long periods on the bench beside the saloon skylight. His hands were placed on his knee, his back upright and his head immobile, like some meditative colossus, frozen just at the point of a decision.

One morning Hoff and I saw him stand up abruptly, walk to the rail and vomit. Hoff grinned and, clenching his tufty hand into the shape of a bottle, tilted it to his mouth. I grinned back in complicity. The signs of Captain Trygg's illness were conveniently similar to the afflictions of a chronic alcoholic.

After this he spent his time on deck during the night watches and the early morning.

He kept Alex nearby on the pretext of allowing the apprentice to rehearse the authority the Board of Trade would no doubt invest him with soon. Whatever the pretext, the result was a subtle variation in Alex's humiliation. Whether it was that Captain Trygg expressed his orders inaudibly or not, Alex hung very close to where the captain sat and so placed himself that he was always in the captain's field of vision. If the captain shifted his gaze elsewhere, Alex sidled self-consciously to where he could again see the captain's face. Somehow these seemed like the manoeuvres of a mentally slow child seeking the attention of an elder.

Once, when two or three of us were adjusting the setting of the spanker, the captain sent Alex forward to the poop rail with an instruction for the remainder of the watch. The acting mate had a tense, over-pitched yell when he delivered orders, more like a voice conveying warning than one confident it will be obeyed. Captain Trygg eyed him as he came back up the planks. Then, when Alex was only a few yards away, the captain turned to Mister Hallet who was standing near the helmsman and said:

'I dislike that boy.' He turned and looked steadily at Alex following this remark. The apprentice looked away quickly. Mister Hallet, I noted, stared straight ahead as if he hadn't heard.

Perhaps we, the apprentices, underestimated the misery that Alex endured at that time. Much of the persecution did not take place before our eyes. When not hovering in the captain's view, Alex went about his work on the ship like a man haunted. Sometimes Jack or Hoff attempted a crack, one of those jokes-of-light-mockery that provide opportunity for the self-imposed exile to re-enter fellowship by laughing at his solemnity.

'Hey, Alex, did she leave you out of her will?'

Alex smiled readily enough, but it was a smile of nervous confusion, and in the end we left him alone. Life in the half-deck was rough-and-tumble, and ship's officers, notably the mates, could be savages. You grinned and you bore it — like everyone else. You grew a thick skin; you toughened quickly. The fact that our chief apprentice was so vulnerable after nearly four years in ships was remarkable — in hindsight — but at the time it ended by arousing indifference in us, and even impatience. Alex was an awkward figure in our midst, perversely blind to our fellowship, long-suffering where a blaze of temper might have done some good.

We had a conversation. I had avoided talking to him for some time, sensing in my weakness that there were only two sides possible: being with Alex or being a part of the rest. However, one day Alex and I found ourselves alone, high up on the fore royal yard, fixing the bindings of the fairweather royal. It was the last of the lightweather sails to go on. The sun was pouring warmly through my shirt as I lay with my belly on the yard and my feet kicking back on the footrope. Far below the *Emilia D.*'s bows made a moving white 'v' in the ocean.

Alex, to my surprise, began it. He asked me what I was going to do in London, and I told him I would probably stay with relatives until I found another ship.

'You'll be sitting for your ticket, I suppose.' Alex shrugged in response to my enquiry. It was the question he had been angling for.

'The captain thinks I wouldn't be much good. Perhaps I should spend another year at sea,' he said.

'You don't want to take any notice of him. What would he know?'

'The worst thing is that he makes me feel like a small boy again,' said Alex, ignoring my remark, 'like I was when I first joined a ship. Back then, say after one of the mates had given me a hard time, I used to try and picture what I would look like now. I pictured myself looking something like Mister Gillard looks. You know...spruce...looking as if I *was* someone.' He stopped and tugged at a binding. Then he added, 'It's as if I've got nowhere in four years. As if I was just the same as when I left Mister Laidlaw's home. I don't think I'll get my ticket this time. Not now. I haven't been able to get any study done for it anyhow.'

'Alex, Trygg means nothing. Gillard's behind you, and I reckon Hallet is too.' I could offer no more searching sympathy than these platitudes. We worked in silence for a while.

Then Alex said, 'You remember Fetherston's sextant?'

'The one he gave you?'

'If anything happens to me I want you to keep it.'

'If anything happens? What's going to happen?'

Alex yanked hard on the finishing knot of one binding, moved along to the next eye in the sail and began threading the cord.

'What's going to happen?'

He made a deprecating expression. 'Accidents. If I fell off anywhere or someone dropped something.' He drew the cord tight, bringing the head of the sail up to the jackstay. This struck me as very morbid talk.

'Not if you follow the correct procedures, Alex,' I quipped. My joke fell on deaf ears. In fact he betrayed a momentary irritation.

'Do you want it or not?'

'Alex, nothing's going to happen to you.'

'Well, it's yours if anything does.'

We worked on with no further exchange. I wanted to tell

him that he had only to stick the captain's treatment for a few weeks, but I was afraid I would let out my secret if I did, so I remained silent. I don't think I was even very grateful for the offer of the sextant. A good sextant was worth pounds, but I didn't believe the offer. I was old enough to realise it was made as a subtle appeal to my allegiance and instinctively I shrank from giving it.

The day was glorious. The sun picked out the whiteness in everything, the bleached hemp and manila of the running gear, the white lifeboats, davits and railings, the arrowhead of the bow wave set in its boundless sapphire field. When we had finished we climbed down and I made the first excuse I could to desert him.

II

Alex was inordinately proud of the sextant given to him by Captain Fetherston. I have mentioned how, during those harbour-bound evenings in Port Chalmers, he would take out the brass appliance from its box, disassemble it, and clean each part meticulously. There was a boyish pleasure to be seen in Alex's fingering of those expertly made components, — telescope, micrometer screw, index mirror and shades, horizon glass and shades. There was a rapture and concentration on his face that had set his interest apart from the negligent attention we paid to our cards and magazines.

The sextant was more than a beautiful precision instrument. It was a badge of rank and a confirmation of promise. Alex now owned a sextant, and as a result he joined the small group of privileged men on board who were allowed to know exactly where the ship was. (We, the rest of the crew, were not kept abreast of the ship's position from day to day for this was considered by Mister Hallet to be idle information; we gained our knowledge by covert looks at the logbook and Mister Gillard's charts, or from whatever Gus overheard and passed on.) The fact that the sextant had been given to Alex by a seaman of Captain Fetherston's reputation could almost be read as an expression of the whole trade's confidence in the apprentice's becoming a conscientious and responsible ship's officer.

There had been little opportunity to use it as the *Emilia D.*

raced before the gales of the Southern Ocean. Both watches had been too busy. Now, however, as the ship stole toward the Line, Mister Gillard would approach Alex wherever he happened to be working on the barque and say:

'It's about midday, mister.'

Then Alex would leave what he was doing, fetch the mahogany box and proceed to the poop, where both he and Mister Gillard would take sightings of the sun, compare their readings, and go below to plot the position. It was a ritual that the second officer inaugurated shortly after our brush with the pampero and which lasted for about ten days.

Seeing the chief apprentice standing next to the second mate — who was barely three years Alex's senior — with the telescopes of their instruments held up to one eye, the other eye squinting, and the sun full on their faces, was to see a formal acknowledgement of Alex's status among us. It was about the last that was left to him. As I have said, Captain Trygg's use of the apprentice as an unofficial mate was a pretext to humiliate Alex, or rather, to let him humiliate himself. The effect of this on his authority over the half-deck was to make him increasingly shy of giving us directions.

So it is tempting to see Mister Gillard's daily request that Alex take a noon sighting with him as an act of redress. It was an act that only Mister Gillard could undertake. Both the mates were no doubt aware of the captain's malice toward Alex, but Mister Hallet's was a character too brusque, too stiff, to extend sympathy to a member of his crew without the risk of diminishing his authority. Mister Gillard's manner, on the other hand, was flexible, and he had a confidence sufficient to allow Alex to flourish a privilege of rank before the eyes of Captain Trygg, who watched the operation (when he was about) with sour disapproval. Mister Gillard was a smart officer, and could not have failed to note this disapproval in the expression of his superior. I suspect it was a small act of rebellion he rather relished.

As I've said, it was a ritual that lasted ten days or so; when we turned in one evening Alex stooped and picked up a small brass screw from the deck near his berth. Immediately he rummaged in his sea-bag, pulled out the mahogany box and opened it. I was able to see over his shoulder. The telescope was missing from its mounting on the frame of Captain

Fetherston's sextant. Alex knelt with the box open on his knee for perhaps a minute, staring down at it, saying nothing.

'What's up, Alex?' I knew already, but was nervous of making my knowledge public. He shut the box abruptly and put it back into his sea-bag. Then, still not answering my question, he got into his berth and faced the wall.

'Is the sextant all right?' Again I could elicit no answer. I watched his hunched form in the bunk for any sign that he had heard me, but he made none. His sextant had been despoiled and he seemed determined to take the shock of that discovery very much to himself.

And it is a shock, finding that among men you know and live with, you are vulnerable; that what is yours, what is *you*, is alienable. This theft, for Alex's humped silence confirmed it in my mind as theft, was so petty, so spiteful. By itself the stolen telescope was useless, and the sextant was useless without it.

As I lay on my bunk I thought it might be a prank of Jimbo's. But it struck me as too petty for that. 'What I do isn't theft, Johnny,' he had said, 'it's opportunity.' This prank, if that is what it was, didn't square with that. Yet who else on board?

We went on watch at midnight and I told Jimbo what I had seen over Alex's shoulder.

'Who would want the thing?' I asked, as we went out for the muster.

'Don't look at me, fellah. What good would it do me?'

'It's so mean-spirited, though.'

'Perhaps he dropped it.'

When Mister Gillard approached Alex around noon the next day, he was told that the tiny screw which attached the telescope to the mounting had got lost, and thus the sextant was not functional. Mister Gillard shrugged and took the sighting himself.

III

'In the first half of the voyage we paint the ship to bring her up to scratch after port. In the second half we paint her to bring her up to scratch *for* port. Important difference,

Johnny,' said Jimbo, deftly wielding his paintbrush around the seizings of the mainstay.

'What is the difference?'

'A fine one, my lad, a fine one.' He didn't elaborate. Alex, who had gone to the bow locker for a fresh bucket of white lead, had come back and was kneeling on the deck stirring the white mixture with a piece of wood. Jimbo looked at me.

'There's an out-of-bloody-work parson on the deck behind me. I wonder if he smiles.'

'Leave off, Jimbo,' I said.

'Excuse me, mate,' said Jimbo, adopting a formal tone and turning to where Alex knelt, 'I wonder if you would be so kind as to smile for us?' Alex stirred the white syrup doggedly and pretended to ignore Jimbo. 'No. He won't flamin' smile for us. No smiles for Jimbo and Johnny. What a pity. Perhaps he enjoys being a walking morgue. And trying to make the rest of us flamin' sympathetic.'

'Leave him alone, Jimbo.'

'Strewth. I'd like to be on the panel of examiners when this bloke goes for his ticket. "Mister Tail-between-your-flamin'-legs," I'd say, "I can't help but feel you're not exactly suited to the life at sea." I'd be trying to be kind of course, Johnny, but we examiners have to weed out the unhealthy specimens, you understand.' I don't know whether he expected Alex to have a good laugh at himself through this outburst, or what was the design of it. The senior apprentice did not falter in his methodical stirring of the white lead. Jimbo turned to me. 'What does he expect us to do? Bleed for him? He makes me puke, that bloke.'

I looked down at the deck, not wanting to answer Jimbo's outburst, or to look at the effect it might have had on Alex. If nothing else, Jimbo's remarks were insubordinate.

Around my feet there had suddenly appeared a galaxy of white specks. They freckled Mister Hallet's precious deck. We had been told not to allow a spot, not a spot, to taint his deck. Our lives depended on it, the first mate had added. Had I put them there? I had been scrupulous. I looked up. Jimbo was staring at me with a fixed, restrained expression on his face. Behind him Alex had risen to his feet and was watching him intently.

'How much of it went on my back, Johnny?' Jimbo asked

quietly. He turned around. On the back of his shirt there was an island of paint from which long peninsulas trailed toward his buttocks.

'There's a bit of a splotch there. Nothing much.'

Jimbo pulled his shirt over his head and held it up. 'Grab hold,' he said, thrusting the garment into my hands. Then, in what appeared to be a part of the same movement he rushed at Alex and swung his fist. It caught the senior apprentice just above the mouth, creating a white patch on the skin and causing his head to bounce slightly like a sprung target at a fairground.

Alex did nothing. He did not so much as put his hand to his face. He glanced once into Jimbo's eye from his two or three inch advantage in height, then looked fixedly at a point somewhere behind Jimbo's shoulder. He stood like a creature that has walked into a clearing watched by enemies and is determined to do nothing rather than make a wrong move. Jimbo was not quite prepared for this.

'Argh, blast you. Are you gutless as well as hangdog?' They stood facing each other, Jimbo with his neck craned forward in provocation, Alex slipping sidelong glances into Jimbo's eye. 'Well you can flamin'-well wash out my shirt.' I had seen one flash of Jimbo's spite on the occasion he had called me a cur. But this was more intense, an expression of enmity rather than contempt.

He took the smeared shirt from my hands and pushed it at Alex. 'Here, take it.' And with that he tried to lodge it in Alex's hands. Alex let it drop on the deck

'You can wash it yourself,' he said.

'Be buggered if I will.'

'Then it stays with paint on it.' Alex turned and walked over to the waterway where the empty paint bucket was rolling and disgorging a tail of white. Jimbo picked up his shirt and followed him, spun him round, and tried to thrust it once more into Alex's hand. Again it dropped on the deck. He tried a third time and the same thing happened. In a spasm of impatience Jimbo pushed Alex from himself and let fly with both fists at his face. His anger was murderous, and though Alex put up his arms to deflect some of the blows, many of them were striking home. Each time they did they made a sickening snap, like a rope that is abruptly pulled tight. Jimbo's anger, and the efficiency of his aggression, were appalling to watch. I feared he might kill the senior apprentice, and I tried to grab hold of his stabbing arms. But they moved with too much force and speed for me to successfully grapple with them. Alex was taking a terrible hammering, and still he made no effort to strike back. His hands were now simply spread over his face to absorb the worst of Jimbo's blows, and there was a kind of martyrdom in his sufferance. Jimbo, seeing his adversary was not going to strike back, was taking more time to aim his blows at the parts of Alex's face unprotected by his hands.

Hoff and a couple of seamen had approached, drawn by the shouts.

'Separate them, Hoff!' My appeal to the Scandinavian must have been strident, for he and the seamen immediately threw themselves on Jimbo. They managed to pin his arms, but as they did so, Jimbo let them take his weight and kicked out with both feet. Alex still had his hands around his face so Jimbo's kick landed squarely in his vulnerable stomach. I saw Alex jackknife and gasp like a man choking. He knelt on the deck, his short hair still surprisingly kempt, his eyes shut tightly, and his torso rocking up and down like a mechanical man as he struggled for breath.

'Iss fockingh coward's hit, thet one,' stormed Hoff, himself more incensed than I'd seen him. He was facing Jimbo.

'Well look what he's done to my flamin' shirt.'

'You are som little boy or sompthingh? You vash your fockingh shirt.'

'No. He washes it. He flamin' did it. Let him fix it.'

'Pah, you vant to grow op som little.' Hoff took the spattered shirt and marched off toward the fo'c'sle with it.

Other members of the crew had wandered over to watch the commotion. I saw Mister Hallet making his way through a group of them. He looked at the paint on the deck and then at the two apprentices.

'Clean this up so it never happened. Then report to me in the saloon. You've got ten minutes.' He turned on his heel. It was at that point I noticed Captain Trygg on the catwalk above us. There was no telling how long he had been there.

'Trouble, Mister Hallet?'

The first mate stopped in his stride and looked up. 'None I

shall not deal with, Captain.' The sun was over and behind Captain Trygg's position on the catwalk, giving his face a darkness it would not otherwise have had. We had to squint against the glare in order to look at him.

He said, 'Whose artwork is that?'

There was a pause before Alex owned to it. 'Mine, sir,' he said clearly. The captain nodded and waited for more. 'I threw a bucket of white lead at his back,' added Alex, and indicated Jimbo. 'It stained his shirt.'

'Murderous tyke, aren't you?' Alex lowered his eyes from the sun's glare and said nothing. Most of the crew must have been standing around the mainmast by this time. Somewhere aft stood the helmsman and Mister Gillard. Somewhere for'ard stood the lookout. The ship lazed through the bland Atlantic. No one paid it any heed. Alex was the focus for all eyes.

'You've started me thinking about your precious reference, son,' stated the captain flatly, and then after a suitable pause, added, 'and that parent who paid your indentures.' Again the voice on the catwalk paused. 'What a waste,' he concluded. Alex's countenance had assumed a stupid stony expression. He stared at a point on the deck as if it held some measureless fascination for him.

'Captain Trygg. A word with you in the saloon, if you please.' Mister Hallet had remained on the spot where the captain's first question had caught him. The Shipmaster-under-God ignored the first mate's request.

'You foul a man's shirt. You can use your own damned shirt to clean up the mess.' Alex's gaze remained riveted on that square yard of decking with imbecile fixity. 'Get it off and do it.' The apprentice made no attempt to remove his shirt.

'A word with you, Captain Trygg.' Mister Hallet had spoken again. The shipmaster looked at him briefly, then back to Alex.

'Your shirt, mister.' Alex stood as though he were impervious to sound. The men watched him. There had developed a suspense in the scene that seemed to have inhibited whatever sympathies they might have had. Mister Hallet's had been the sole voice of protest.

'Do you need help with it?' This last utterance was barked

more than asked, and it seemed to jolt Alex into action. He began to fumble with the buttons of his shirt.

He had not succeeded in undoing two of them before Mister Hallet had marched forward, put a restraining hand on the apprentice, looked up at the man on the catwalk and shouted:

'I shall not see this man humiliated.' Then he strode to the ladder that surmounted the wall of the forward deckhouse, scaled it with that feline agility I had noted on my first day aboard, and in a moment was face to face with the captain and talking to him in a suppressed voice. From below it was not possible to hear what was being said.

As I recall it now, what strikes me about the episode is how utterly civilised the conversation between Mister Hallet and Captain Trygg appeared to be from my perspective below them on the main deck. There were no fisticuffs and, apart from their parting remarks to each other, no raised voices and no interruptions. They were like two men in professional conference. Their talk lasted perhaps three minutes. There was no guessing at the content of their exchange, or the charge of feeling that underlay it. At the end Mister Hallet turned and bellowed at Alex and Jimbo:

'Get that cleared up. MOVE!' Then he strode away toward the poop, as if drawn by important business there.

Captain Trygg called after him: 'I'll be taking you to task for that, mister. Mutinous is the word for it.' The first mate stopped and regarded his captain from the distance of ten yards he had covered.

'You're not a fit man to command a vessel. People shall be informed when we reach London. I promise you.'

The captain smiled slightly and began to stroll after the mate. 'Not an appropriate thing for you to judge. You in particular, I think, Mister Hallet.' They passed out of sight behind a lifeboat.

IV

Mister Hallet's 'MOVE' had succeeded in penetrating Alex's trance-like stare at that square yard of deck which he had seemed to want to make his own. It galvanised everyone else who was waiting around too. Sea water was drawn and sloshed about wherever paint had spattered. I was surprised by the number of willing hands. The restoration of the deck to its pristine condition became everyone's business. Seaman and apprentice alike got down on their knees and scoured the boards. Within ten minutes there was no physical evidence of the fracas between Alex and Jimbo, and the two apprentices went aft to report to Mister Hallet in the saloon.

Jimbo rejoined us within a couple of minutes. He hurriedly took his paintbrush from the billy of paint and went back to work on the seizings with great show of industry, looking back over his shoulder every now and then toward the poop. Someone had given him a scare.

'What did you get?' I asked in one of those awed voices that anticipates the worst.

'Nothing much. Strewth. Hallet was black. I've never seen him so dark. He told me that if I step out of line just once between here and London he'd see I didn't get another ship. Ever! I don't think he likes me much.'

'What's happening to Alex?'

'I dunno. Hallet saved him up for last. Trygg was in there with Hallet and was watching what he said like a hawk. I don't reckon he liked what Hallet said about him on the catwalk. I reckon they'd had words.'

We did not have to wait long for Alex to emerge. He passed us, walking quickly for'ard. His face was turned away from us as though he were hiding it.

'Hey, Alex, what did you cop?' I shouted. It was hardly tactful. He took no notice, and disappeared into one of the heads that stood on either side of the break of the anchor deck. At the same time, behind me, Mister Hallet was bellowing from one of the poop doors:

'Jack Bell! Report to the saloon.' Jack hurried past and shrugged when we looked at him questioningly. Three minutes later all was clear. Alex had been relieved of his responsibility for the half-deck and Jack had been appointed the senior apprentice in his place.

Jimbo was unimpressed when he heard the news. 'Tch tch,' he said. Alex's dismissal dismayed me, as did Jimbo's callous response to it. Jimbo was as much to blame for the incident as Alex. He had provoked it. The inequality of the two punishments meted out was outrageous, and perplexing, for they issued from Mister Hallet. The outcome of the morning's disturbance seemed to be less punitive than sacrificial, as if calculated to isolate Alex further. At each new instance of his distress I felt a spasm of pity for him, and I did so now. But it was a strangely barren pity. Alex was a victim, and somehow this was appropriate. And the fact that he attracted pity somehow made him odious. Jimbo was right; it was disgusting.

I buried that revulsion deep. But it was there. I recalled how protective and well-meaning Alex had been to me throughout the voyage, how dogged his good intentions were and how transparent an appeal they made for my friendship. These things made him and his plight the more pitiful, the more repulsive.

I have no way of knowing whether these feelings were shared by Hoff, Jack, or any of the fo'c'sle crowd. It was midday and we went for our dinners. Alex made no appearance. No one said very much over that meal. Three of us at least had sufficient fellow-feeling to be aware of how deeply shamed Alex in particular would be by the loss of his responsibility and status among us, and the awareness made us despondent.

'This place is as much like a morgue when he's here as when he isn't,' observed Jimbo.

'Sometimes iss good if you shut your mouth som little,' said Hoff. 'For one day you make enoff troble, I think.'

Jimbo left Hoff's rebuke unanswered, but forked the hash into his mouth rebelliously. I had finished and decided to go and look for Alex.

He was not along the rail, nor, so far as I could see, was he aloft. I tried the door of the latrine into which I had seen him go earlier. It opened an inch or two before a foot was pressed against it from the inside. I stood back.

'Alex?' I asked, tentatively. There was no answer, which confirmed the occupant must be the apprentice. 'Alex...are you all right?' Again no answer was forthcoming. 'You can't stay in there all day,' I reasoned. 'You'll be missed at the muster.' I was aware that if any seaman happened to pass by and see me standing outside one of the heads conducting a one-voiced argument, I would look ridiculous. 'Alex?' I said desperately.

He was determined to keep his peace. Whatever misery and

shame had come down on his head from the morning's incident he was resolved to take into himself and share with no one. He may have been weeping, or he may have been grinning broadly at the bitter hopelessness of his life at that moment, but whichever it was I was not going to discover it. I went in search of Jack, and found him coming out of the deckhouse with the two other apprentices.

'You may have to do something about Alex, Jack. He's been sitting in the heads for half an hour or more. I couldn't shift him. I couldn't get a word out of him. He'll be missed.'

'Let him be, fellah. He'll turn up when he's ready. People get knocked down a rung all the time. He's just got to take the rough with the smooth.'

Alex had not turned up by the time of the evening meal, though the head was now vacant. Mercifully the captain made no appearance during the afternoon, and the two mates did not notice, or affected not to notice, Alex's absence. One of the fo'c'sle crowd reported seeing him squatting down behind the windlass. 'Taking a well-earned break, sailor? I said to him. Surly bastard. Said nothing. Even looked the other way. He wants his bottom smacked, that one,' said the seaman.

We were on deck for the eight to midnight watch, and Alex emerged to join the hands at the break of the poop. He stood carefully outside the two pools of light cast by the lamps above the poop doors. Jack went up to him while we were waiting for the mate's orders.

'Don't take it hard, fellah. It happens to the best of us.' Alex looked away, resolved to show us that he did not want to hear. Jack persisted. 'Trygg'll probably have me out on my ear for something equally small before we reach London. That's the way it goes.' Alex shunned Jack, and the latter gave up. Besides, Mister Hallet had materialised out of the darkness aft with our instructions. He rapped them out in a tone that suggested his mood was volcanic.

In the days that followed Jack had only one challenge to his authority in the half-deck. We were sitting as a group in a puddle of sunlight on the main deck the morning after Alex's dismissal. There had been some items of gear that had chafed and been sent down for overhaul. We worked, re-serving, re-parcelling the intractable wire cordage, putting in new splices where necessary. It was the kind of work at which Alex had always excelled, and now, caught out among us in that strong tropical sunlight he worked at it as if he feared that by stopping he would be compelled to look up and meet a face of a fellow human being and be impelled back into our loose fraternity. No one had spoken for several minutes. Captain Trygg and his two mates were nowhere to be seen.

Jimbo may have been feeling reconciliatory toward the apprentice who had showered him with white lead. Or he may have been simply mischievous. At any rate he said:

'You'd have to agree with me that Trygg's a flamin' snake now, wouldn't you, mate?' He was looking up from his work at Alex, but the latter behaved as if he hadn't heard. 'What d'you reckon, Alex?' He pronounced the name with an awkward friendliness.

Jack stopped what he was doing. 'You can shut your mouth and put that serve on as though it looked like what it was supposed to be,' he snapped. Jimbo was taken aback.

'Don't let your new-found responsibilities go to your head, Jack-my-boy. Or you'll be in danger of losing your good looks.' Jimbo grinned and touched his chin with his fist.

'I'll rearrange yours if you don't get on with that pendant without yapping,' said Jack. The two inseparables looked at each other for some moments. The jocular smile seemed to drain from Jimbo's countenance He got to his feet, hunched his shoulders and strolled over to the rail. Here he leaned over the side, and spat. Jack watched him. Jimbo looked out to sea for perhaps a minute, then came back, his hands deep in his dungarees pockets. The smile was back on his face.

'He's a hard bastard, this one is,' he said, then knelt to finish off the serve.

During the course of this interchange Hoff and I had stopped work and watched the tension between the two apprentices with bated breath. Not Alex. He did not raise his head from his task the whole time. He would not be seen to be one of us, not even in the smallest and most reflexive of his responses.

V

Gus had genius. Though it may be a harsh thing to say about the only man from the *Emilia* days with whom I kept up an acquaintance, for as long as he was on shipboard Gus was a natural lackey. His instincts (while under the scrutiny of his superiors at least) all led in the direction of service. His genius was to go about his duties in such a manner that he was present and not present at the same time. It was a trick of profile. Men felt able to talk in the presence of Gus with no more thought to his overhearing what they said than they would give to a sofa or a decanter overhearing.

When Mister Hallet left the shipmaster and strode aft along the catwalk he was heading for the saloon where the steward was laying the table for the midday meal. There was a great deal that was about to be said in that saloon, and the part that Gus overheard shook his equanimity considerably — sufficient for it not to pass out of his mind in a hurry. I rely on it, for my picture of what happened in the after end of the ship after the deck fight is constructed entirely from what Gus passed on to me at unguarded moments in the days and weeks that followed.

Through long practice Gus's ear was attuned to the different intervals of each officer's gait as it sounded on the deckboards above his head. He identified the stride of Mister Hallet as he placed the knives and forks, the condiment cellars and the jug of water on the saloon table. The mate's shoes rapped along the length of the poop, stopped somewhere near the helmsman where some words were spoken to the second officer. Gus could not hear what was said. The poop hatch was opened and Mister Hallet's legs came down the companion, until the whole of the first mate was visible, very erect and, Gus thought, looking rather agitated. It occurred to the steward to ask Mister Hallet whether he knew what the captain's dining arrangements were to be this day, but something in the mate's countenance prohibited enquiry. Besides, Gus had identified the more laboured gait of Captain Trygg on the deckboards, and moments later this officer also appeared, feet first, down the poop companion. Gus laid each item of cutlery with a discreet lack of clatter, but his presence was not noticed by the two men. They were far too absorbed in each other's company, it appeared.

'I could sack you for that little speech of yours out there, mister,' said the captain. 'Do you know that?'

Mister Hallet was disinclined to reply. Gus went from

saloon to pantry, leaving the pantry door ajar. Neither officer took his eyes off the other, and Gus watched both through the crack in the door.

'Do you know that?' repeated the captain.

'I know it.' Mister Hallet's reply was shot out rather than spoken. Gus was impressed by the size of the two men in that narrow confine. Both had to stoop to avoid the overhead beams and this had the effect of craning their heads forward in an aggressive posture. They seemed to fill the whole room. Captain Trygg was the huger of the two, and the older by about ten years.

'I shall want some restitution out of you,' stated Captain Trygg. The first mate's face was like the blaze of a fire, said Gus when he was describing the scene to me weeks later.

'Your malice toward that boy has been atrocious. I shall tender a report to the owners. You should not be given command of a vessel.'

The captain sat down, took his flask from his pocket and poured some of its contents into one of the tumblers Gus had set out. He drank the stoup in two quick gulps, but it was a while before he spoke. When he did so his voice was quiet and his words were chosen.

'Consider, Mister Hallet. If ever there is a choice between accepting my word or yours, you will not be believed.' He paused before adding, 'It is known that you have blotted your copy book.'

'What the hell are you inferring?'

'A man who lies once for convenience will do so again. That is a rule of thumb where enquiries are concerned. I am familiar with your run-in with that seaman over a killing some years ago. It created quite a splash, didn't it?' Mister Hallet did not reply to this, though the captain provided opportunity before continuing. 'So you see, I want some restitution from you. Your conduct out there prejudiced the authority on board this ship. Why, you had the entire crew taking an interest in what you had to say. Well, you must make amends, mister. You must be seen to make amends.'

The first mate stood as still as a monument, staring unflinchingly at the seated captain. Gus had the impression that there were signs of shock on the mate's face, but he maintained his silence. The steward himself was most indignant on Mister Hallet's behalf. 'I had a mind to go out there and tell that boozing good-for-nothing where the real authority in the ship lay,' he told me. But his instincts as a snoop triumphed, and he remained observantly in his pantry.

The captain spoke again. 'One of my apprentices threw a pannikin of white lead over another. A serious breach in the good order of this ship, that. You tell him he's not the best man to run the half-deck. Appoint someone else. Tell him today's little episode goes on his record...and will be passed on. Tell him that. Your behaviour out there was partisan, to say the least. You need to re-establish your...coolness, I think.'

'And if I don't?' Mister Hallet's voice had become very quiet, matching that of the captain's.

'I sack you.'

Mister Hallet did not say anything immediately. Then he said: 'What kind of pleasure is it? Hounding a boy over the side?'

'You are being theatrical, Mister Hallet.'

The two men continued to stare at each other. Gus remembers a long interval at this stage in the proceedings during which nothing was said. Then the captain put his question quietly.

'Do I get my restitution?'

Gus saw Mister Hallet take his eyes off Captain Trygg momentarily, then fix them again on that blotchy face.

'I think your kind doesn't deserve life,' he stated simply. Gus had an idea that the captain smiled at this last remark, but the angle he stood at from the captain revealed only the latter's profile. He could not be sure. At any rate no words were exchanged for another long interval. Then Gus heard shuffling in the corridor outside the saloon. There was a knock on the door.

'You'd better sit here, Mister Hallet.' The captain surrendered his seat at the table and went to sit on one of the couches. He seemed to sit down very carefully, maintaining the same upright posture that he preserved on the skylight bench through the night watches. It was as if to move his torso out of the vertical occasioned him pain. He watched Mister Hallet very carefully. The mate had remained standing in the middle of the room. There was another knock on the door. Abruptly he went to the table and sat down.

'Come in!' The two apprentices marched in and stood before him. 'I'll take you one at a time. You, wait outside,' he said, motioning Alex back outside the door. Then he turned his attention to Jimbo. The voice with which Mister Hallet directed his watch had an impersonality about it that implied it did not matter who you were. It was harsh, but dispassionate. The voice with which he spoke to Jimbo was unlike the one Gus was familiar with.

'I've got you summed up, laddie. You're trouble. If you want to fight on my ship, you take me on. Got that? Because I'll maim you without blinking an eyelid. Understand me?'

'Aye aye, sir,' said Jimbo. He looked at a patch of wall on the other side of the mate's head.

'Now, if you step out of line by one fraction between here and the time I throw you off this ship in London, I'll see you never get a ship again.' The mate paused. Then he said: 'Get out!' and the two words sounded like the crack of a whip. Jimbo vanished.

Mister Hallet called Alex in. His tone for the senior apprentice was formal, but there was anger and resentment behind his address, said Gus.

'You have behaved in a manner unbecoming the position you hold. I am relieving you of your responsibilities in the half-deck. Your conduct today is likely to be mentioned in any report sent to the Board of Trade as to your suitability for a second mate's certificate. Get out.' Mister Hallet's second 'Get out', Gus thought, sounded wearier than the first. Alex shot out, 'as though he had been given a ten-second start in a run for his life,' commented Gus. The mate rose, strode down the corridor and bellowed for Jack. By the time the latter arrived Mister Hallet was sitting behind the saloon table again.

'You take over the seniority of the half-deck as from now. Make a job of it.'

When Jack had gone, Captain Trygg spoke. 'Very impressive, Mister Hallet.'

'You are a disgrace. A disgrace to the service. We shall see what is to be done.' The first mate had risen from his chair and these words were shouted. No doubt they were heard by the helmsman and the second mate at their stations above. Gus then heard Mister Hallet's footsteps bang up the companion. He heard him address four words to someone whom he presumed was Mister Gillard.

'Come with me, mister.' The footsteps of the two men receded down the quarterdeck.

When they had gone, Gus remembers a great stillness in the saloon. Captain Trygg remained on the couch without moving, and Gus remained stock-still in his pantry for fear of upsetting that sudden lull. It lasted for two or three minutes, then the captain's shoes banged up the companion. Gus looked at the stacked provisions in his pantry, the tidily arrayed crockery and cutlery on the saloon table, with the one tumbler from which Captain Trygg had drunk out of place. He held a tureen in his hands and for some moments he could not remember what he had intended to do with it. He felt suddenly afraid. 'Of whatever it was, Johnny. The *thing*. It was on the ship, and there wasn't going to be any peace until it had worked itself out . . . or we left. That's what I thought at that moment with that tureen in my hands. And I was right, wasn't I?' he said to me perhaps three weeks later, somewhere north of the Azores.

VI

When the *Emilia Denholm*'s apprentices filed in for their dinner that day, some of them took note that Mister Hallet and Mister Gillard were in conversation at the poop rail. The two men stood facing for'ard, their hands resting on the rail, the taller man bareheaded, in grey shirt, dark trousers and braces, the second officer in sun helmet and a white tropical suit. The sea sparkled all around them, the ship rose and fell in lazy motions on its progress northward. From the half-deck door there was nothing unusual in that conference. A small breach in the ship's discipline had been dealt with. A schism between the ship's captain and first officer had been taken aft to the hallowed precincts of the poop accommodations where, we presumed at the time, it had been resolved. There was nothing in that conversation that might attract the interest of the casual observer.

Weeks later, when I heard from Gus what had passed

between Mister Hallet and Captain Trygg in the saloon, it became clear to me that the former's talk with Mister Gillard, whatever its content, was not an idle one. Fourteen years elapsed before I discovered what was said.

I should say that the idea of writing this account formed slowly in my mind. The events that took place on the *Emilia Denholm*'s voyage from Port Chalmers to London in 1913 hurt and changed me. They excluded me forever from the shelter beneath which I had lived for the first sixteen years of my life. In the course of a lifetime it is not unusual to experience bitter, heartbreaking labour, to see a death or two, or to be a witness to the destructive agency of some malicious spirit. But mine was a crash-course. I was not brought to adulthood so much as wrenched into it. The pain of that wrench subsided in time. A war intervened in which, I confess, I had less emotional stake than most men of my age. But what happened on this, my first voyage, continued to perplex me long after the shock and pain had gone. I wanted to talk it out, hoping that in the process I might be able to determine whether what happened was avoidable.

I was prepared to do some research. On two or three occasions during the twenties, when my ship was berthed at a British port, I went to Denholm's in London and consulted the *Emilia*'s logbook for 1913. This document gave me little more than dates and positions. Of character and motive there was nothing. Why was it that Alex attracted that malice to himself? Why was he so unprotected at the end? I traced Captain Trygg's sister to an address in Preston. I knocked on a door and made enquiries, but ten years after his presumed demise my questions about Captain Trygg were received coldly. I was not invited in. I visited Gus on his patch in the Midlands and picked his brains for all he knew of the ship's officers and apprentices. He could tell me nothing I did not know already about Captain Trygg, and little useful about either Mister Hallet or Mister Gillard. We stood in the greengrocery he had bought when he retired from the sea, the boxes of fruit all around us. Gus tinkered with the ancient brass scales that were on the counter.

'He should have put a stop to that cruelty. He should have put his foot down sooner. He was the one to do it. A tower of strength was Mister Hallet. He should have acted,' said Gus, shaking his head.

I had formed the idea that the first mate did act, or had tried to. I was mystified by that conversation he had with Mister Gillard after leaving Captain Trygg in the saloon. It became important for me to find out what was said in the three minutes or so after Mister Hallet had addressed his brusque 'Come with me, mister,' to the second mate. Thus, whenever I had opportunity, I tried to track down Mister Gillard. Gus thought he had gone into the Royal Navy in 1914 and served in destroyers. I went to the Naval Records Office. There were several Gillards serving in destroyers. I was informed that my Mister Gillard had not only distinguished himself, he had survived the war. But the records could give me no information as to what happened to him after his demobilisation in 1919.

I chose to believe he returned to sailing ships and tried several shipping offices that I knew still chartered the odd deepwater sailer for a coal or a grain cargo. I was wrong about sail. A tip from a man in one of these offices sent me to the premises of one of the big Oriental shipping companies. Yes, they had a Mister Gillard working as the second officer on the company's flagship, the *Cathay*, a very modern liner that plied between Southampton and the Orient, with visits to the major Australian ports every second voyage.

'A smart young fellow that,' said the elderly official, a plump, kindly man who seemed to know each of the officers in his company with some degree of intimacy, perhaps because he was responsible for the company's filing system. 'He'll be made the first officer of the *Cathay* at the end of the next voyage. He doesn't know it yet. The man's scarcely thirty-four. There's plenty of older men think he's jumping the queue. He'll captain *Cathay* one day, I shouldn't wonder.'

It was a year or two before I caught up with Mister Gillard. In 1927 I had the second mate's berth in a barque that was loading coal in Newcastle, New South Wales, for Antofagasta in Chile. I had been watching the shipping columns in the newspapers for the *Cathay* and, as luck would have it, she was due in Sydney. I sent a wire to her first officer via the agent's office requesting a meeting, and a day after the ship docked I received an invitation to meet Mister Gillard on board.

I travelled down by train and arrived at Circular Quay in the early evening. The *Cathay* was an impressive sight. Every porthole was lit and shone like a blazing rivet. The effect of the thousands of decklights on her white paintwork was to make her resemble a fabulous palace of enamel and glass. Bunting fluttered from stem to mastheads to stern. I went aboard and met Mister Gillard in the central foyer of the ship. Despite the fourteen years since we had last set eyes on each other, and despite the fact that I had been only a pip-squeak apprentice at the time, he recognised me immediately. He always did have a very clear head.

I looked forward to the meeting. Had he not been the affable one, the popular Mister Gillard? I was led through several large and luxuriously furnished lounge rooms to a smaller sanctum where there was a bar decorated with mirrors and coloured globes. He ordered brandies and waved aside my offer to pay for them.

We sank into some expensive upholstery and he sat regarding me. I decided to break the ice between us by conjuring up common memories. The first officer of the *Cathay* smiled with polite forbearance but it was clear he was disinclined to engage in reminiscence. He was a decade and a bit older, yet his face still showed that youthful brightness and that smiling dispassion I remembered it had upon it in 1913. Its effect was icy. Yes, I had looked forward to meeting an old shipmate again, as I chose to think of him, and I was egotistical enough to believe he might feel the same way. Nautical men who had done some time in sail were becoming fairly thin on the ground by 1927, and there was little other than nostalgia to keep us together. He raised his glass and drank, then regarded me with a look of expectancy. He wanted me to come to the point.

I obliged. I told him how the events on the *Emilia Denholm* had troubled me for these long years. I may have mentioned that I wanted to write something down about them, for I remember feeling I had bared my soul and was embarrassed by the aloof, slightly indulgent way in which, I thought, he regarded me. In short, I concluded, there was a conversation he had held with Mister Hallet at the poop rail immediately after the dismissal of the apprentice, Alex Holt, from the seniority of the half-deck, and I had a notion that things were said in it that may have affected the outcome of what eventually happened. I was ready with dates and names if his memory needed jogging.

It didn't. He remembered the voyage well. 'Captain Trygg knew from Port Chalmers that he was dying. I think he rather hoped to be buried at sea. Why else take over a ship when you know you're a goner? Still, it's not the most pleasant knowledge to harbour in yourself for five months, is it?'

I agreed, and suggested it was a pity we didn't bury him somewhere off the Falklands.

Mister Gillard said, 'I've wondered, since, whether we can blame him for what happened. We heaped blame on him at the enquiry and the trial, of course. Old Hallet insisted upon it, and by then it didn't make much difference to the captain. But perhaps a dying man can be excused certain things. What, after all, did he do that was unusual?'

I wanted to blurt out that he'd had an unusually powerful effect on the course of at least two lives. But I doubt Mister Gillard would have been impressed. Instead I returned to the point.

'Can you tell me what Mister Hallet said to you in that conversation you had with him after Alex Holt's dismissal?'

He looked at the contents of his glass and swirled them about a bit. He seemed to be making up his mind about something. At length he said: 'Mister Hallet wanted to know whether I would lend him my support. After the brawl on the deck you described there had been an argument in the saloon between him and Trygg. It must have been fairly unrestrained because the odd insult was carrying up to where I was standing near the helm. This Captain Trygg had stated that he would dismiss Hallet — there and then — if he didn't connive in the humiliation of the apprentice. That was Hallet's version of it, at any rate. He said the captain had a leverage over him, something to do with that unfortunate murder enquiry he, Hallet, had got mixed up in. He told me that he was convinced that the captain's treatment of the apprentice, what was his name — Holt, thank you — of Holt would end up with something nasty happening. There was only one thing to be done, he said. Lock the captain up in his cabin until London, and do any explaining that needed to be done then. He thought the crew would support the move, but my agreement in the matter was essential.'

'So he was contemplating mutiny?'

The future captain of the liner *Cathay* looked at me with

what I thought was approval. 'When the fancy explanations are taken away, that's what it was. He told me any enquiry would exonerate us once the unusual conditions on the ship were revealed. The man Trygg could not be trusted, he said. He had neglected his responsibilities. He was promoting disaffection; wilfully promoting it. He was out to ruin a boy. It was up to us to do something about restoring the good order on the ship. He had a case.'

'Could you have approached the captain? Warned him off?'

'Old Hallet thought it was too late for that. I'd seen him angry before, but there, at the rail, he was...agitated. He liked things straightforward, he said. Agitated. Most unlike him.'

My next question was the delicate one. 'So you decided against it?'

'Against what?'

'Against lending him your support...in locking the captain up at least.'

Mister Gillard did not reply immediately. He looked into his glass, from which he had drunk very little. And he looked at me. I think he believed himself to be under attack.

'I thought the situation required coolness.' He stopped and considered for some moments. 'Certainly that captain was a malicious individual. He was a sick man also, though no one, I think, guessed at that stage that he was actually dying. Perhaps if I had fallen in with Hallet's plan the ugly incident that followed might have been avoided. It's easy to be wise in hindsight.' Mister Gillard paused again. 'But I had a different view from Mister Hallet. It's one thing when matters come to a head at sea. You can point to the passions and sympathies that are moving people. It's quite another thing in a court-room where a Board of Enquiry is sitting. They have the law. They discover the facts. They tally the one against the other, and if they don't fit, someone's career goes up in smoke. I had to think about that. Of course I disliked the humiliations being inflicted on that boy. I made a bit of an effort to buck him up at one stage. But he was a rather solemn, defeated sort of character, if I remember. In the end there wasn't much I could do. As for the mate's idea of locking up the captain — that was madness.'

'It was the only hope of protection Alex Holt had in the

end. It had come to that. There was nothing us fellows in the half-deck could do. The more he was shamed in front of us, the more he withdrew into himself. Mister Hallet's taking steps was Alex's last hope.'

The ex-second mate of the *Emilia Denholm* disagreed with me emphatically. 'That's nonsense. He had himself to rely on. His own strength of character. It couldn't go on forever, after all.'

I wanted to say that Alex didn't have the strength, not *that* kind of strength, that cheeriness and that instinctive power to throw off discouragement. That was simply not Alex's character. But then it was not in the character of Mister Gillard to believe that. The rings of gold insignia on his jacket cuffs affirmed it. He looked at his watch.

'It was a long time ago. I don't think it makes much difference now.' He smiled and stood up. There was a reception being given by the captain of the *Cathay* that he was expected to attend. Would I excuse him? It had been a pleasure to meet up with me again. He held out his hand and I shook it. Then it occurred to me to ask:

'Do you think it would have made a difference if you had backed old Hallet's plan? To you, here, I mean?'

Mister Gillard looked at me for a moment, unsure as to whether to treat my question as impertinent or not. When he spoke, I sensed he was on the defensive again, though a little less patient now.

'Let me be frank with you, Mister Boult. I was ambitious in those days. I wanted to get on. I still do. But I also believe strongly in observing the forms. When things go wrong, and the choices are no longer clear, I stick to the book. Not because it's the easiest course to steer. Not because it's always the most just. But because it's usually the least dangerous in the long run. I regret what took place on the *Emilia Denholm*, but if you want my opinion, Mister Hallet was off his rocker to suggest such a course of action. Abandon the protocol on a vessel and you let anarchy in. Whatever Mister Hallet thought the apprentice might do — and at the time he thought he was more likely to jump over the side one night — he should have known that. Now, if you will excuse me.'

He smiled one of his icy smiles and walked off among the sofas, leaving his brandy half-drunk. The second officer of the *Cathay* had allowed me barely half an hour of his valuable time. Perhaps my questions had offended him in some way. But I had paid for a railway fare from Newcastle. Anticipating an evening of nostalgia, I had booked into a boarding house. He was of course a busy man, but as I drained my brandy glass, I felt more than a prickle of resentment towards the popular Mister Gillard.

VII

The suggestion that Mister Hallet put to Mister Gillard at the poop rail was the last attempt anyone on the barque made to deflect Captain Trygg's malice toward Alex.

The ship dawdled toward the Line.

For a day or two Alex gave up eating at our table in the midshiphouse. His intention may have been to spare us the melancholy influence of his company, of which Jimbo had made him acutely conscious. He came in with the rest of us at the beginning of each meal-break, spooned some food on a plate, filled his enamel mug with black tea, and went out to consume the meal sitting on the cargo winch in front of the mainmast, a place where he could not be spied from the poop.

It did not last. Shortly after he had gone out one morning he reappeared with Captain Trygg. Alex went to a place on the bench and sat down. We had stopped our banter on the arrival of the captain at the doorway, and looked down at our plates in expectation of the berating that must inevitably follow.

'Breakfast is eaten at table on my ship,' said Captain Trygg.

Alex rose from his seat, half faced the captain, and with his eyes lowered, replied, 'Aye aye, sir.'

'I wonder whether you're old enough to be on a ship at all. You foul it with white lead. You wander off and eat your muck wherever it suits you. That parent of yours has got some explaining to do, mister.'

'Aye aye, sir.'

'You can take over the slopping-out duties until further notice.' The captain left the doorway. We finished the meal in silence.

It was the custom for us each to take a week of 'slopping-out' and this particular week I was on roster. The job consisted of washing up the breakfast, dinner and supper things for the entire watch, and cleaning out the heads with a long iron plunger and buckets of sea-water.

'I'll give you a hand, Alex,' I told him at the end of breakfast, and commenced to scrape bacon rinds into the scrap bucket. I was on roster, so I would not be missed from the watch for three-quarters of an hour or so. Alex took the plates from me coldly.

'If you don't clear off and leave me to do this by myself, I'll hurt you,' he said. I must have hesitated, for he elbowed me out of the way. 'Clear off,' he snapped. I shrugged and left him to it.

Each morning when he had finished he laid the assortment of cutlery and crockery on a patch of sail spread upon the deck outside the galley door and went to fetch Captain Trygg from the skylight bench. His handiwork was then inspected, sometimes cursorily, sometimes minutely. Frequently the heads were not up to standard, and Alex might spend an hour in their fetid atmosphere, scouring and sluicing. It was a repulsive task.

It is likely his new duties had one compensation. They effectively removed him from our company for an hour after each meal, and I suspect this helped to alleviate the torturous self-consciousness he felt in the presence of other people. The night watches were easy for him to get through. It was dark, and he could move among us without being too heedful of being observed by us. But the remainder of the day watches must have been a torment to him. He never spoke now, unless he was spoken to. He answered questions in monosyllables, and shrugged his shoulders at those enquiries he could evade. There had been an earnest young man who had told me all about dolphins as we leaned on a fo'c'sle rail, and there was this abject boy. I could not believe they were the same person.

CHAPTER 7

Crossing the Line

I

There had been no movement — no perceptible movement anyway — from about four degrees south of the Line. On some days the sea lay like a sheet of extravagant porcelain, the only dark patch upon it being the short reflection of our bulwarks and yards. We could watch the reflections of our faces, as we leant over the rail, distorting languorously in the negligible swell twelve feet below where we stood. Sometimes there was a shimmer on the sea, stippling it like the scales of a fish and deceiving us into thinking there was the ghost of a breeze that might lift our sails and carry us away.

But there was no breeze. There was no movement. Our sails, every sail we could bend, hung like the curtains of a room that has been undisturbed for years, and indeed, though the whole sky and ocean were around us, the feeling we had was of suffocating enclosure. The heat was intense and it was impossible to look up into the sky or out upon the dazzling sea without the eye being offended by the unrelenting glare.

Little relief to the discomfort came at night. Darkness fell suddenly. Every corner of the ship's accommodation — half-deck, galley, fo'c'sle — had been invaded by putrid odours that rose from the ship's bilges, and these seemed to be at their worst during the night. We slept in our makeshift hammocks out on the deck beneath the stars during our off watches. Whatever we lay our backs upon stuck clammily to our skins. Alex, persistent in his avoidance of our company, slept alone in the half-deck.

It seemed a place where the winds expired, where ships stood like monuments on a flat plain, invisible to each other, until each in its time rotted and sank below.

One day we saw a ship on the horizon. The sun popped

over the sea rim and rose in its arc, and there, in the distance, it revealed three masts. For an entire day they stayed in the same position on our quarter. Without a telescope it was impossible to tell whether the vessel was bound in the same direction as we were, or in an opposite direction. The next morning they were gone, and we were again the centre of that featureless plain.

Following his one unsuccessful intercession on Alex's behalf, Mister Hallet pointedly ignored the captain's relentless harassment of the apprentice. The first mate had stuck his neck out on Alex's account further than any of us knew at that time. Now, as he watched the sufferer go about the work of the ship, his eyes avoiding all human contact, a scowl of distaste would lodge itself upon the mate's lean features.

During our time in those Equatorial latitudes, when we existed in a stupor of futility from day to day, when even Mister Gillard's wakeful head was seen to drop upon his chest in the middle of an afternoon, the first mate carried out his duties of sailing the ship with the savagery of a man possessed. He would move the becalmed ship, if by no other means than his own fury. At the faintest zephyr, at the least flutter of the limp ensign at the peak of our spanker-gaff, Mister Hallet was in our midst, roaring us from our hammocks or from our daytime tasks. Then, for half an hour or so, we hauled the great yards around one by one, while the mate glowered nearby, poised to spring on any hapless seaman who did not pull his weight. We hauled. We sweated until our faces and torsos were maps of aggravating rivulets. We swore. We belayed and coiled the falls of the braces. We returned to our daytime work of repairing sails, wire-splicing, painting, grateful to be able to sit once more in shade and doze as our hands moved. And within the hour Mister Hallet was among us again, bellowing us to the braces as the illusion of a breeze came from another quarter. The sheaves in the blocks squeaked as the cordage ran over them. The trusses groaned as the yards swung through their quadrant, and we cursed to blazing heaven for a proper wind, for movement, for change of any kind.

Mister Gillard informed us reliably that we were making progress: ten miles, thirteen miles, eleven miles and so on for the twenty-four-hour periods between sightings. But this was theory, or so it seemed to us, who could discern no physical change in our condition.

So far as I know, no one apart from Jimbo and myself were aware that the captain was dying by that time, although it was no longer possible for him to disguise from the crew that he was ill. He seemed to have a troublesome cough which caused him to make delicate plosive sounds in his throat every few minutes. Now and then, during periods at the helm, I saw him trying to ease what appeared to be a pain in his left shoulder. He walked, if not with labour, then with deliberation. Most obscene of all was his stomach. What Hoff and others had smirked at as an alcoholic's paunch was developing into a grotesque swelling. His abdomen was growing daily, like a balloon, and now could scarcely be concealed by the tropical jacket he wore.

The period he chose to be seen on duty was from about midnight to the beginning of the forenoon watch at eight. For most of those long hours he sat bolt upright on the bench where Captain Fetherston had taught us our seamanship. He drank from his flask with the negligence of a patient swallowing a frequent treatment. He exchanged no words with the duty officer. His head, held upright in its attitude of concentration, might jerk once or twice in those small hours, or he would turn abruptly to the helmsman and ask:

'How's her head?'

'North-west by north, Captain.'

'Come up a little.'

'Aye aye, sir.'

And the ship would be brought a point or two toward that quarter imagined to be our windward. These instructions may well have been decorative. It was marvellous with what clarity voices carried from the skylight to where our hammocks hung on the main deck in that Equatorial stillness.

In the hours between sunrise and breakfast I used to sneak glances at him. It struck me his face was growing more yellow each day. But then the world was filled with yellowy light, as though air and mast, deck and human flesh had been tinted with sulphur.

The last duty he took upon himself to perform each morning was to accompany Alex to the patch of sail outside the galley door. The two of them would stand over the ranks of plates and mugs. They might have been two men at a bazaar chatting about prices. The captain would be observed picking up a plate and pointing out something to the apprentice who, like a shopkeeper, would take a corner of his shirt tail and polish vigorously.

We watched this morning ritual from afar. We were impartial about it by now. The captain was to be endured. Alex had to take the brunt of it. That was the situation. The apprentice had successfully discouraged our participation in his ordeal. The averted eyes, the fastidious minimising of his contact with us, stated plainly enough that he regarded this as his affair. So be it. Had Alex suddenly turned on the captain one morning and biffed him a couple of times I dare say we would have been roused out of our equanimity. But there seemed little prospect of this. His whole nature seemed to have adapted wonderfully to the subservience that was required of him. Captain Trygg's choice of a victim, if he had made a choice, had been shrewd.

When the breakfast slopping-out duties had met the standard, Captain Trygg retired below and remained there until evening. There were days when he did not follow this procedure, when he remained on deck for thirty hours or more. At such times he set Alex to removing tar stains from the deck, and the apprentice might spend the entire day on his knees, conspicuous by the isolation of his job and the frequent attention he received from the Shipmaster. He was mercilessly bullied, but crueller still, he was made a focus. With the ship stationary, the air windless, the sea a mirror stretching in all directions, what Alex might do, or might have imposed upon him by Captain Trygg, was the one feature of our lives that contained any promise of development. Fellow-feeling ordained that we should be indignant or sympathetic towards what we daily witnessed. In fact we were entranced by what might happen.

When not working we sat in the shade under the lifeboat davits, reading, or rather, falling asleep over the page, whittling aimlessly at a lath of wood scrounged from the carpenter's cubby. Hoff and a seaman baited a line with a scrap of salt pork and sat astride the bowsprit fishing for shark. There was a yell from them once and we crowded the fo'c'sle rail to see what they had caught. A medium-sized hammerhead was on the line, its hideous lateral head breaking the surface of the water, its body thrashing a white turbulence in the sea immediately below where the two fishermen manipulated their line. The creature escaped, taking the shark-hook with it.

'Took one flamin' look at this ship and buggered off. I don't blame it,' observed Jimbo.

II

Jack was killed on April the ninth, 1913, a few minutes of latitude south of the Equator. For some weeks afterwards I held myself responsible for his death. Even now, twenty years on, there is no avoiding the fact I sent him to it.

The bow locker of the *Emilia Denholm* was a capacious compartment beneath the anchor deck. It contained many of the carpenter's, bosun's and chandler's stores; items such as spare blocks, paint ingredients, marlin spikes, serving mallets, shackles, as well as larger pieces of the ship's equipment. As part of the preparations for our arrival in London it was to be painted, and to this end Mister Hallet detailed the apprentices in his watch to clear it out shortly after breakfast on April the ninth.

Already the day was hot and would become hotter. As we went forward after the muster we passed Alex with his pail of sea water and his stack of soiled plates. We filed past him without attempting to speak, though Jack stopped and looked on for a moment as if trying to think of something to say. Alex worked on stonily, not raising his eyes from the pail of cloudy sea water.

'We'll make a chain of it,' said Jack, when we stood outside the bow locker. 'You fellows get in there and throw me out the smaller things. Johnny, you stand there and make a stack of them when I pass them to you.'

The work became a game. Jack stood in the entrance to the locker and deftly caught the objects that were thrown to him from the dark interior. From where I stood beside my growing pile I could occasionally catch the gleam of sweaty arms and torsos.

'Here, Jack. Catch.' A heavy anchor shackle came spinning out into the sunlight. Jack stepped aside and caught it.

'Strewth. What kind of googly was that?'

'You cetch these vons, Jeck?' Three single purchase blocks came flying out in rapid succession. Jack took each in his cupped hands and in the same smooth movement tossed them toward my pile. I fumbled each of them.

'How good are you, Jack?' A serving mallet came corkscrewing out towards Jack's head. He ducked and put up his hand to catch it.

'Good enough for you blokes, anyway.'

The game changed subtly. From making their missiles hard to catch the two occupants of the bow locker attempted to strike Jack's person with their projectiles. The latter warmed to the challenge. I heard Jimbo's voice call out:

'Hey, Jack. You want to take a look at what's behind you.'

Jack grinned and did not oblige, which was as well, because Jimbo's call was followed by a series of three-inch shackles flying out of the darkness like bullets. Ping, ping, ping. Each of the shackles was caught and tossed onto my pile. No doubt if he had been wielding a cricket bat in his hand he would have slammed them toward the horizon.

For that is the picture that is in my mind now. Did he tell me he came from a town somewhere out on the Western Plains of New South Wales, or was that someone else at a later date? By and large there was little interest taken in what our origins were. I have no idea where Jimbo or Hoff came from. I could not say where Mister Laidlaw's home for boys was situated. I could not even name the continent. Yet now, as I contemplate the last two or three minutes in which Jack was alive, the image comes of him slamming a cricket ball over corrugated iron sheds in some hot township on the Western Plains, superb, watched by the odd shopkeeper, sending a mob of admiring youngsters after the soaring leather ball.

I describe this picture, not because I have any authority for saying that Jack was a cricketer — as I say, it may have been another, later acquaintance — but because the fragmentary pictures I do have of him from that morning conjure it up in my mind. I remember watching the electric reflexes of his limbs and torso as he fielded each of the missiles that flew at him. There was a surpassing grace and athletic beauty in the speed and confidence with which he moved, his back and arms bared to the sun with his tattoos like proud bruises on his biceps and forearms, his belly and chest facing the hole from which Jimbo and Hoff hurled all manner of awkward objects. He stood there, lit in the Equatorial sunlight, one hand on a hip, waiting for the next projectile to come flying at him, flaunting his invulnerability. This is the picture that distils in my memory out of these fragments, simpler than the person or event was, certainly, but sufficient as an image of its original.

'What are you gawping at, fellah? Here!' He lobbed at me a heavy snatch-block.

The game petered out as heavier items such as the hold ladders, spare tarpaulins, a leather fire hose were manoeuvred through the bow locker's entrance. In my patch of sun I daydreamed. It was so hot. My lids felt heavy. There in the yellow light were Alex and the captain. The eating utensils lay in their ranks at the feet of the two figures. Alex had his neck and head craned forward like a blind man waiting for a familiar to lead him somewhere. His arms hung by his side with the fists loosely clenched. He was listening to a thing the captain was saying, and though they were scarcely fifteen yards off I could not distinguish any words in the captain's undertone. I saw Alex walk over to the pinrail below the foremast shrouds and take a spare belaying pin from its hole. There were two kinds of belaying pin on the *Emilia Denholm*, those made from lignum vitae and heavier ones made from brass. Alex took a brass pin and returned to where the captain was watching him. As I say, it was hot, oppressively so. My state of mind was somnolent. It may have occurred to me that the apprentice would strike the shipmaster, but if it did I was sufficiently drowsy not to feel alarmed at the prospect.

Of the various utensils we ate with, most were enamel, though a jug in which we mixed our powdered milk and one or two bowls for keeping sugar or the tinned margarine we occasionally had were made from a thick glazed clay. Alex knelt and smashed these one after another with his brass pin. He then looked up at the captain's face intently for a moment or two like a very little, as yet unsocialised, child scanning the face of a parent for signs of approval or reproof. The captain made no effort to restrain him, but stood, his hands in the pockets of his unpressed white jacket with the thumbs hooked over the pocket hems. Alex swung the belaying pin down upon a stack of enamel plates and a dozen went clattering and spinning across the deck. Alex had gone overboard, I realised.

'Jack! Jack! Alex! Look. He's gone off his rocker.' It was probably something like this that I shrieked. In any case the tone of my voice was sufficiently strident for Jack to turn and peer towards the commotion. 'Do something, Jack. He'll hurt someone,' I said. I sent him to it.

Jack said 'Strewth,' and advanced toward where the apprentice was standing, casting about for the next object at which to lash out with his weapon. Curiously he never made the slightest menacing gesture toward the captain, and that man clearly perceived no danger, as he held his ground without flinching or removing his hands from his pockets.

Jack was some five yards from Alex when he said, 'Ease it off a bit, fellah.' In twenty years I have not decided for certain whether what Alex did next was murder. As if the very sound of Jack's voice was a trigger, Alex turned and flung the belaying pin with all his force. Jack had time only to avert his head slightly and the brass missile struck him on the left temple. The force of the blow knocked him over like a ninepin at a fairground. He fell on his back and lay on the scrubbed deck in the ferocious sunlight, an incongruous sight, like a man sprawled dead drunk in a city square. When I reached him his eyes were slits and his mouth was formed in a slight grin. From his expression it might be thought that he had just seen something ridiculous. That expression is the only picture I am able to summon of Jack's face. He had been killed instantly.

When the mind receives a massive shock I believe the memory retains the information of the senses, not as a coherent picture, but as a series of burn-marks almost, difficult to connect up with surrounding experience. I remember seeing the captain with his hands hooked into his pockets. I remember seeing Alex with his head craned forward again in that curious attitude of sightlessness. People were starting to make noises. I suppose the fellows had come out of the bow locker. I think I must have simply stood in a kind of white daze. Somehow both Mister Hallet and Mister Gillard were present, and I recall Captain Trygg saying, as the first mate hurried past him:

'Your man seems to have done a mischief.'

I was being pushed hard in the small of the back by Mister Gillard and told to grab a hold of Jack's legs. I must have fumbled, for the first mate was shouting, 'Help him, blast you,' and a seaman had taken one of Jack's legs from me. Hoff had picked him up under the arms. Mister Gillard was leading Alex aft by the elbow. The captain had disappeared.

III

Jack was buried at sea late in the afternoon of the day he was killed. The haste in disposing of the dead apprentice was practical and ghastly. In that remorseless Equatorial heat it was thought that Jack's body would not keep long.

He lay for a morning in the carpenter's quarters. After we had laid him on the floor in that room, Mister Gillard took Hoff and me by the shoulder.

'You boys stay away from here.'

During the morning we saw the Scandinavian sailmaker go into the deckhouse with a length of canvas under his arm, and later an able seaman went in carrying four heavy crowbars. Behind the mainmast shrouds a hatchboard was set up between the rail and two large drums. Mister Gillard hurried here and there, his white-suited figure somehow deeply troubling as it crossed and re-crossed my field of vision.

Everything, it seemed, was being taken care of. There was a procedure. Those whose turn it was to take the helm, did so. The routine did not alter. Chaos did not fall upon the ship. I suppose Hoff, Jimbo and others were beside or around me through those hours, but I can recall no one saying anything nor any consciousness of their presence. I was locked into my own state of shock, of disbelief. I remember being able to visualise Jack coming around the corner of a deckhouse with his smile and his swagger far more readily than I could visualise his imminent burial. My mind perceived that there had been some kind of dire event that had taken place in the early part of the forenoon watch. But that Jack should no longer be cónspicuous among us, that his place at our table should have been vacant at dinner time, that was merely temporary, surely.

'All hands.'

We were called to the weather mainbraces in order to back the mainyards arìd take any way off the ship. The ship had no way, but the order was obeyed nevertheless; the initial procedure in the formality of burial. We were sticking to the book. We hauled and belayed the falls. Then we were summoned to the main rail where the hatchboard had been set up.

Six able seamen brought Jack out of the deckhouse. What they carried was a ghastly canvas parcel, bearing little resemblance to the shape of a man. They placed it on the board and I heard the clink of the crowbars as it was set down. Mister Hallet descended from the poop and stood next to the bier with a Bible in his hands. He read something from the Epistle to the Corinthians.

The moment arrived and two seamen canted the hatch-board. The white package shot over the side with what seemed great speed. I was resolved not to watch. I heard a splash and could see in my mind's eye the whiteness of the mummy turn green and grow smaller as it sank into the still ocean. Everyone stood for a moment or so, silent, their caps or hats in their hands. Neither Captain Trygg nor Alex were in the gathering.

We were given the order to square the yards around again, and did so. It made no difference. The ship did not appear to move, and it seemed to me it remained for many hours over the spot where Jack's body had entered the sea.

CHAPTER 8

'Home? Not in Your Life, Laddie'

I

What did I expect? Turmoil? An avenging disorder to commence upon our ship? The truth of the matter is that Jack's death upset very little in the daily life on board the *Emilia Denholm*. For another week the winds continued to baffle us. Such breezes that blew up were invariably disposed to flow from the direction in which the barque's head was pointing, compelling us to bear off west-south-west toward the Orinoco delta. If we tacked the vessel, the breeze would die. The sailmaker sat on his stool in the shade under the lifeboat skids, aproned by a snowy expanse of canvas, and shook his head in sad disbelief. He had never been on a ship that had so much ill luck with its weather, he said. But luck was too impersonal a word. Luck, after all, could change. In those oppressive calms we sensed a closer intervention, as though whatever power arranged our progress watched us attentively and prolonged our limbo with a delicate malice. Yet we never actually went backwards and after an interminable time we picked up the north-east trades six degrees north of the Line.

For the balance of the voyage Alex was confined to one of the small cabins off the saloon which were reserved for the odd passenger the barque might carry. Once each day he was brought out onto the main deck by Mister Gillard for a period of half an hour. These visits were to allow him to take exercise, but usually he chose to stand at the weather rail and stare fixedly at the water that slid past the ship's side. It was feared that he might try to throw himself overboard, and to prevent this the carpenter was instructed to fashion a single manacle from a disused boom-iron. This was fitted to Alex's wrist on his visits to the deck, and a leash of some ten yards in length was held, very self-consciously, by Mister Gillard. The manacle did not appear to trouble Alex in the least.

I had a horror that I might have to speak to him. He was no longer a person in trouble. What he had done had been enormous. He was taboo. He had outcast himself irreversibly from our little company. He could not sit at the half-deck table with us again. Ever.

Luckily we were not encouraged to go near him. Hoff tried to exchange a few friendly remarks on one occasion, but he could elicit no response from the manacled apprentice, and as soon as he noticed Hoff hovering near Alex at the rail, Mister Gillard told the Scandinavian to clear off.

Three times a day Gus took in Alex's meals. The door was unlocked by the second mate, the tray deposited on a chair and the door locked again. The steward made a point of passing cheerful, neutral comments, but as with Hoff, not so much as a sign that he had been heard was forthcoming from Alex, so in the end Gus gave it away.

The only man on board able to communicate with the prisoner was the second mate. We overheard him using the soothing sounds a man might use to a horse or a dog, cajoling him to walk the length of the main deck, or informing him it was time to return to the cabin. Alex followed Mister Gillard meekly, but we never heard him say anything in reply.

Mister Hallet entered Alex's cabin once shortly after the slaying. For a quarter of an hour Gus overheard the indistinct monotone of the first mate's quizzing of the apprentice. Each question was followed by a period of silence. At last he heard the first officer's voice raised in exasperation. 'What makes you think you're special, laddie? You'll hang by your neck for this. Think about it.' Then a door slammed, a key clicked in a lock and shoes banged on the poop companion.

Between the time he dismissed Alex from the seniority of the half-deck and the midnight when the *Emilia Denholm* was nudged to her berth in the West India Dock in London some six weeks later, Mister Hallet's furious driving of us did not abate. We chipped and scraped, painted and oiled, made minute adjustments to the trim of the ship by shifting the galley coal or the fresh-water tanks from one position to another. It kept us busy, but it did not speed us.

Once, I think it must have been the day following Jack's death, the first mate took me by the elbow and led me into the midshiphouse, shutting the door behind us. He questioned me closely on what I had seen.

Then he said, 'Was it deliberate?'

I stammered that I didn't know. 'It could have been,' I said.

'Damn you, laddie. You saw what happened,' shouted Mister Hallet.

'I can't remember, I can't remember,' I repeated stupidly. I had realised that Captain Trygg and I were the only two people on board who had witnessed what had happened.

There was a tyranny in Mister Hallet's hounding of the crew that was more than the professional reaction of a ship's officer to a demoralised company. There was a frustration, an angry sorrow in it, and an inference that all of us were somehow in collusion with the principal mischief-maker. He was always present, bawling, rousing us, berating us. He became not so much an individual intruding on our lives as an abstract condition of them. Life was one alarm after another, a moment-to-moment misery that was wiser in its design of diverting us from another kind of demoralisation than I had years to understand at that time.

The mate became the effective shipmaster. When Captain Trygg walked out of that sulphurous Equatorial light after informing his first officer that 'his man' had done a mischief, he went to his cabin and did not appear above deck until he was carried onto the dockside in London. To the best of my knowledge he did not set eyes on Alex again, though a mere eighteen feet of the saloon's floor divided the doors behind which each lived. After that morning on the Line Captain Trygg evidently decided to retire from the sea, and he played no further part in the direction of the vessel.

It was clear that he had no interest in the death, accidental or otherwise, of one of his apprentices. His cabin door remained shut and the two mates shunned it. It was Gus who became the sole channel of information in regard to the sick captain. He took in three meals each day, and collected the virtually untouched plate an hour later. We gathered that the shipmaster no longer had sufficient strength to come to the door at the steward's knock, so Gus went in and placed his tray on the table. On most of these occasions he found the man sitting in that curious upright position he adopted. Sometimes the volume illustrating the Australian parrots was open on the table before him. Usually there was an empty tumbler and a half-empty bottle in evidence. No words were exchanged between them.

At one period, whenever he went in, he found the captain bulkily wrapped in oilskins and sweaters, shivering uncontrollably at the same time that his face was greasy with the sweat of fever. The steward recognised the signs of pneumonia. If asked, he told us, he would have provided what succour he could. Gus knew his duty. But he would not offer. No, definitely not. The captain had done nothing that might inspire solicitude.

The cabin stank of vomit. There was a hand-basin near the bunk into which, Gus supposed, the man retched. It was kept scrupulously clean, presumably by the captain himself.

Captain Trygg's own supply of liquor gave out and he began using the ship's provision of rum. One night, during the second dogwatch, Gus woke to hear a key rattling in the door of his pantry and the sound of liquid being poured from one container into another. Someone at the cabin stores. As I say, Gus knew his duty. He got out of his bunk and stood in his cubicle with the door ajar a few inches. He heard the key rattle in the pantry lock again. He saw a huge shape pass within a foot of his eyes. He glimpsed a face, or rather he sensed a face, and the impression the steward formed was that the lines of that face had pulled themselves tight around the most acute physical agony.

'He's not a guzzler, boys,' he told Hoff and me in a whisper a day or so later. 'He's dousing some terrible discomfort. He's in a low state all right. That face!' He screwed his own face into an emphatic grimace. He had discovered what Jimbo had guessed in that strange interview with Captain Trygg, that the liquor was nothing more than a crude anaesthetic to kill a monstrously growing pain.

While he walked the catwalk, or turned up in unlikely places, it was not possible for me to readily credit Jimbo's claim that the captain was dying. Now that he was decisively removed from us and the only news we had of him came via the awed and murmured snippets Gus passed on to us, it was easier to believe. Some three weeks or so before our arrival in London it was generally known among the crew that the *Emilia Denholm* carried a dying captain.

Hoff wept when Jack was buried. I remember looking up and seeing him among the small funeral audience, the tears flowing freely down his cheeks and into his blonde beard. There was something immensely moving about Hoff's tears that afternoon. They were tears of plain grief, and they were tears of acceptance too. I did not weep. Jack's sudden, almost casual extinction was too perplexing. I did not understand it. I did not believe it.

No one in the half-deck or the fo'c'sle was ever heard to voice any recriminations against Alex, but most, like me, regarded him as outcast. Hoff did not, and it is a witness to the generosity of his soul that he made the one, albeit short-lived, attempt to communicate a sympathy to the shamed apprentice.

In the weeks that followed Jack's death no one was appointed as chief apprentice. With only three of us now living in the half-deck there was little point. Besides, we were too subdued by what had happened, too beset at the same time by the attentions of Mister Hallet, to require any regulation by one of our number. But Hoff took such lead as was necessary. His natural cheerfulness restored itself more rapidly than either mine or Jimbo's. There was tact in it too. Most particularly he stood by Jimbo.

The latter's reaction to Jack's death had been curious. They had been the inseparables. Had they not served together on numbers of ships before joining the *Emilia D.?* The recounting of their japes and scrapes had provided the colour at many a meal-table. In the days and weeks that followed that brief ceremony at the ship's rail I noticed Jimbo kept his eyes lowered to the deck for much of the time. At meal times when he sat with us there was a rebelliousness expressed in his features that was more suggestive of guilt than bitterness. Indeed, for the rest of the voyage Jimbo wore that appearance of refractory sulkiness; it was like the face of a chastised child convincing himself of his innocence. I had feared he would be the angriest in accusing Alex. He never mentioned him, or Captain Trygg. He spoke very little, discouraged others to talk to him, and only suffered Hoff's presence in his vicinity as a man might suffer the attentions of a well-meaning but slightly tiresome attendant.

There was little enough time for talk. The removal of two apprentices and the ship's captain left us shorthanded. Two or three days before passing the Azores we took down our lightweather sails and bent the storm canvas once more. For a short time we were propelled by some helpful westerly gales, but these were followed by more tedious calms, and south of the Scilly Islands the weather turned easterly. The last leg of our voyage into the English Channel was fought for cruelly with every yard braced against the stays and the helmsman making every point to windward that the vessel and the weather would allow. For several days we stood out into the Atlantic on a course almost at right angles to the direction we wished to make. Then back toward Ushant Island off the French coast. It was as if the malign power that had resided with us for so long was determined the *Emilia Denholm* should not reach her haven. Only when we had entered the Channel itself did the easterly gales abate, and the wind haul round to the west-south-west.

Shortly before dawn on the 14th of May the Lizard lighthouse became visible on our port beam, a prick of light set on the cobalt sea-rim. By the time the sun had risen we could see the southern coast of England some eight miles off to port.

The winds were light and the sun shone. For a day the coastline flowed beside us, light blue against the blue of the sea. At four-thirty on the morning of the 15th all hands were called to reduce sail, and at five twenty-five a.m. the *Emilia Denholm* hove to some mile and a half off Dungeness. As soon as it was light Mister Hallet sent his signal advising the shore authorities about the captain's condition. A further signal was sent requesting a pilot. Shortly after six this gentleman had stepped aboard and, it having been decided not to remove Captain Trygg until the ship docked in London, we sheeted home our sails again and stood away for the Thames. Off Deal we took on board the tow-rope of a tug, furled the sails of the *Emilia D.* for the last time, and laid the mooring hawsers out along the deck. The onset of darkness and the great river closed like a funnel upon us.

I stood with Hoff at the fo'c'sle rail while he pointed at the clusters of lights that winked from either shore and named each: Gravesend, Tilbury, Dartford.

'What's London like, Hoff?' I asked.

He shrugged. 'I neffer been there.' He was silent for some moments as we contemplated the dark river water swirling below our hawseholes. Then he added, 'Iss no goot you ask me what is Melbourne like either. I neffer been there. O.K. I get ferry dronk in Melbourne vonce. First time dronk in Melbourne.' He grinned. 'But Melbourne, London, San Francisco, for me and you it iss same place. Vee are seamans now. Seamans neffer go no place. Change shippe, neffer change place. Neffer haf place.'

There were no stars and no moon. The river was busy with traffic. The buoys of the fairway winked. Launches chugged across our path showing their red or green navigation lights. We passed a string of long barges being towed by a very small tug. A large steamer with the portholes of its bridge superstructure eerily aglow slid past us with its propeller blades thrashing the water. In moments it was lost to seaward.

There were delays while lock-gates were opened and closed. We passed lines to men in the darkness who stood, as if by magic, along the lock-gates. A few minutes before midnight on the 15th of May we were nudged to our berth in the West India Dock. Again there were men on the wharf ready to receive our mooring lines. That we should have been expected by human beings we had no knowledge of, who slipped our hawsers over bollards and signalled us in a familiar way was vaguely astonishing.

We were stood down. The following morning Captain Trygg and Alex were taken off the ship.

II

The day the captain and apprentice were taken from the ship was also the day on which it was visited by a representative of Mister Denholm. In company with the first mate he inspected the vessel and it seems he was favourably impressed by the high standard of her maintenance. But as we watched him nod his head vigorously at each of the points Mister Hallet indicated to him there was a suggestion that the man possessed some item of information unshared by the lean mate. The representative of the shipowner had a manner of showing his interest that conveyed to an onlooker the impression that here was a man owning the essential facts already. His attention to what the first officer had to say was dutiful, and this gave him a subtle authority over Mister Hallet. It broke a spell in my mind. I had known the *Emilia Denholm* was one of Mister Denholm's fleet, but I had felt the ship to be the property of Captain Fetherston, and then the property, ostensibly of Captain Trygg, but in practice of Mister Hallet. I had equated authority with ownership.

One of the crew overheard and passed on a snippet of their conversation.

'To put it bluntly, mister...no longer a real proposition. Too slow, too expensive...afraid you've proved that this voyage...She's the last of our sailers to go. Sad; very.' The first mate's reply was not heard, but he escorted the shipowner's man to the gangplank very soon afterwards and then disappeared aft. By supper time the entire crew had learned that the *Emilia Denholm* had been sold to a Norwegian concern and, as soon as her wool cargo was unloaded, the barque was to be towed across the English Channel to Dunkirk where her new owners were to take delivery. Her present crew were to be paid off immediately with the exception of we three apprentices and one or two of the more experienced seamen who were to stay on for as long as it was necessary to send down the sails and a good proportion of the running gear.

So most of the fo'c'sle crowd departed, each with their few pounds. Mister Hallet had spoken with the dock authorities and it had been decided that it would serve no useful purpose to detain them for the impending enquiry into the apprentice Jack Bell's death. We who remained unbent, unshackled, sent down and sent below the gear from daybreak to dark. We did so with little enthusiasm. Though the *Emilia Denholm* was not the prettiest vessel to have been slipped from the Firth of Clyde, she had been our home, or the nearest thing we could call a home. And here, while we were still actually occupying her, she had been sold to foreign owners. We had not been consulted. Of course we would have left her anyway, but there was something proprietorial in our attitude to the barque. We had worked her, from one hemisphere to another, through conditions of heartbreaking difficulty. And without so much as a by-your-leave, she had been sold. The manner of it was offensive, but what lay behind it was a fear, the fear that this trade we had entered was disappearing as fast as the ships in which it was practised, and that it would not be long before it vanished from the earth. Homelessness and redundancy were, for us, the same thing. Listening to the scathing remarks Hoff had to make about landsmen in the half-deck that evening, I was encouraged in the sense of cabal all seamen feel when contemplating landsmen and the doings of landsmen.

On the morning of our third day in London we were told that we were to be granted shore leave that evening.

'Johnny! You, me, Jimbo, vee go for a spree. All get dronk. I know somvare in Chinatown vare no von vorries to ask vat age you are.' Hoff had just joined me with his news where I was laid out on a topgallant yard passing down the buntlines. I had been in the city of London for fifty-six hours and so far my experience of it was confined to the sight of the roofs of the warehouses that stretched like angular grey dunes across Millwall and the Isle of Dogs.

'I'll be in it. I've never been drunk before.' This was not strictly true. I had babbled happily enough after a few mouthfuls of the rum issue down in the Southern Ocean. Nevertheless Hoff was thrilled with my disclosure.

'Iss goot.' Gleefully he explained the course the evening would take. 'You drink, you laugh. You drink more, you fight. You drink more, you are sick efferyvare. You drink more, you schleep goot. Then you vake op, you are man...' He grinned and added, 'A man vith bad head.'

'It sounds like fun.' Jimbo, when we saw him, nodded assent to the plan.

We were released from work an hour or so earlier than usual. Within five minutes we had donned our shore clothes and plastered our hair down with water. Mister Gillard put his head through the midshiphouse door.

'You're nightwatchman, son,' he said to Hoff. Then, noting our preparations for going ashore, he grinned and added. 'It has to be someone.'

'Fockingh damn,' exclaimed Hoff when the second mate had gone.

'We'll give the idea away, mate,' said Jimbo. 'I'm not much in the mood for a spree anyway.'

Hoff was vehement. 'You fockingh go. Shonny most be made dronk. Here.' He put a couple of coins into Jimbo's hand. How he had managed to produce them was miraculous. The half-deck was, by definition, penniless.

'You're crazy,' said Jimbo, looking at the coins.

'You com back here fockingh dronk,' said Hoff. We set out for the dives of Chinatown.

Our spree was a cheerless affair. From the start Jimbo was moody. We seemed to do a lot of tramping down sparsely lit streets in search of establishments he assured me existed. 'Charlie Brown's', 'The Tiger', 'The Prospect of Whitby'. I began to wonder if Jimbo knew where we were supposed to be going. We entered one premises that was material enough, a large smoky chamber packed shoulder to shoulder with men. Jimbo led the way through the press, placed his elbows confidently on the bar and ordered. The barman regarded the two of us, then shook his head. Jimbo remonstrated.

'You boys cut along or I'll have you thrown out.'

Jimbo spat on the floor, then eyed the barman. 'Put you in a real job and you'd blow away, you bastard.' The man behind the counter smiled. He had all the cards. We left.

A second place refused to serve us. We tramped down more streets. Jimbo's animosity became unpredictable.

'I reckon it's your girly face that's the trouble, fellah,' he said on one occasion.

It was getting on for closing time. We arrived at a third establishment and Jimbo approached a rotund, jovial-looking individual who was standing near the door with a group and exchanged some words with the man. The latter contemplated the features of the artful James Wichelo, apprentice, for some moments, then nodded, took the coin that Jimbo proffered and disappeared.

We waited. No jars arrived. Jimbo went to the door and spoke to the group the man had been with. All at once I saw him being pushed down the steps. A burly man, with a comical droopy moustache, followed him a pace or two. There were raised voices.

'You want to take care, son. Pushing your weight around.'

'That bastard's got my money.'

'You're not allowed here, sonny-boy. You know that. You're under age. Now push off before I break your arm.'

I pulled Jimbo away and we retreated, with him hurling insults over his shoulder. There followed a period when we wandered aimlessly through the streets of what I learned, much later, was Wapping. Jimbo fulminated against London, landsmen and Creation for a time. Then he suggested we go in search of a brothel. I said I'd prefer to go back to the ship. I found the idea repelling.

'That'd be right,' he said. 'You probably couldn't raise it anyway.'

We walked on in silence, a silence in which I could sense his hostility had been diverted from London and landsmen to me.

'We might have taught that bastard a lesson if you hadn't hung back,' he said after a while.

'Don't be crazy. There were half a dozen of them.'

'You still flamin' hung back.'

'You told me my face didn't help.'

'Yeah. Yeah. Always handy with a flamin' excuse. I should've come on my own. You're a killjoy, you are. I reckon it's been bad luck ever since you came on board in Melbourne.'

'What's the matter with you? We're supposed to be on a spree.'

'Some flamin' spree with you hanging about like the smell of a dead dog. Ah, Christ you make me puke.' This conversation had been conducted as we walked down a long road. The odd cab clip-clopped past us with a silent driver perched on top of it. Otherwise there was no humanity. We walked on without further exchange for a minute or two. I had been taken aback and wounded by his antagonism. I was looking for a way to retaliate.

'You're the one who caused the trouble,' I discovered myself saying. 'You stole the telescope from Alex's sextant. I know you did.' We walked side by side. Jimbo did not respond to my accusation. 'Outside of Trygg there was no one on the ship nasty enough to do it.' Still there was no response from Jimbo. It was possible to believe he wasn't listening. 'And I reckon you deliberately provoked that brawl with Alex. Jack might have been alive now if you hadn't joined in with Trygg.' I was saying things I hadn't realised I believed. 'Call *me* bad luck. You're worse. You do cruel things for the fun of it.'

Even before I had finished I noticed my left ear was stinging slightly. It had been boxed. And Jimbo had said, 'You want to be careful what you say, Johnny.' Then he quickened his pace up the street. Clearly he did not expect to get boxed back.

'It's true, isn't it?' I called after him. 'You were the one who wrecked his sextant.' There was no answer. I ran and caught up with him. We turned into an adjacent street. He was walking very fast. I stole a glance at his face. 'You're blubbering,' I said. It was true. There were tears coursing down his cheeks and his gaze was fixed ahead unseeingly. He made no sound. I found it hard to keep up with him. Abruptly he turned and sat down in the gateway of a house. It was a narrow, terraced abode with an iron railing fence and with heavy damask curtains in a downstairs window behind which was a chink of yellow light. The evening was growing dark around us. Further down the street a group of children stood around two who swung a skipping rope. The rope flicked rhythmically on the cobbles and the children chanted in time with it.

Jimbo's head was lowered, but I could see tears splashing on the gate step. He sniffed loudly and began rolling himself a cigarette.

'Why did you do it?' I asked quietly, rather awed by this behaviour. The hunched figure in front of me shrugged. When it spoke the voice was crumpled.

'As a kind of favour to Trygg.'

'A favour? Did he ask you to steal it?'

'Yeah. No. Not in so many words.'

'What did he say?'

Jimbo looked past my shoulder, blinking away the tears as though they were troublesome motes of dust.

'He said he couldn't see the harm in testing Alex's mettle a bit. Him going for his ticket. Would I keep an eye open . . . for ways of getting to him . . . to Alex.'

'Was this when he caught you in his cabin that time?'

Jimbo nodded. 'And so he said he'd shop you for being there if you didn't?' Jimbo shook his head. The cigarette glowed red.

'He didn't threaten?'

'Not in so many words.'

'Why did you do those things then?'

There were some moments of silence before he answered. 'The idea of tormenting old Alex...I don't know... appealed to me...at the time.'

'Appealed?'

'Oh, it wasn't just that...but it did...appeal. I couldn't...I couldn't resist, having a go at him when I could.'

I was silent for some moments, then I said, 'What else was it?' I remember I pronounced the question very coldly. All that I had blurted out in my desire to retaliate against Jimbo had turned out to be true. I was not yet seventeen. People hurt each other because it appealed to them, because they couldn't resist it. I was expected to grasp this.

Jimbo said: 'Trygg told me he needed something to divert his mind from what was happening inside him. He had some growth in his belly — you saw it. Why not make a job of getting this ship to London, I said to him. I was cheeky, but he'd been encouraging me to say my piece: I reckon he appreciated the company. He replied that he'd had his fill of that. Mucked about in ships all his life, he said. Now suddenly here he was without any life left over. So, he told me, he had decided that he wanted to do something that was all his own — one last thing. He was going to make something of Alex — that donkey-faced fellow, he called him. Make or break, he said, it didn't matter much, so long as he could know it was all his own work, and that the fruits of it would outlive him. When he told me this I rather liked him — Trygg I mean. That voice coming out of the pitch blackness. It was as if I suddenly saw all of him. I couldn't think he was a snake after that. Hell, I'd started to admire him. I don't know why. The way he went on, it was clear he didn't like the idea of dying much: he seemed, I don't know, almost to blame life, to blame all of us, for the fact he was done for. Going under without a ripple, with everyone else bellowing and jumping and running about, while he couldn't spoon down a meal without puking, or even stand up or lie down without getting an awful pain in his gut. He couldn't sail the ship without thinking what an idiot business it all was. And when he saw other people being serious about things, small things, it just made him angry, he said. That's probably why he was always on Alex's back. I was impressed. He wanted to live. But he couldn't. So he decided to do the next best thing and take a hard kick at life before he went.'

Jimbo had spoken in a low monotone with his head lowered as though he were addressing the step on which he sat. I remember feeling no sympathy for what I'd heard.

'Yes, well his kick killed Jack,' I said. The bent head nodded. 'And it'll probably get Alex hanged.' Again the head nodded. 'You helped.' I believe I shouted those two syllables. The head was still this time but I could see fresh tears making little asterisks on the scoured gate step. I became aware of the presence of some of the children who had been playing with the skipping rope standing in a group behind me, watching the two of us with an awed curiosity. Jimbo dragged quickly on his cigarette.

'When Alex gets put on a charge of murdering Jack, you should be put in the dock as his accomplice. You and Trygg.'

There was another long silence before Jimbo said quietly. 'Trygg'll be dead, if he's not already.'

I was perplexed. Captain Trygg may have been our common enemy, but Jimbo had been a shipmate and Alex's fellow apprentice.

'You tortured Alex. Or helped to. Deliberately. Why, Jimbo?'

'Bugger off back to the ship, Johnny,' he said. The children stood impassively behind us.

'Answer my question.'

The lowered head seemed lost in contemplation for a minute or more. Then again I heard that voice from the face I couldn't see. 'Because I wanted to at the time. I didn't think about it.' We said nothing to each other for a while, then Jimbo said, 'Bugger off back to the ship. Leave me in peace. Please, Johnny.'

I had never heard pleading in Jimbo's tone before. It brought me back to where we were with a jolt. I stood watching him for perhaps two or three minutes. He appeared to be oblivious of the seven or eight children who formed our audience. His cigarette was smoked down to its last half-inch and almost immediately he began to prepare another.

'I can't just leave you here,' I said at length. He didn't answer. 'You might as well come with me back to the ship,' I tried again, but I had no success. So I walked away toward the docklands, leaving him sitting in the gateway of that suburban house, knees drawn up, head drooping, suddenly looking like an old and derelict man. A cigarette burning incongruously between his fingers, he was the object of the frank curiosity of a group of children.

I don't know how long he sat there. I was not awake when he returned to the half-deck. Suffice it to say he was back on board and ready to start work at first light. He was subdued, but otherwise looked none the worse for wear. In the next two days we exchanged hardly a word, and the conversation we had in that Wapping street was the last real one we ever had.

At noon on our fifth day in London we — the three remaining apprentices and the couple of seamen who had stayed on after the discharge of the rest — stood beneath the poop rail waiting for the first mate to appear above us and speak the formal words that would end our duties on the *Emilia Denholm*. All the sails and gear had been stowed below. The last of the wool was coming out of the ship's holds. Mister Hallet appeared.

'Thank you, gentlemen. That'll do. Report to the saloon for your pay and references.'

We went aft and stood in a queue in the corridor outside the saloon. One by one each of us went in, took his pay and reference, shook hands with each of the mates and returned to the main deck. Being the most junior member of the crew, I was last.

When I entered, the saloon door was shut behind me. The first mate gave me my slip of paper and my few shillings, and Mister Gillard handed me a box. It was Alex's sextant.

'He said he wanted you to have this. It's about the only thing he said the whole time he was locked up. It's got no telescope on it so it's not much use until you get one. But it's yours. He won't need it.'

I took the box. Then Mister Hallet asked me what I was

intending to do. I answered that there were relatives I could stay with until after the enquiry. After that I supposed I would be looking for a ship.

The two mates looked at each other briefly. Then Mister Hallet said, 'You won't be needed at any enquiry, laddie. And another thing; if I were you I'd get clear of that pal of yours — Wichelo. He's trouble.'

'Aye aye, sir.'

'I might be able to find you a ship. Give me your address in London.' I wrote it down for him.

'Would it be a ship home, sir? To Australia, I mean.'

'Home?' said Mister Hallet with the suggestion of a smile. 'Not in your life, laddie.'

With that I said farewell to the lean mate and to Mister Gillard, and went out onto the main deck where Jimbo and Hoff were waiting. There were goodbyes, even some chiacking from Jimbo though I don't recall what was said. Hoff pumped my hand vigorously. We swore to meet up again, after which the two of them went off together. I collected my bag from the half-deck and left the *Emilia Denholm*. When I looked back at her outside the dockyards, all I could see were her upper masts and yards, already barely distinguishable from the masts and spars of other sailing vessels berthed in the West India Dock.

For a week I was the victim of fond and lavish hospitality offered by a branch of my mother's family. Then one morning a cable arrived for me. It was from Mister Hallet, and read, 'Report barque *Methuselah* comma York Dock Belfast stop.' There was also a date, which was within the fortnight.

That unequivocal telegram probably kept me at sea. There was no arguing with it. I travelled by train to Liverpool and caught the overnight steamer to Belfast. Here I joined the *Methuselah*. Within three weeks of docking in London I was on another ship beating down the Saint George's Channel, bound for Bahia Blanca in the Argentine.

III

And that was the end of it. I was allowed simply to sail away from consequence, to duck the problem of having to make up my mind about what I had seen that morning on the Equator. It necessitated, as I later learned, that Mister Hallet perjure himself before an enquiry for the second time in his career, but this, it seems, he had determined to do by the time the ship tied up at the West India Dock.

So the truth was adjusted and the result was that Alex did not hang. The Board of Enquiry that was convened to investigate the death of the apprentice, Jack Bell, listened to the evidence that was given by the first mate of the *Emilia Denholm*, read the report of the incident he had made at the time, and found that Alex was answerable to a charge of manslaughter. He was committed for trial. When asked to state how he pleaded he was heard to pronounce the word 'guilty'. The evidence of the first mate was heard again and was corroborated in detail by the very smart second officer of the ship. The charge was considered proven and Alex went to prison for four years.

Gus, who sat through the entire enquiry and trial, was impressed by how close to the truth the first mate's testimony was. The background to the slaying was described with faultless accuracy, the illness of the captain and the resulting uncertainties in the command of the vessel, the unnatural malice the late captain had shown toward the apprentice, and the dogged, patient way in which Holt had borne the daily degradations to which he had been subjected, until, of course, the event of that morning on the Equator.

As to the event of that morning, had he, Mister Hallet, not seen it? He had been on duty at the poop rail when his attention had been drawn by a clattering coming from somewhere near the galley. Noise carried with peculiar clarity that morning. The ship was in the doldrums; the sound of the sea and wind were all but absent. From the poop rail it was possible to hear the odd call coming from those boys working in the bow locker. That sudden clattering of plates was distinctly odd. Mister Hallet had leapt to the conclusion some frolic was going on for'ard. He had descended the poop companion and there he was in a position to see the origin of the rumpus. Captain Trygg and the apprentice Holt were standing in the vicinity of the galley door with various of the crew's eating utensils on the deck about their feet. (The first mate had explained how Holt had been put on slopping-out duties indefinitely for incurring the captain's displeasure at some juncture.) Mister Hallet noted with surprise that the apprentice was laying about himself with a belaying pin, smashing things and sending them scuttling across the deck. Equally surprisingly, the captain stood with his hands in his pockets making no attempt to restrain the unbridled apprentice. If anything, oddly enough, the captain's attitude expressed curiosity. The first mate had proceeded forward to put a stop to the disturbance. Evidently the senior apprentice, Jack Bell, who had been standing at the door of the bow locker supervising the work of the three other apprentices inside, had seen the commotion and been taken with the same idea. He was nearer than the first mate to the two men, so had reached them first, had approached Holt and tried to restrain him and, in doing so, had been caught by a blow on the temple as the instrument was swung wildly about. The blow had killed Bell instantly.

Could the blow have been aimed deliberately?

Mister Hallet stated that he did not believe so. He gave an exact description of the manner of it. He pointed out that the force of Holt's anger, if anger it was, was directed at the utensils on the deck. Bell had been caught by a negligent and misadventurous swing of the brass pin. Besides, added the first mate, the author of the apprentice's grievance stood by the whole time and was shown no violence. Mister Hallet said that he had formed the impression the apprentice's behaviour was more in the nature of the desperate airing of a grievance than in the redressing of one. This may have sounded strange, but the circumstances on the ship were quite unusual.

The sober gentlemen on the Marine Board of Enquiry found them not only unusual, they found them astonishing. They were astonished that events aboard a vessel of the merchant marine could come to such a pass. They were astonished that a shipmaster could behave in such a perverse manner. What was known about Captain Trygg's record on previous ships? Not much, it seems. The gentlemen were not happy about the shortage of witnesses to the event. Surely a ship's deck just after breakfast is a hive of activity? There must have been some members of the crew who observed what happened, surely?

There was none, Mister Hallet replied, almost truthfully. All had been questioned most carefully by himself and the second mate. A description followed of where the crew had been at the time such that there could have been no witnesses.

A great deal came out in that enquiry and the succeeding trial. For instance, in explaining the occasion when he had attempted to put a stop to the captain's victimisation of Holt, the first mate was compelled to explain why the captain was able to thwart the attempt. The subject of the Tate Enquiry came up and one questioner on that Board tried to make much of this. Mister Hallet trod some very thin ice for a while. But it was a line of questioning that was not pertinent to the issue. The monosyllables, those that were decipherable, that Alex himself gave under questioning *were* pertinent. They agreed with Mister Hallet's account at all points. He had not known how Jack Bell had come to be lying dead on the deck. He did not remember having struck him. He supposed that he had. He just did not remember. He appeared to co-operate with the court and with the evidence that had been presented. I suppose there must have been some hard talking on the part of the first and second mates at some juncture during the weeks the barque made her northing after crossing the Line. And something of this must have been successfully communicated to the confined apprentice. But whatever arrangement of the facts they made, for once Gus heard nothing. And their arrangement saved Alex from hanging.

I was pleased and relieved to hear this news on the occasion I visited Gus for the first time toward the end of the war. Alex did not hang. That was good. It was intolerable to think that someone I had known, shared the half-deck table with, who had leaned over a rail beside me as dolphins rocketed through the water below, who had discoursed at length on those engaging sea mammals, should have his neck abruptly broken at the end of a rope. I was glad the truth could be adjusted, on that occasion at least.

But I'll not say the idea hasn't worried me sometimes, the idea of bending what happens to suit what you think ought to have happened. It is an opportunity the closed life of a vessel makes possible — more, makes tempting — when things start to go wrong. I don't believe Mister Hallet was an untruthful man. I don't think he cared much one way or the other about truth. He was an instinctively *just* man, and a practical man. The past for him, I believe, was a trove of practical experience. The present was a circle of fastidious alertness. He was a seaman. This was his trade and this was his character. An apprentice on his ship had been subjected to unnatural humiliation to the point where he had lashed out blindly and desperately. That belaying pin was aimed. Alex had wanted to cause injury, and if a man dies, in law that is murder. But Mister Hallet had been right in one thing, I think. Alex's action had been demonstrative, not vengeful. And it had been provoked by a man who could not be brought to account. Alex had killed a man. He would have to pay. But not with his life. This was how Mister Hallet saw things, so the facts were adjusted minimally and one man's idea of fairness was achieved. It depended on our convenient isolation upon the high seas. But like the sea it was capable of being arbitrary and dangerous in its effects. It had been proved wrong on one occasion and men who had bundled one of their number over the side of a ship had gone off casually into the world as though nothing untoward had happened. As a result Mister Hallet had placed a formal restraint on himself. He had not accepted, and would not accept, a position of shipmaster. But he had not brooded. He was a practical man.

And if things had turned out differently; if, at the age of sixteen, I had been told to tell some lies to an enquiry as I stood in the gloom of a deckhouse with the lean mate gripping me fiercely by the elbow, I would have done so blithely. Now, at thirty-six, I don't know. I would be too nervous about ramifications. I would feel jittery about telling lies under the hard gazes of several maritime gentlemen sitting at a bench. But then he was a forceful man himself, Mister Hallet.

When Gus left the *Emilia D.* in London he left the life at sea. Kindly soul that he was, he visited Alex in prison on one occasion. The visit was not welcomed. The ex-chief apprentice sat opposite the ex-steward and stared at his hands for the entire period of the visit. Gus kept up a patter of gossip in a tone, I can imagine, of well-meant heartiness.

The change Gus witnessed in the ex-apprentice's appearance was a sad one. The prison clothes he had been given were outsized, and they gave the impression that the once kempt and tanned Alex had shrunk in stature within them. There was a regulation cap, clownish in character like something designed for a child's birthday party, and this sat ridiculously on his head and seemed to accentuate his ears. He was, Gus had been told, a model prisoner, a little too eager to please, if anything.

At one stage in their meeting the ex-steward asked whether his mother knew of his present circumstances.

'She thinks I'm still at sea,' replied Alex, without looking up.

Only once, when he left the room, did the ex-apprentice slip the ex-steward a furtive look.

'It looked like the expression I saw on some of the other faces in those corridors and yards, Johnny,' he said, when telling me of it. 'As if he had no...regard for himself.' Gus shook his head sadly. He was prepared to share quite some few of the world's troubles, except that for twenty-five years his discretionary position as a steward in the merchant service had offered him no scope for taking the initiative in such matters. He served, he watched, he relayed the gossip, because this was the one outlet for his charity and the one weakness in his discretion.

Over the following years he wrote to the prisoner a few times, though he never had any letters in return. Shortly before my visit Gus had received one of his letters back with a note from the governor of the jail saying the prisoner, Alexander Holt, had been discharged and was now, so the governor believed, working as a porter on one of the London railway stations, having been found medically unfit for military service.

Neither I nor Gus heard of him again. Whenever I came ashore in London and found myself catching a train, I kept an eye out for him. Would I have spoken to him if I had seen him? I don't know. I suspect my watching out for him was prompted more by a morbid curiosity to see for myself the transformation that had come upon him. What would we have said to one other? I had his sextant. I had replaced the telescope and the instrument had brought me advancement and a cabin aft. But why should Alex have had an interest in that? Anyway, I never saw him. The promising candidate for a second mate's certificate, who at one time may have wished to throw himself over the side of a ship, presumably survived, and continues his existence to this day pushing trolleys and handling baggage on some large railway terminus.

I gathered from the ex-steward's account that Captain Trygg was dead by the time the enquiry began. It was about the only convenient thing that huge man accomplished for us. The date and the place of his death I do not know. His ambulance took him off into the London streets and oblivion just as the launch had brought him from oblivion to our ship's accommodation ladder on the still water of Otago Harbour. He disappeared from my life and the lives of the others in the same abrupt way in which he had entered them. So I never heard exactly what his illness was. But I have described to the odd medical man I have met the symptoms we all saw during the weeks aboard the barque, and I am told that Captain Trygg undoubtedly had cancer; of the stomach, or possibly the pancreas.

In the end I cannot determine what was behind his particular malice. Was he simply an ill-disposed man? If so, there's not much hope for any of us. Besides, I write as one who once lay broken on a saloon sofa watched over by the Evil One with an attention approaching tenderness. Or did I dream that? Was his malevolence a way of diverting his mind from the fearful things that were happening to his body, as Jimbo had suggested? Or a way of kicking life for the mean trick it had played in curtailing his? There was something in these two ideas. Did he, like Jimbo, simply not think about it much at the time? Yet, even as young as I was then, these various reasons struck me as inadequate. And I still find it hard to accept Captain Trygg's own account, to Jimbo, that it had to do with making a man out of Alex, or with producing some sort of 'effect'. He may have said that purely for Jimbo's benefit. It doesn't square with how unremitting his cruelty toward Alex was, or with the pleasure he presumably derived from it.

Then again, perhaps Alex had attracted malevolence to himself. Are there human beings who are prone to do this, who even generate it, all unwittingly? There was a truth in this idea I was not prepared to face for a long time.

Whatever the cause, I was not permitted to know how Captain Trygg came to be what he was. I only know that he spent some weeks among us, and that he was not one of us. Certainly he was human enough, with a sister in Preston, and a cancer that ate away his life before our eyes. But he was not one of us because there was nothing in our lives he could take seriously. We had all our options. Time and opportunity were before us. Was not Alex expected to pass his examination for a second mate's certificate with flying colours? Trygg had no time. No wonder he looked through us. And having no time, he was hardly a man any more. He belonged elsewhere.

It is a strong temptation to remain on the straight and narrow when you know that you will have to live with unpleasant consequences if you don't. The shipmaster had outgrown consequence. The certainty that he was about to die had conferred on him a frightening privilege. And he had used it. The life of one young man had been extinguished, casually. The life of another had been crippled. Whether the man was intrinsically malignant, whether he had given free rein to some foundational conviction of the contemptibleness of all men and all human purpose, I cannot say, but the idea of singling out a man — a boy rather — and subjecting him to an unremitting humiliation in the eyes of his fellows until he lashed out beneath the pain had clearly appealed to him, had been irresistible. Because he was dying, he had suddenly found himself with the insouciance and the powers of a god. It must have been intoxicating, that realisation of being, effectively, beyond sanction.

I did not see Jimbo, Hoff or Mister Hallet again. The Great War swallowed them up and I have no notion of what became of them. My inclination is to believe they survived. They were seamen, and for those four terrible years the sea was, for the most part, a safer place than the land for an able-bodied soul.

And I survived. Twenty years ago I joined a barque, impelled by a romantic urge and, in fairness to myself, a more practical and enduring love of sailing ships and the graceful machinery associated with them. In the course of a voyage I was shoved into adulthood. I got my first taste of work. I saw death and perversity too. A great deal of powerful experience was concentrated into those few weeks, and the years that followed were, if not dull, tame by comparison.

But the life I had chosen was obsolete, even then in 1913. Now it has all but disappeared. Apart from the odd grain carrier plying between Spencer Gulf and Europe, the masts and yards have been taken down and stowed below. The hulls are rusting in forgotten corners of dockyards. Here and there a small boy clambering among the piles of a wharf might spy with the shock of novelty four masts and a spike bowsprit anchored in the bay. How had they got there? If he were to watch for long enough he might see those spars shake out their white foliage, lean before the moderate breeze and shrink away toward the horizon. It is a sight that the boy will not forget. It is a sight that conjures a powerful longing, a longing that is both exhilarating and sad in its character; and ancient beyond memory.

But this is romancing, and romance, be it looking forward or back, anticipation or nostalgia, is the one voluptuous possession. It shies at what the actual moment brings. This is 1933. I must look for employment.